TRIANGLE

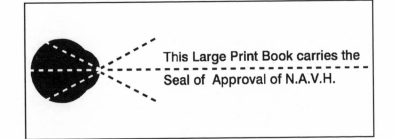

This Large Print Book carries the
Seal of Approval of N.A.V.H.

TRIANGLE

KATHARINE WEBER

THORNDIKE PRESS

An imprint of Thomson Gale, a part of The Thomson Corporation

THOMSON

GALE

Detroit • New York • San Francisco • New Haven, Conn. • Waterville, Maine • London • Munich

THOMSON
GALE
™

LIBRARY OF CONGRESS CATALOGING-IN-PUBLICATION DATA

Weber, Katharine, 1955–
　Triangle / by Katharine Weber.
　　p. cm. — (Thorndike Press large print core)
　ISBN 0-7862-8977-5 (alk. paper)
　1. Triangle Shirtwaist Company — Fire, 1911 — Fiction. 2. New York (N.Y.) — Fiction. 3. Women clothing workers — Fiction. 4. Large type books. I. Title.
　PS3573.E2194T75 2006b
　813'.54—dc22   2006018325

Published in 2006 by arrangement with Farrar, Straus and Giroux, LLC.

Printed in the United States of America on permanent paper
10 9 8 7 6 5 4 3 2 1

In memory of my grandmothers:
Pauline Gottesfeld Kaufman (1887–
1969), who finished buttonholes at the
Triangle Waist Company in 1909, and
Kay Swift (1897–1993), who made
wonderful music

SHIRT

The back, the yoke, the yardage. Lapped
    seams,
The nearly invisible stitches along the
    collar
Turned in a sweatshop by Koreans or
    Malaysians

Gossiping over tea and noodles on their
    break
Or talking money or politics while one
    fitted
This armpiece with its overseam to the
    band

Of cuff I button at my waist. The presser,
    the cutter,
The wringer, the mangle. The needle,
    the union,
The treadle, the bobbin. The code. The

infamous blaze

At the Triangle Factory in nineteen-
eleven.
One hundred and forty-six died in the
flames
On the ninth floor, no hydrants, no fire
escapes —

The witness in a building across the
street
Who watched how a young man helped
a girl to step
Up to the windowsill, then held her out

Away from the masonry wall and let her
drop.
And then another. As if he were helping
them up
To enter a streetcar, and not eternity.

A third before he dropped her put her
arms
Around his neck and kissed him. Then
he held
Her into space, and dropped her. Almost
at once

He stepped up to the sill himself, his
jacket flared

And fluttered up from his shirt as he
  came down,
Air filling up the legs of his gray trous-
  ers —

Like Hart Crane's Bedlamite, "shrill
  shirt ballooning."
Wonderful how the pattern matches perfectly
Across the placket and over the twin bar-
  tacked

Corners of both pockets, like a strict
  rhyme
Or a major chord. Prints, plaids, checks,
Houndstooth, Tattersall, Madras. The
  clan tartans

Invented by mill-owners inspired by the
  hoax of Ossian
To control their savage Scottish workers,
  tamed
By a fabricated heraldry: MacGregor,

Bailey, MacMartin. The kilt, devised for
  workers
To wear among the dusty clattering
  looms.
Weavers, carders, spinners. The loader,

The docker, the navvy. The planer, the
   picker, the sorter
Sweating at her machine in a litter of
   cotton
As slaves in calico headrags sweated in
   fields:

George Herbert, your descendant is a
   Black
Lady in South Carolina, her name is
   Irma
And she inspected my shirt. Its color and
   fit

And feel and its clean smell have satisfied
Both her and me. We have culled its cost
   and quality
Down to the buttons of simulated bone,

The buttonholes, the sizing, the facing,
   the characters
Printed in black on neckband and tail.
   The shape,
The label, the labor, the color, the shade.
   The shirt.

                     — Robert Pinsky

■ ■ ■ ■

PART ONE

■ ■ ■ ■

ONE

This is what happened. I was working at my machine, with only a few minutes left before the end of the day, I remember so clearly I can still see it, that I had only two right sleeves remaining in my pile — my sister Pauline, she did the left sleeves and I did the right sleeves and between us we could finish sometimes as many as twenty-four shirtwaists in an hour, three hundred shirtwaists on a good day, if the machines didn't break down and if the thread didn't break too often, and if nobody put a needle through her finger, which happened all the time and the biggest problem then was you didn't want to bleed on the goods but you didn't want to stop work so you took a piece of scrap and you wrapped your finger tight and you kept working — my sister was a little faster than I was and sometimes her finished pile would be high because she did her sleeve first and then I would take from her pile to do the right sleeve but I have to say my seams were the ones always perfectly straight.

And then when I was done, the waist would be finished except for sewing on the buttons and trimming the loose threads, and who did that was the little girls over in the nursery, that's what we called that corner, the nursery, some of those girls were only ten or eleven years old already working and working, poor things, but what other life did they know? Those little girls would sew on the buttons and cut all the loose threads and then the waist would be ready for pressing.

It was payday that day, it was a Saturday, and the pay envelopes had just been handed out, and before that for a few minutes there was a break and my friend Ida Brodsky, she died, she was a wonderful friend to me, she made a cake for a surprise because of my engagement to Sam, because we had just said a few days before we would get married, we didn't even get a ring yet, and people were happy for us, all the girls working together, it was so cheerful sometimes even with the hard work. I had my pay envelope and my sister's also, to keep for her, we each got maybe six or eight dollars or sometimes less, except in a good week,

14

and once we each made twelve dollars for a week's work but that was an exception, but you could live on that money we made and send some home, too. We thought we were doing well, we were happy enough with what we had, even though the unions told us to get more and told us we shouldn't be so happy, and they were right, but we were never hungry, we were so young and healthy and strong, and it felt like a chance to get ahead, so we didn't mind the long days and the terrible loud noise of the machines and the smell of the oil everywhere.

That oil, they had to use it, to keep the machines going, but they could have opened those dirty windows for even a breath of fresh air, it wouldn't have made us work slower and who knows it might have made us work better, but all the windows were always kept closed tight — and I remember I just took a moment from my machine to tuck the pay packets for both of us into my stocking to be safe like always, I took them both from our boss, Mr. Jacobs, so my sister could keep working for every minute left — and the next day would have been our one day off in the week, so we were looking forward to that — and then there was a big noise behind me, while I was still bending down, like nothing I had ever heard, and I thought, What could that be?

So loud, like an explosion and something breaking all at once! So I turned around, and my sister next to me, she turned around too, and what did we see? Flames! They were just outside the window on the Greene Street side, they were right there behind me. The flames were coming up from the eighth floor but we didn't know everybody on the eighth floor was already in a commotion and escaping because that's where the fire started, and a lot of those girls got out before that big noise which was the windows breaking from the fire, mostly they got out from the eighth floor, but we were on the ninth floor, that's where I worked already for a year with my sister, we learned English so fast and we had these good jobs and our life in America was a big adventure for us. We thought it was fortunate to work on the ninth floor where the bosses gave a little more pay and the really skilled girls, the fastest workers, they had their machines. Maybe that was never true and it was the same on the eighth floor but this is what we thought. Nobody on our floor knew what was happening right underneath us until those windows blew out. More people could have got out if we knew, but nobody told us. They knew on the tenth floor and they all got out, but one. A lot of people below us and everyone above us got out. Only on the ninth floor it was unlucky to be, because nobody told us.

And so first we had this big explosion and we saw these flames and the girls all around me started to shout and scream, my sister also, and everyone was in a commotion and the flames got bigger at the window and then the flames, they were inside with us, coming along the wall and across the floor like water flowing, I've never seen anything like that and I am thinking this is very bad — and the next thing you know the flames were around us, and right next to us, and we can feel this heat like a furnace and at first there was the screaming but nobody was moving, everybody was frozen for a moment, but then there was a rush of all the girls trying to get across the room at once, but they were blocked by the machinery because the big rows of sewing machines were on these long tables with no gaps, they took up so much space and there was no way to pass except at the ends of the rows of tables, and some girls tried to crawl under but there was no room with the pedals and the machinery and they were pushing and there were girls climbing across the tables with their long skirts bunched and getting caught in the machines and they were falling and shoving and everyone was shouting and pushing and grabbing and calling out, and the Italian girls were praying and screaming to each other.

Mr. Grannick, one of the garment cutters, a very nice little man, he stood up on a chair and tried to make the girls listen but a lot of the girls couldn't see him because now there was so much smoke, and people were screaming and coughing and choking and nobody could hear what he was saying with the noise — he was one of the ones who got out — and I saw a girl with her hair on fire, and then another one running with her clothes all burning up and so I pushed my way past these two Italian sisters, I think one was called Rosalie, she was the young one, they were just standing there screaming and crying without moving, their faces were all red and their eyes were all red and they were in my way and I never saw them again, I'm sorry, God help me and God help them, but I pushed past them and I saw there were too many girls at the door and nobody could go out that way, it was a terrible thing, but nobody's fault, because the door, it opened in, didn't we all know that already, it was a narrow door we all used it to go out, because it was the only way out, it had to be, so we could pass by the guard who inspected us to make sure we weren't stealing any of the goods — some of the girls took scraps home to make things, and some of them even stole finished waists, one girl, she was new, she tried to hide a waist tucked into her hair in a big rat — that was a style and that was what we called it, a rat — but she was caught, it was just the week before, her name was Ella something Italian like Piacentini, something like that, and she was crying and she promised never to do it again but we didn't see her any more after that day and we were sorry for her — who would know how lucky she was to be sent away in disgrace from the Triangle that week?

The fire was getting hotter and it was everywhere, on the machines and the tables and all our work was burning up and the smoke was so thick and the smell was just terrible, black from the oil and the burning goods and the smell was so strong, and everyone was coughing and gagging and choking, and there was also the very horrible smell of burning hair, and all those girls were pushing and pushing together, it was just so terrible I can't really describe it, they were all pushing at once and the girls in the front maybe even got squeezed to death from the pushing but nobody could open that door.

I had an idea about another door — sometimes the bosses went in and out this other door, we were never allowed to go that way on the weekend when the freight elevators weren't running — it was by the back side of the building instead of the Washington Place side, they would go on these other stairs by the freight elevators to walk up to the tenth floor where the offices were, so I had this idea — I don't know why nobody else thought of this but everyone was in a big panic and maybe everyone assumed the other door would be locked like always but you have to try, and I'm sorry to say this about all those poor girls who didn't make it but nobody else thought to try — and I pulled my sister by the hand to go with me over there, across the room, but it was like running towards the flames and it probably didn't seem right to go towards the fire and all the black smoke to get away, but that's how a lot of people got out from this building in one way or another, running into the fire to get through, and my sister, why did she pull back, I don't know.

And meanwhile there were girls at the passenger elevator door trying to crowd into the elevator, too many of them, and it was smoke everywhere, and the windows were breaking on both sides and there were girls with their hair on fire and their dresses on fire — screaming, screaming like you can't imagine, like animals, not like people anymore — and they were standing in the windows screaming and then they were jumping and the girls watched the ones who jumped, and then they were in the window after them, and then they jumped, in rows, it was like they waited their turns, it was just so terrible.

I never thought about jumping, to tell you the truth. I don't know why, I just somehow thought I could escape this and live some more. I was foolish and so young I didn't know that it was almost impossible and so I thought I could try to keep alive. But other girls were just as young with their lives ahead of them too, like me, and they didn't see a way to get out like I did, so maybe it was just I was lucky. Because it was then I saw Mr. Jacobs, he was the contractor my sister and I worked for, I saw him with a waist around his face so he could breathe with all the smoke and all you could see were his eyes, they were red from the smoke, and he was coughing like everybody, and I saw him go to this other door I mentioned, the door by the freight elevators to the stairs we aren't supposed to use on weekends, and he had a key and my sister was right behind me, and I saw him unlock the door and I went to follow him, but my sister wasn't right behind me anymore.

I should have held her hand tighter, but I didn't, because I thought she was right behind me, and then she wasn't there, and I saw her, she was going through the flames the other way, because the flames were everywhere now, and you couldn't tell which way was which, and where she was going, I found out, even though I didn't know it right then, where she was going was to my fiancé, that was Sam, Sam Gottesfeld, he was twenty, and like I said, we were going to be married, and he was at the corner window on the Washington Place side, and he was helping the girls.

And she went to him, my sister went to him, I don't know what she was thinking, and I don't know what he was thinking, staying by the window where nobody could get out, why he didn't try to go to the stairs or the elevator, or try that terrible fire escape hardly anyone could go on, I don't know, even though he wouldn't have lived anyway if he did that, because so many girls tried that and they died, but I don't know what he was thinking staying there by the window, not even trying. I called her, I called to my sister, but she didn't hear me, and everyone was coughing and screaming so loud, and I tried to go closer and keep calling her name, but she didn't hear me with all the screaming, and the noise was so terrible from the fire roaring and the little girls wailing, there were some little girls, nobody was helping them and they were burning, and they were coughing and gagging, it was pitiful, and they were crying with the smoke, the smoke made everybody cry, there was so much smoke, and I tried to get to my sister but the flames caught on my hair, and I was getting burned, and I had to go back, so I went back to that door Mr. Jacobs had unlocked, and he was gone, there was nobody else near me now and there was nothing behind me but flames, like a wall of fire, and I went through, and I fell down, but then I got up and I saw that you couldn't go down the stairs with the fire so I went up the stairs to the tenth floor and there was nobody there, they had all saved themselves already.

It was full of smoke but I saw a ladder that was there, and it was going up to an opening in the ceiling and I went up that ladder to the roof, and there were firemen on the roof and when they saw me one of them said, "Here comes another one, must be the last one," and then they grabbed me and shouted at me I had to crawl across a ladder over a big gap to a building on the Waverly Place side and they helped me climb up onto the ladder and I did this somehow with my dress burned and my hands burned, and I had broken ribs, it turns out, but I don't know how that happened in the commotion, and I kept my eyes closed, and it was like another nightmare inside this nightmare, but I did it, and there were some students who helped me over the wall, and then they helped me stand up, and then I walked down the ten flights of stairs to the ground floor of that empty building, and I was by myself and it was like everything was normal and quiet for a minute. But then I went out on the street and a policeman ordered me across the street, like I was just a busybody, because there were bodies falling everywhere and he said I could be killed.

So I crossed the street, and there were all these people looking up and so I looked up, and what I saw was so terrible, the girls jumping, jumping from so high up, they weren't like people, it was like watching insects or animals do something they have to do because they can't think for themselves, this one girl jumped and she tried to keep herself straight, I could see her trying to stay in a line, moving her arms like she thought she could just fall straight and land on her feet and be fine, but she died. Some of the girls were still on fire, lying there on the sidewalk, and the firemen turned the hoses on the bodies to put out the fires, and then one girl jumped and her skirt caught on the sign pole sticking out from the fourth-floor business, it was Blum, they had trimmings and notions, and she hung there screaming, and she was burning up, and then her skirt burned away and dropped her from that sign pole and she fell on the sidewalk, and she was still burning, and the sound was so terrible when she fell, like a bag of wet laundry falling. Some people on the street, they said afterwards, thought they were throwing out the goods to save them, in bundles, when they saw the falling girls, but it wasn't bundles of goods falling and making that terrible sound.

So then I walked to the corner where I could see the sidewalk on the Washington Place side because I was looking everywhere for my sister, where she would have fallen, and there were bodies everywhere and I was looking at them to see her but I didn't see her. I saw so many girls I knew in the street like that, and some of the men, the machinists, the cutters from over by the window where the flames came in. Some of the girls I knew only a few days but others I knew for a while and it was such a big shock, one would be burned black like a cinder but I would know the boots or the dress, and then another would be perfect and still beautiful except dead from the fall.

There were ladders for the firemen, but they didn't go high enough so they were useless, and there were firemen with another useless thing, a big net they were holding in the middle of Greene Street, and next I saw three girls at once, these girls were jumping into it holding hands, but they went right through this foolish net feet first, all together like that, and they hit the pavement and the force of the falling girls flipped all the firemen right into the net on top of the dead girls, it was just craziness — and then everyone was shouting and pointing and I looked up and I saw Sam, my fiancé, in the window, it was all broken, there was nothing left of the window, just the big opening, and he was helping girls. He was still alive but I didn't see my sister.

I had to sit down on the curb, I was so weak, and there was blood running past me over my shoes, it was water from the fire hoses mixed with blood, it was like a river of blood running past me, it was so terrible, and I just sat there letting it run over my shoes and I couldn't even open my mouth anymore like I forgot how to talk English and I just watched. Everywhere on the street there was money. Coins from everyone's pockets, because it was payday and so in their pockets and their stockings they had their money, and it fell out from the pay packets or wherever they were carrying it, and it was all over the street. They told us before we came here, in America the streets are paved with gold, and this day it was true, but so terrible, to see this money in the gutter. For what did they work so hard, but to have this money?

There were three girls Sam helped to step up onto the sill, one at a time, it was like slow motion suddenly even though it was all in a minute, and it was very narrow, not such an easy place to stand, and you could see there was hardly any window ledge, and there were flames behind them shooting out of the window, and he helped each one of them get up to the sill, he would give her a hand and help her to stand up straight and calm and steady and then he would let go each one of them, and each girl would just fall away and then the next girl would come in her place, and they were just falling out that window, one after the other, with Sam to help them, three times he did this, and then I looked at the window again and what did I see but Sam, he was a good man, such a decent man, and there was my sister standing beside him. And he helped her up and then she waited for him and he got up onto the ledge too, and he took her arms and he put them around his neck like to hold on in the ocean, and he put his arms around my sister, and they kissed each other, and then together they jumped.

That's it. I have said all I remember about that terrible day until the next thing I know, when I am waking up in the hospital with the pain and there are all the clean white sheets on me, and the doctors and the nurses are telling me how lucky I am to be alive, how lucky it is that my baby is safe inside of me, and also they are telling me what I already know, about Sam, and about my sister, that he is dead and that my sister Pauline is dead, and I am alone.

— Transcribed recollections of
Esther Gottesfeld, from
*Remembering the Triangle Factory
Fire Fifty Years Later,*

28

March 25, 1961, commemorative
booklet published
by the ILGWU, New York City

Two

George Botkin didn't answer his telephone. When he was working, which was most of his waking hours, he turned on his answering machine (the kind that was so old it used those tiny tape cassettes). Sometimes he was inspired by the mechanical noises of the answering machine. The outgoing message was an unfinished waltz melody of his own, and though he had the ringer and the sound switched off so he couldn't hear the outgoing recording or the voice messages people left, if he wasn't working out something new at the piano or listening to a playback or a CD or some strange recording of something that interested him, or solving a counterpoint problem by tapping out the interlocking rhythms on his practice pad or on one of his African drums, then it would be quiet enough for him to hear the tiny sounds of the answering machine taking a call.

Just hearing the machine clicking and whirring made George think of his unfinished composition being played, which often inspired him to turn from the work at hand, no matter how complex and involved, and jot a few more notes toward the completion of the waltz on the crumpled, coffee-stained sheet of music paper assigned to this piece. Somehow, that perverse interruption — the urge to add a little more to the tune just because he knew that the waltz melody was being played, though he couldn't hear it — didn't distract him the way that speaking to another person, dealing with another person's voice and mood and wants, even for the briefest moment, could ruin the entire day, composition-wise.

So perhaps every time Rebecca called — and this was the sixth attempt in three hours — it had provided a little creative tickle. If he was there. But she was eager to hear his voice right now, not the damned waltz. She needed to tell him about her grandmother, and she wanted George to say something surprising yet soothing, the way he usually did when she was upset about something. The first notes of the musical signature that heralded his message began yet again, rendered in a pretty little flute solo. (George claimed he couldn't really play the flute and was only fooling around with the flute he had found sticking out of a trash barrel on Horatio Street one night, and his fingering was just whatever clumsy, made-up guess at the right placement had come into his head, though his playing sounded very sweet and pure to Rebecca's untrained ear.) Though she usually liked to hear it, Rebecca hung up rather than leave yet another message. She had been trying him all afternoon, and now it was almost evening. The nursing home had called about her grandmother at three, and she desperately needed to talk with George — her lover of twenty years, her partner, the man in her life, her mate, her consort, her significant other, whatever the hell you want to call what he was to her — both for real comfort, just for the steadying sound of his voice, and for the practical necessities of planning.

Answer the phone, just this once! Damn his contrarian, geniusy refusal to have a cell phone like everyone else. Damn his unwillingness to look at e-mail more than once a week. Damn his lack of concern about his useless, broken fax machine. Answer, please, answer.

Rebecca was usually tolerant and understanding of George's eccentricities, as was he when it came to her very different (and admittedly far less imposing) quirks. Right now she wished he lived in a somewhat more predictable fashion. She wished she could depend on him a bit more. She wished, in other words, that he were just a little bit more of a grown-up. It's not that he was unreliable or untrustworthy. He was possibly the most honest and straightforward person she had ever met, in fact. It was just that he could be anywhere, doing anything on this beautiful September afternoon, inevitably in pursuit of some new material for his music. Maybe he *was* sitting right there working beside the answering machine, inspired by the clicking, like an autistic child mesmerized by a dust mote, making more of the exquisite music that had won prizes and made his a household name.

Genius flowed from George Botkin, or rather, everything in the world somehow flowed *through* him and came out transmuted into sounds that were unlike any music, unlike anything anyone had ever made on earth before. If what Flaubert said is true — that "language is like a cracked kettle on which we hammer crude rhythms to make bears dance, while we long with our music to move the stars," then George

Botkin's music was what all of humankind longed for with every spoken word.

Why did his music stir people so powerfully? Why did it have such universal appeal? What made it work? Everyone recognized that George Botkin's music was overwhelmingly beautiful, but *why?* Many critics and scholars had pondered these questions for years. Writing in the *Times,* a certain critic famously began his review of the historic debut of the *Protein Rhapsodies* with the words, "Why do we admire a sunrise? Is truth beauty, or beauty truth?" George Botkin's music was called, by various critics at various times, lucid, transparent, muscular, vividly distinct, confoundingly jazzy yet classical, strangely intimate, deceptively accessible, formally brilliant, outrageously melodic, and profoundly odious (a minority viewpoint).

There was something childlike in George Botkin's energy and creativity. Rebecca secretly thought he resembled his music, the energy and charm of it. Because George was confident and believed in his talent, there were people who thought him self-centered. But this wasn't really fair. He simply knew what he could do.

George played the piano very naturally

starting at the age of five. His musical memory was impressive, and from a young age he could reproduce almost anything he heard — to the consternation of his parents, who weren't always entertained by his renderings on the piano of the NBC chime, a truck downshifting on a hill, the piercing laugh of the next-door neighbor, or gulls screaming at a garbage dump. His strange, perpetual singing made him an agreeable if noisy child. As he grew older, he was disappointed that other children didn't have their own songs, though they were often happy to copy his. On the first day of school, proud to be a first grader at last, George spontaneously sang a joyful song about the smell of new chalk, to everyone's laughter. He learned to keep his music private for several years after that. Smells and colors, street lights, words, clouds, the thud of the newspaper hitting the front porch, the lumpy seams in the toes of his socks, everything and anything always stirred musical patterns in his mind. How sad that most other people didn't seem to have their own music at all.

By high school George had discovered that he could teach himself to play almost any instrument with surprising ease. His abilities made him popular at parties, where he would improvise witty musical caricatures of his friends on any instrument at hand. (*Music & Art Botkin,* a casual, top-of-the-piano recording of a dozen musical impressions of faculty at a performance at the Thanksgiving variety show, when George was a junior at the High School of Music and Art, would circulate years later and become a collector's item.)

The origins of George's mature work could be traced back to his first student compositions at Yale in the 1970s. He was torn between his two possible majors, chemistry and music, though not terribly dedicated to doing the actual work to acquire the necessary credits toward a degree in either subject from semester to semester. By the end of spring term in his sophomore year, when he had mostly majored in smoking pot and dabbling in other recreational drugs — as he would freely admit whenever interviewed or asked for public reflections on his life and work — he was also in desperate need of a new strategy to avoid failing every class. George began orchestrating amino-acid sequences of polypeptides, composing his first musical work that drew so much attention, his now-famous *Protein Rhapsodies.*

The saving grace in George's otherwise

carelessly completed chemistry labs had always been his uncanny ability to see connections and anticipate consequences that eluded the average chem lab student. He was like a natural chess player who can take one look at a board and see all the moves and consequent moves at a glance.

George recognized that his were unusual abilities — to see and hear patterns, to perceive the samenesses and the differences that other people didn't notice, and to transpose those patterns and contrasts into musical forms. His lifelong experience of making mental music to match the way the wind blew, the way a dog barked, the way the light flickered through the trees as his mother drove him to school — as far as he was concerned, this music in his head had always been part of the simple pleasure of being alive, but it had never before occurred to him to write it down for any purpose, let alone make it the central element in his life's work.

To George, now driven by the alchemy of panic and fatigue, those amino-acid sequences had suddenly been apparent as pure melody. The equations and formulas resonated on the page as entire nuanced musical figures, the way a cloud formation can suddenly reveal itself to be the familiar form of a man's hand. He could hear them, he could feel them — and so he seized them whole, broke them into manageable parts, and reassembled them on a musical staff. The *Protein Rhapsodies* flowed onto the page so easily and completely that when he was done, George worried momentarily that he had simply transcribed some existing work of music from the recesses of his memory and superimposed it on the patterning of the amino-acid sequences that had beckoned him. It had been a very long time since he had permitted himself to be overtaken by the music. Writing it down, embellishing and deepening the patterns, George allowed himself to make it into something big and powerful.

He played the *Rhapsodies* for his mentor in the department, the pianist Russell Moore, who was floored by the authority, the subtle optimistic clarity, and the uncloying melodic inventiveness of his music. Moore assured him that what he had composed was something entirely new and worthy, a work with the gravity and proportion of Bach's First Prelude, but it wasn't an imitation of Bach at all, that wasn't what he meant, he assured George. The only thing it sounded like was Botkin.

George met Rebecca in 1981, the same year his *Sea Change Symphony* — based on arrangements of the sonification of tide tables around the world — won the Rosanoff Award at the international competition in Prague. By the time George and Rebecca had fallen in love and joined their lives together in the complex arrangement that worked for them and mystified everyone else, George had discovered that Rebecca's knowledge of human genetics (she was at that time writing her Yale dissertation for her public health degree) could provide a lifetime's worth of inspiration. The first weekend he spent with her in New Haven, George had been so fascinated by the beautiful forms of the graphs in her doctoral thesis, concerning a study she was running on heritable predictors of high-risk pregnancies and labor outcomes, that he asked for copies to take back to New York, where he spent most of the summer writing a string quartet based on her charts of the progression of natural labor contractions as compared with the artificial contractions of labor induced by the drug Pitocin.

The first time *Parturition* was played publicly, by the Tokyo String Quartet at the summer music festival in Norfolk, Connecticut, in 1982 (the performance having come about because it had won a minor composition prize), a pregnant woman went into labor in the fourth row when her water broke during the final "Crowning" movement — and she delivered a healthy baby just a few hours later at a hospital in Torrington. When, at a subsequent performance, another pregnant woman left in early labor during the "Pitocin" movement and gave birth the next day, the coincidence was played up by a feature writer in the local newspaper. Then the story was picked up by several television stations for the evening news, and it ran on the national newswires. Both women had been past their due dates, George had pointed out to the reporters who telephoned him for comment, so it wasn't exactly a miracle that either one of them had given birth, but that sort of attitude wasn't newsworthy, and the coverage continued to emphasize the extraordinary effect of his music.

By the last night of the Tokyo's eight scheduled performances that summer, looking out at perhaps ten hugely pregnant women scattered through the audience in the big, resonant barn, all fanning themselves with programs before the performance was to begin, the members of the quartet realized they had to change their program to include one final impromptu performance of *Parturition* instead of the scheduled Fourteenth Beethoven Quartet in C-sharp Minor. Two women in that audience (both past their due date and one actually in early labor before the performance began) gave birth within hours of the concert.

Once the piece was recorded, first by the Tokyo but subsequently by several different string quartets, so many women claimed that they had gone into labor soon after listening to the music that many midwives and obstetricians routinely began to provide their patients with a *Parturition* CD at thirty-eight weeks, once the cervix was noted as ripe and beginning to soften. *Parturition* stories ran in newspapers and magazines, and there were endless interviews on television and radio, throughout which George kept pointing out that all pregnant women go into labor and have babies after forty weeks of pregnancy, regardless of the music they hear, although he certainly didn't mind if these women had found his music helpful to the process. His modesty and logical insistence on crediting the ordinary course of human biology and not the music only enhanced the legend.

Even before the success of the quartet, George had continued to explore all sorts of formations found in nature for their musical possibilities, especially genetic codes and cell structures. Now the public eagerly waited for the next composition, and the next, which was a new kind of pressure, but it meant that whenever he deemed any composition finished, there were performers waiting to play and record the work. The danger, had he been temperamentally different, was that it could have meant a constant temptation to declare a piece finished far too soon, but George wasn't constitutionally capable of persuading himself that a work was finished when it had reached a difficult stage of development or when he was bored and no longer sufficiently challenged by its newness.

Sometimes his work was only a playful riff, as when Rebecca's naturopath friend Sharon gave George some echinacea capsules to palliate symptoms of a terrible, plaguing head cold, and he was inspired to arrange a soothing and strangely familiar (the way a half-remembered dream has strangely familiar elements that slip just beyond the reach of your conscious mind) flute sequence based on the amino acids of echinacea. The James Galway recording of *Echinacea Serenade* soon became standard background music in thousands of holistic healing centers and treatment rooms of naturopaths, acupuncturists, and chiropractors around the world. It wasn't George's best work, but it was simple, people just loved it, and it became the Botkin standard, the opening diminished-fifth interval making it instantly recognizable in two notes.

In the winter of 1986 George's best friend, Stark Whitely, a jazz musician with many appealing obsessions (among them Scottish history, presidential kitsch, repudiated members of the royal families of Europe, Jayne Mansfield, Krazy Kat, chutneys of the world, and Bix Beiderbecke) whom he first encountered in a tedious modern German history class during their sophomore year at Yale, told George and Rebecca that he had lymphosarcoma and had been given a pretty grim prognosis.

"Ironic, isn't it?" Stark said. The three of them were at Pepe's Pizza in New Haven, a favorite, worth the chronic lines out the door. Stark was a large man, and though he was big and soft and had all sorts of unhealthy habits, he was robust in his own foppish way, and it seemed ludicrous to think that he had a disease that could kill him. "I thought I dodged a bullet when I tested negative after Steve got sick four years ago," he said. "When every time I would see a different friend with new KS lesions, I would feel so lucky. And now I've got this. Everyone will assume I died of AIDS, won't they?"

They assured him that he wouldn't die, but neither George nor Rebecca could look him in the eye when they said it. They had both noticed how pale and unwell he already seemed, and they knew that he noticed their discomfort, because he changed the subject gracefully a moment later. The evening was long and strained and sad. They all tried to enjoy their white clam pizza, and Rebecca labored with an almost frantic cheer to introduce things to talk about — politics, gossip, the movies, the wonderful performance a few days before by their mutual friend Denise the mezzo-soprano as Dorabella in an otherwise ragged Opera Studio production of *Così fan tutte* — anything but what they were all thinking about.

For most of that February, George experimented secretly with a dark piano sonata based on the polypeptides of lymphosarcoma, though he was meant to be working on a lucrative commission that didn't interest him very much, a jazzy theme for a Japanese car commercial starring Tom Selleck. The work on the sonata drove him into a chronic unpleasant mood, and both he and Rebecca were plagued by nasty sinus headaches that wouldn't quit. Rebecca's headache was so severe and unrelenting that she missed entire days of work, which was terrible because at that point she had just started her new job in clinical genetics at the Yale School of Medicine.

They canceled a long-planned five-year anniversary weekend on St. Lucia, though it would have done them a lot of good. They fought horribly for the first time, over inconsequential things, the details of which they could hardly recall a day later, though the bitter mood lingered on and on like a bad smell. Their sex grew infrequent and angry. In March they came close to breaking up, and they might have done so if it wasn't for George's attachment to Rebecca's grandmother. Sitting with her one dark afternoon, he grew ashamed, imagining her response if he actually put in motion the destruction of the connection to Rebecca he thought, until that moment, he had wanted. Stark grew sicker; no treatment worked. It was painful to see him, painful to avoid seeing him. Rebecca knew that visits to Stark, now in a hospice outside New Haven, were the only reason George came up from New York at all.

Finally, in April, when Rebecca, ordinarily a very principled respecter of privacy, felt an uncharacteristic urge to snoop around George's desk one unhappy gray New York morning while he was in the shower, her first glimpse of the hieroglyphics headed "Lymphosarcoma polypeptides" — scribbled all over with musical notations in George's familiar emphatic scrawl — was all she needed to understand with sudden clarity what George was working on, day in and day out. She made him stop, and she made him put it away unfinished, every scrap of paper with notes for any of it, in any form, and he agreed, reluctantly, recognizing her wisdom through his fury at her prying.

When their headaches vanished and the air in their rooms seemed to brighten by the day, they both recognized the dangerous and powerful possibilities for his gift. "That was such a close call! Now I want you to burn those folders. Every bar of that music. Every note. Seriously. You must use your power only for good from now on," Rebecca admonished.

Stark had taught a jazz theory seminar in

alternate semesters at the Yale School of Music, and when he died, in May — unaware of George's attempt to create a work of music inspired by the insidious disease that killed him — the memorial service, at which only Brahms and some Beatles songs were played, by an ensemble of Stark's students, was held in Battell Chapel, on the Yale campus.

At the sad little reception afterward, across Elm Street in the Calhoun College master's house, where Stark had been a fellow, George sat down at the piano and idly, unthinkingly, began to play through a few doomy bars of the unfinished sonata. The effect was instantaneous. A dropped glass shattered. Everyone stopped eating, cookies suspended halfway to open mouths, teacups poised. Conversation faltered and died out. George, oblivious, stopped and started again. As he played, a palpable gloom rolled out like a fog, curling into corners. Everyone felt it. The department registrar began to sob quietly as she swept up the pieces of broken glass. Students began edging toward the doors. The Calhoun master's wife, an ordinarily demure and proper writing tutor from Alabama, could be heard distinctly to say, "What the fuck just happened?"

Rebecca abandoned a conversation with

Andy Manzer (an old boyfriend of Stark's she had heard about but had never met before, who had become something of a success as a casting director in New York these days), whose face had contorted in sudden grief as the clammy black notes of George's music rained down on them, to rush over and drag George away from the piano.

"What were you thinking?" she hissed at him, pulling him off the bench and slamming down the keyboard cover, as if sealing the piano would help contain the toxic music from seeping further into the atmosphere. They made their way toward some of the remaining students predictably clustered near the tea and cookies in the dining room.

"Sorry. I just wasn't thinking. It came to mind."

"No kidding you weren't thinking. How could you do that?"

"Sorry."

They looked at each other for a long moment, and Rebecca felt her tears welling up yet again as another wave of grief swept over her. George put his arm around her while reaching with his other hand for an oatmeal cookie. The feeling of the gathering brightened again. He took a big bite of his cookie, like a little boy; someone laughed out in the kitchen, and ordinary conversation slowly resumed. Rebecca looked around for Andy, but he was occupied now, chatting with animation among some eager theater studies students. Stark had admired a great deal about Andy, she recalled, including his ability to seduce sexually confused students of either gender (which tended to leave them only more confused). She wondered which one he would choose.

Stark's mother was in conversation with Oswald Simon, a tedious pianist and professor at the School of Music, who was just finishing his declaration of deep appreciation for Stark. In fact, Rebecca knew Ozzie had campaigned vigorously against the department decision to reappoint Stark for another term, and had spread some AIDS rumors. (He himself was deeply in the closet, waxed mustache and all.) They moved across the room to her side, and Edwina Whitely reached out and took George's arm, to reserve him for the next conversation momentarily, without turning away from Ozzie, whose absurd shoulder-length white hair Rebecca studied while recalling Stark's description of the last Oswald Simon piano recital in Sprague Hall.

"The only way the audience could really

understand the feeling of the music was by watching his dramatic head tosses and all the body English, all the swooning and writhing and flinging about of wrists," Stark had reported. "The playing itself had absolutely no feeling, no nuance at all, but most audiences don't realize they're not reacting to the actual sound when they're watching someone like this onstage. I told my students to observe this, to watch for all his ridiculous empty gestures, and they were mightily entertained."

Her conversation with Ozzie Simon concluded at last, Edwina Whitely thanked him politely and turned her attention to George and Rebecca, a tiny, Stark-like ironic smile playing at her lips. She told George how much Stark had truly admired his work, and George explained that he had been trying to write something celebratory to honor her son's life, because the unfinished work he had just been playing was too dark and too much about her son's death. She cried unabashedly when he said this, without even attempting to dab her streaming tears with her napkin. Rebecca understood in a new way that the kindest thing you can do for someone in mourning might just be to witness the tears, simply to accept the person's grief any way it comes. Sometimes she rushed people out of her office on the grounds of efficiency and consideration for the next patient who was being kept waiting, when she knew it was really because sometimes she simply needed to shut down the flood of grief and misery that punctuated her working days.

When they took her to the train, as she got out of the car, Edwina said something about wanting to send George a personal object of Stark's, for which he thanked her. Back in Rebecca's Willow Street apartment, there was nothing more to do or say about Stark Whitely on this day. He was truly gone. George and Rebecca got into their bed and clung together under the quilt, crying, their arms wrapped around each other. They became still at this darkening blue hour, listening to the odd yet comfortingly familiar noise of the upstairs neighbor, Al, a solitary copy editor at the *New Haven Register*, who seemed to spend his waking hours patrolling the perimeters of his apartment in hard shoes, with pauses only for the mysterious dragging sound that suggested the regular movement of large steamer trunks across bare wooden floors. They dozed briefly, not speaking, and then their embrace segued from a simple and comforting holding to a marvelously charged and erotic connection, with every touch a provocative invitation to touch more purposefully, more teasingly, more daringly. They began to make the particular kind of urgent love ignited by grief.

Moving over her, George looked down into Rebecca's eyes and saw his own sadness. They rocked together, slowly, with the languid luxury and privilege reserved only for couples who know each other this thoroughly and profoundly.

"Larghissimo," Rebecca whispered. They moved in a kind of deliberate and inevitable harmony, their two-part invention as new and familiar as always. They came together, and then subsided into a deep doze for a few moments, only to be woken by the upstairs neighbor's renewed dragging sounds.

"We're alive," Rebecca murmured. "And I'm starved."

"It's the best thing to do after a funeral," George whispered into her neck.

A few weeks later, when Rebecca and George had both pretty much forgotten about Edwina Whitely's promise, Stark's alto saxophone arrived by UPS. George had at that moment become preoccupied with a little lullaby inspired by the molecular structure of valerian (though he would soon abandon it in favor of a paradoxically jazzier yet effectively soporific lullaby based on the patterns of certain neurotransmitters and endorphin receptors). The saxophone sat untouched in a corner of George's loft for a couple of months, and then Rebecca had a thought.

Without mentioning it to George, she took the mouthpiece away with her one Sunday evening, carefully bagged. She brought it to work the next morning and asked one of the lab techs who liked her if he could get a DNA sample good enough for a complete off-the-books profile, using the new PCR amplification technique. "What do you think this is, toots, a private forensics lab?" he had complained, but in fact he could and he did.

When Rebecca arrived at George's loft the next Friday evening, she presented him with the printout of Stark Whitely's DNA profile. George hardly ate or slept for the next forty-eight hours, their weekend plans abandoned, until he had finished the outline of the opening for *Requiem for Stark Whitely,* his famous first individual portrait composition and the only one composed for piano, alto saxophone, and cello. He completed it within the month, and it was performed in a student workshop at Yale that autumn by three of the students who had played at Stark's memorial service.

Fortuitously, Ornette Coleman was visiting on campus and sat in on the workshop. His performance of the Requiem at a jazz festival in Montreal the following spring was the public debut of the piece, and then came the Miles Davis recording that made it truly famous the following year.

To hear that recording is to feel that you knew Stark Whitely and you knew the way he played his saxophone — the clever quote from his quirky rendition of "Satin Doll" in the opening bars made sure of that — but beyond that, well beyond that, you knew the resonance and timbre of Stark Whitely's voice, the force of his handshake, the smell of his hair after a day at the beach; you knew how he liked to drown his pancakes in maple syrup and that he was partial to nasty boys with tattoos who took his money, as well as to rebellious debutantes who would nevertheless end up just like their mothers; and you knew the sound of his footsteps on the stairs when he was growing up in a small town in North Carolina. To hear this music was to know that you missed, you desperately, deeply missed with all your heart, the way he held his knife, his love of P. G. Wodehouse and Thomas Hardy, his fondness for bow ties, the way he danced 'til three — and to hear this music was to know that you loved this man, you really loved him (and you loved George Botkin too, for writing the piece), and you would mourn Stark Whitely every day for the rest of your life. George Botkin won a MacArthur the following year.

Between patients, Rebecca tried George's phone yet again. She found the waltz soothing, but she had to take another call before it reached its witty conclusion, which landed on the identical B-flat tone of the answering machine's beep. She didn't need to leave another message anyway.

Countless other musicians had, of course, by then begun composing a formless kind of music based on DNA and other natural structures in hopes of imitating his success, if not the ingenuity of his music, but most of what they produced was devoid of the innate rightness in George's music, the quality that Ned Rorem called "Botkin's trademark surprising inevitability." A public willing to be entertained rather than moved didn't necessarily take the trouble to distinguish the synthetic work of the followers from a true Botkin composition, and an entire industry of nature-inspired musical composition soon sprang up, for which George was unfairly held responsible. From Gershwin to Copland to Ives to Botkin, wasn't this imitation — and the consequent vague dilution of the public's appreciation for the original work — the fate of genius, an inevitable aspect of the marketplace of the great American musical tradition?

At best, the work of imitators sounded exactly like thin, second-rate Botkin. At worst — and the electronic people were the worst of the worst, George thought, obsessed and seduced as they were by the brilliance of the technology and the cleverness of whatever robotic system they had devised to transpose data into sound waves, rather than being guided by any deep sense of actual musicality — the music of the imitators was the sound track for fever dreams, music written by those who had only ever heard rumors of music. The music produced by all the Botkin imitators is the formless, tuneless, relentless music you will not be surprised to hear piped in just before your plane crashes.

George's compositions in recent years were built around his invention of a simple universal amino-acid musical scale with which any DNA could be expressed musically.

"If I had this system ten years ago," he had complained not long before to Rebecca, "I could have written Stark's Requiem in an hour."

"So what? I know a thoracic surgeon who can repair a torn aorta in ten minutes, while complaining about the expensive repairs on his Saab and what's wrong with his second serve, but it took him decades to get there. Anyway, you wouldn't have developed this system if you hadn't written Stark's Requiem first," she pointed out with her usual logic. "And the techniques for mapping DNA hardly existed. You know that." He knew that was right. He knew he couldn't have written the Requiem even two years before he wrote it, whether or not he had the DNA patterns to work from. From that first inspired leap of faith when he wrote down the *Protein Rhapsodies,* George had always found that the time wasn't ripe for certain elements in his work — until suddenly it was.

At age fifty-one George Botkin had at last learned to trust the convoluted and often frustrating process of finding his way toward the next big idea. It had been six years since he had completed devising an eccentric ensemble for these new DNA compositions, using vibraphone, harp, flute, guitar, piano, and oboe to represent the different tones of the peptide bonds. It was a system that seemed to offer endless and beautiful possibilities. Having the peptide bonds represented by these specific instruments was so clear and obvious, inevitable to his ear now, yet it had taken him years to find this simple format.

George believed that his most original work lay in the future. He felt as if his own sensibility, that deep feeling of musical connection to the damndest things — which some people who had investigated his work called synesthesia — was growing in intensity, ripening and mellowing and expanding all the time. One organizing system that fascinated him, and he knew it would lead to at least one ambitious symphonic composition, was the way Fibonacci numbers and their forms are found in nature (although he was worried that art inspired by Fibonacci numbers had suddenly started appearing everywhere, a great deal of it fuzzy-headed and second-rate, which made him mistrust his own attraction to the form). There was also something that clicked about the proportions of the golden rectangle that called out to him, maybe just for one concise little concerto. Beyond that, in another year or two, once his understanding had deepened, the most exciting thing of all lay on the horizon — the infinity of possibilities in fractals and Sierpinski triangles. In a deeply significant way, as a competitive runner might look years ahead to an Olympic race, he felt that he was training, saving up, building up his abilities for this challenge.

Sierpinski triangles appealed to George especially because there was something exquisite about them and also because hardly anyone outside mathematics was messing around with them, as far as he could tell. They weren't all the rage like Fibonacci numbers. Only one or two people seemed to be applying these calculations to music, and those individuals tended to be heavily into theory rather than composition. Did anyone care what music actually sounded like anymore? So much post-tonal composition. Too much.

And then there were the aleatory composers. George didn't understand what drew them to music at all. They wrote a kind of music by a process of random selection, either by the composer or by the performer at the moment of performance. Every decision, including key, dynamics, tempo, sometimes even the order of the movements, depended on the outcome of thrown dice, drawn playing cards, or computed mathematical laws of chance. Some people called this "chance music" and compared some of George's work to the best of the Boulez aleatory creations. But this was wrong — George left nothing to chance. And he found most of these contemporary compositions ugly and misshapen, devoid of musicality, music only by definition. Yet he was slotted into this category of new music just about every time his work was reviewed. It was rather discouraging to be so misunderstood; it was never a good sign when references to aleatory music crept into critical writing about a Botkin composition, as this tended to reveal the mind of an unpassionate critic whose head was too easily turned by theory, no matter what the music actually sounded like.

Which was not to say that theory didn't interest George. Some new form or system would inevitably provide the starting point for something rich and strange. He was always searching for the next grain of sand to grow a pearl. Though found mostly in nature, once you know where to look for the forms (most ferns, the subcontinent of India), one way to locate a Sierpinski triangle is to play the "chaos game." In this game, any three points are chosen on a plane. The points don't have to be equidistant. Any point x may be chosen in the same plane, inside or outside the figure. With the roll of a die, a point is made halfway between x and the vertex indicated by the die. This process is repeated endlessly, each time from the most recent point. Although you might expect, after a while, to see a randomly dispersed field of points, what you see instead, inevitably, is a Sierpinski triangle.

George had spent months working this out on the floor of his studio with some guitar picks and lengths of piano wire, and the marks were still there in the floorboards as reminders, but whatever the form could mean in his work, he didn't feel ready to take it on just yet, so he had put it all away carefully to mature, like a potentially great wine vintage.

Fractals and Sierpinski triangles had been of considerable interest to George when he was an undergraduate, experimenting with repetitive downward arpeggiated three-note chords to create a series of scherzi with both ternary and binary forms. He had discovered, dwelling as he did for those years at the intersection of science and music, that iterating binaries are common in dances, from the Renaissance all the way through the Classical period, when iterating ternaries were dominant up through the Romantic period. In his junior year he had written a very long term paper about Sierpinskis and fractals, accompanied by a tape of exemplar piano sketches (recorded on a mediocre tape player that belonged to a strangely hirsute cellist from Indonesia named Marianthe whom he had met at the snack machines in the hideous "machine city" dungeon beside Cross Campus Library, in one long, speed-fueled all-nighter in a practice room in Hendrie Hall). The paper had squeaked him through to a passing grade for an advanced geometry course he had otherwise neglected. George was fairly certain that his professor hadn't grasped the meaning of his paper entirely, and might not have even played the tape all the way through.

Although it had been a while since George had thought about fractal forms or Sierpinski triangles in a very focused way, the allure of fractal forms had returned one muggy night just this past August, when he was too hot to sleep and had been up listening to some vinyl from the sixties, Alfred Brendel's Vox cycle of Beethoven sonatas.

He had suddenly heard the form, all at once, with astonishing new clarity, in the third movement of Beethoven's Piano Sonata no. 15 in D Major, op. 28.

George hoped his life would be long enough to do all the work he carried around in his head in tiny, ungerminated forms that he could sometimes feel just floating there in his frontal cortex like some minuscule yet vast private reference library of ideas. He wasn't afraid of dying so much as he was afraid of not living long enough. He thought about this all the time because Huntington's disease ran in his family and the threat of the disease hung over him. George's mother died of Huntington's when he was sixteen and a senior in high school. It was the last year he lived at home. There had been a dark decade of struggle and dwindling presence for Martha Botkin, who spent her final four years in a nursing home, imprisoned by this relentless disease. George always felt terrible visiting her and even more terrible not visiting her.

Where had it come from? Her father, George's grandfather Max Jacobson, had, in all likelihood, begun to develop Huntington's symptoms before his death; they would never know for sure, because he died of a heart attack at age fifty-two. But family stories of his rages, his accident proneness, and his rapid decline in ability to manage his shoe store — which had led to rumors of secret drinking in the year before his sudden death in the stockroom of Stride Rite Shoes on Austin Street in Forest Hills — made it a likely supposition. A cousin at the funeral told the family he thought his grandfather, Max's brother Morris, might have had the same illness, whatever it was, though at the time, no doctor had ever put a name to it. He had died in a fire, the family said at his funeral, though since then two different aunts had confided in this cousin that Morris's death had in fact been a suicide.

Whenever George tripped or dropped something or cut himself with a paring knife that skidded off an apple, he was reminded of his mother's early, inexplicable symptoms — she had for years blamed herself for her increasing clumsiness, especially in the kitchen — and he wondered if this was the beginning, if it was all going to start slipping away, quite literally, from that moment on.

Meanwhile, he had far too many commissions hanging over him for his brilliantly economical little musical portraits based on an individual's DNA. It had become a problem. The first one had caught him by surprise, the year after Stark's Requiem was recorded, when Ted Turner had phoned to ask him if he would be willing to compose a Ted Turner concerto.

"I can have my DNA profile delivered to you in an hour," Turner added. "Name your price."

"Um," George had replied, not quite certain that he wasn't the butt of a practical joke that would soon reveal itself.

"For full orchestra," Turner had added. "I loves me some violins."

"A million dollars?" George ventured.

"Done. My lawyers will draw up a contract," Turner had replied.

It was insane. When in 1988 the piece was premiered, ridiculously, in Los Angeles, conducted by James Levine, it was news everywhere. There was a profile in *The New Yorker,* an article in *Vogue,* another in *The New York Times Magazine,* and then there was the famous Letterman appearance, and after that more narcissistic rich people than he knew existed on earth were all clamoring to commission a Botkin musical portrait. Trump, of course. Soros. Various members of the Goulandris family. A lot of absurdly wealthy athletes with absolutely no familiarity with classical forms of music (one seven-foot basketball player referred to having enjoyed the "prinkle-prankle music they played when the little mice ran around" during the vintage Saturday morning cartoons he viewed in his childhood). A Saudi family wanted a symphony representing the DNA of fourteen family members, all of them men, and was willing to pay ten million dollars for it.

After the first two commissions George grew less excited with the work, despite the money, having learned from each one a little more about what he wanted to do next, and having discovered, too, that it was very difficult to compose a portrait of an individual who didn't interest him. (And it was impossible to compose a portrait of someone he disliked, which had made for a very unpleasant exchange with Donald Trump when George returned his check.)

By 1998 George had limited himself to one commission a year, which in itself provided worlds more money than he knew what to do with, so by this time he had endowed fifty generous Stark Whitely scholarship programs at music schools around the world. The waiting list for a George Botkin musical portrait grew longer every year, and as rumors circulated that he would soon stop writing these portraits altogether, rumors also circulated that large sums of money had changed hands in order for certain people to swap places on the waiting list. It was like a huge joke, mostly, though at times George wished he had never taken that first commission from Turner. He had never even gotten to meet Jane.

"You can do occasional business with the devil without selling him your soul," Rebecca would remind him whenever he spoke of ending the commissioned work entirely. She cared more about the money than he did, and she was alarmed when he talked this way.

"Kind of," George would reply.

"It's important to keep expanding the Whitely scholarships, isn't it? You don't have to put your heart and soul into each piece, do you?" Rebecca had asked him the last time they had this conversation. "Can't you just write something that's good enough? They wouldn't know the difference. It's not as if these pieces get a lot of public play. Or you could recycle some of the material from other pieces that didn't work out."

His aggrieved look had been his only reply.

Rebecca made the last two calls necessary

to reorganizing her calendar of Friday appointments in the Clinical Genetics Department. As a counselor, she was good at her job, genuinely compassionate yet sufficiently detached to be able to offer patients the information and guidance for which they came to the Yale School of Medicine, one of the best genetic departments in the country. She was still at her desk at the hospital, though her workday was long over and nobody else in the department remained. She had been able to reach most of her scheduled appointments, or had left messages canceling or reassigning patients, and she had managed to catch up to all of her paperwork as well, so her absence would be less problematic, and then came the weekend. Rebecca worried that she might miss Monday, or Tuesday as well, who could say, but of course she couldn't plan a timetable. Nobody could predict how long it would take for her grandmother to die, or even if her grandmother was actually going to die this time. Nobody could expect Rebecca to know this. She could only deal with a day at a time. If there was no change over the weekend — if Esther had not yet died but seemed to be imminently dying — then she would simply have to call in Monday morning and throw herself at the mercy of Jan, who ran the department scheduling desk.

Rebecca's grandmother, Esther Gottesfeld, had lived for the past twenty years in the West Village Jewish Home, which was not too far from where Esther had lived for forty-five years before that, in a small third-floor walk-up apartment on Bleecker Street. Rebecca had grown up there, after her parents died when she was eight. Esther had managed on her own until she was eighty-six and the stairs had become a serious problem with her arthritic knees, not to mention the crack addicts sleeping in her lobby, though they didn't bother her as much as they concerned Rebecca. ("They're just looking for a warm, safe place, and who isn't?" Esther had shrugged, though even she was not so thrilled about the powerful stench of urine in the corner of the lobby by the mailboxes.)

The Jewish Home was also just a few blocks from George's loft on Tenth Street, so Rebecca wanted to let him know that, unexpectedly for a Thursday, she would be taking the train into the city to spend the night. She hoped he would be free to have dinner with her. She hoped he would be in a mood to go to a restaurant. But if not, not. She knew she wouldn't have to ask him to go with her to Esther's bedside. He adored her grandmother, who adored him back. He had probably seen Esther more recently than had Rebecca, as he often dropped in for a quick visit, which always perked Esther right up.

"A very talented young man," Esther would always boast to the nursing staff and any of her hallway neighbors who happened to be in range when George came to call. He often sang to her — strange, scatty renditions of his works in progress, which she tolerated with a certain amount of interest, or show tunes from the thirties, which made her face light up as she hummed along. In the stale, linoleumed social room down the hall, there was a horribly out-of-tune piano, with a broken sostenuto pedal and several keys missing, like bad teeth, their ivory veneers. The room was used mainly by the bridge and poker crowd, as well as the illicit smokers, residents and staff alike, who congregated by an open window down at one end, and sometimes he played for her there, which always drew a small crowd of residents and staff.

"Talented! Ach, like you wouldn't believe. A Mendelssohn. Like two Mendelssohns."

Rebecca and George had met because of

Esther. It was now five years since George's beloved great-aunt Molly died, just short of her eighty-sixth birthday. A sweet-faced tiny woman who stood well under five feet in her prime, Molly Rozencweig had been resident in the Jewish Home for decades — ever since the death of her equally tiny husband, Sol Rozencweig — plagued all her life by the effects of the polio that had struck the summer she was eight. (Molly got sick first, but her little sister Dora, then six, had come down with a more severe case and died overnight. Their older sister, George's grandmother Eva, had been spared entirely.)

In the nursing home, Molly had lived across the hall from Esther, and the two had formed an immediate alliance (which was needed with the likes of Ruth Sussman and Milton Schernfuss on the floor, each of them having more unfortunate opinions and personal habits than the other, and let's not even begin to consider the undesirable traits possessed by a certain Frieda Rosenbloom, who made everything unpleasant whenever she could, which was why nobody liked her, not even the most patient member of the staff) from the spring day Esther made her reluctant move from her apartment.

Just a few days after Esther was settled in,

Rebecca's visit to her had coincided with George's visit to his aunt Molly. There had been some pleasant chat in the hallway. Two weeks later, when George and Rebecca coincided again, the two old ladies had insisted on being taken out for a walk together, and the four of them had spent most of that afternoon sitting at a table in a neighborhood café, drinking iced tea and talking about Molly's life and Esther's, and the coincidence of Rebecca and George both having a Yale connection. They found out later that Molly and Esther had schemed this match from the first hour Esther had been on the premises, when Molly had espied Rebecca systematically helping her grandmother organize and unpack. They also discovered that Molly and Esther had known each other years earlier, from Workmen's Circle meetings, though Molly was years younger than Esther. "The kid," Esther always called Molly, and she even commissioned Rebecca to get a birthday cake decorated with the words "Happy Birthday to The Kid" for what turned out to be Molly's last birthday, her eighty-fifth, the year Esther herself turned a hundred and one.

Rebecca and George fitted together in an eccentric and harmonious living arrangement that none of their friends, not even their closest friends, really understood, not completely. Their friends also didn't understand why they weren't married, or why they never had children after all these years together. George lived and worked in the West Village. Rebecca lived and worked in New Haven. Each of them had learned to accommodate the other's requirements, whether it was the good bedside reading lights Rebecca brought to George's unaccountably dim bedroom so she could read in bed comfortably, or the enormous drenching showerhead that George spent a strained and exhausting weekend installing at Rebecca's to replace the puny, ineffective dribbler that she had somehow lived with in her Willow Street apartment until then. (They had come to agree, over time, that it wasn't really his fault that the old water pipe cracked as he tightened the fitting, causing a literal cascade of disasters that flooded the apartment below.)

Neither of them would have strayed into a romantic involvement with someone else; no one had been even remotely tempting for either one of them for many years. The time they spent apart wasn't about anything like that at all. Maybe theirs was a slightly more theoretical and intellectual — and less passionate — connection than some couples have, Rebecca sometimes considered when she thought about what she knew of the way other people conducted their lives. But how could it be? Their attachment was fierce, if played out in unconventional counterpoint. It worked for them. She was pretty sure they loved each other at least as much as more traditional couples seemed to, and the years in which they might have had children had passed without her ever wanting a child for more than an hour or two, never long enough to make her even begin to contemplate all the hazards of artificial insemination or adoption, even though every adopted Chinese baby girl she knew (and she knew five) was irresistibly sweet and bright.

In particular, their friends Aaron and Scott from the School of Music had a charming Chinese baby, Mya, who struck Rebecca as a virtual advertisement for adopting Chinese baby girls. The last time they had come for dinner on Willow Street, Rebecca had brought out a Scrabble set to give Mya something to do when she became restless at the table. Not quite two, Mya had set herself a series of tasks, first sorting the letter tiles into matching piles at the four corners of the rug, then arranging the wooden racks into perfect geometric rows, to which she added playing cards sorted by suit, and backgammon pieces, organized in alternating colors, interspersed between the nonsense words she next spelled out with deft precision, using all the Scrabble tiles.

"What's the plan, sweetie?" George asked Mya respectfully, stepping carefully over her little form on his way back from the kitchen, where he had gone to get the second bottle of wine. She had taken some of her stacked letter tiles and was now repositioning them purposefully on the coffee table to spell out more meaningless words. "Are you practicing to be the next Jenny Holzer?"

"She's going to grow up to be a taxonomist," Aaron said proudly.

For every wonderfully healthy baby in her life, Rebecca knew fifty babies with neurodegenerative diseases about which absolutely nothing could be done. Every pregnant woman who had ever sat in her office was carrying a baby with something horribly wrong — spinocerebellar ataxis, trisomy 18, Rett syndrome. Nature usually got it right, Rebecca knew, but those fetuses didn't come her way.

On their second real date that spring night twenty years ago, when they first ventured out unsupervised by the old ladies, they had meant to go to a movie, but instead they spent the entire evening in a little Greek restaurant on MacDougal Street. George had revealed his Huntington's background to Rebecca as he had never revealed it to anyone else in his adult life, and this unexpected and rare show of confidence, in its way a herald of their growing attraction, had been rewarded by a long description from her on the Huntington's study on which, ironically and coincidentally enough, she was working that same summer, conducting clinical interviews for a long-term study of individuals with Huntington's disease in their family. The disease fascinated Rebecca. So much and so little was known about it. She was avid to discuss it with him, as much as he could tell her. She was completely oblivious to what he was feeling until his eyes suddenly brimmed with tears.

"I'm sorry," she said, stricken. "I'm an idiot. A complete idiot."

"No," he said. "I'm an idiot for trying to pretend it's not a possibility in my life even though I think about it every day. Every hour, some days. So, do you want me in your study?"

Rebecca's summer job started right after

that, on the first of June. In that week, every single one of her interviews went badly. She didn't have the right tone. She was too sympathetic, or not sympathetic enough. Too hasty. Too ponderous. Each of her interviewees lived with the possibility of this awful disease and had seen family members sicken and die of it. Many of them walked in the door cheerfully enough, but as the questions progressed, they rapidly revealed themselves to be angry, depressed, sarcastic, bitter, despondent. They needed good friends, and therapy, vacations in the Dordogne — anything but her prying, cold-hearted questions for the damned study.

Although she should have had someone else — her supervisor, anyone else — conduct the interview, given the circumstances, George was Rebecca's final appointment that Friday afternoon of her first week, after his meeting with someone in clinical genetics to review his family history, the results of his blood test, and all that could be surmised about his own situation. She had decided on her lunch break, during which she had taken a depressing walk through the ugliest, most blighted part of New Haven, behind the medical school, that she was going to quit the study, even though she needed the job both for the money and for the experience, which was essential for her graduate studies in public health. It was just too hard, too grim. Now it was almost five o'clock, and the previous two patients had taken extra time to placate and mollify and baby through the survey questions, so he had been kept waiting for nearly an hour. George didn't complain to her as he sat down in her little office, which set him apart from almost everyone else she had seen all week. But she wasn't about to start sleeping with any of the other patients.

"So, I have to ask you these questions like you were just anyone else, okay?" she began apologetically, after taking a moment to glance over the basic profile questionnaire he had filled out in the waiting area, to make sure he hadn't skipped any details. She read the first question off her clipboard, though by now she knew all the study questions by heart.

"Do you understand your health profile? That the blood test revealed that you do carry the genetic marker on chromosome four, but without access to other family members this is an ambiguous result?"

"Yes. No. I mean, yes, I understand what it means, but I have no idea what it signifies," he replied. "Do you?"

Her pen poised over the yes and no boxes

for question 1, Rebecca had glanced up and looked at George. She would always remember this moment, though she couldn't really say why. It seemed all wrong to have him sitting there across from her this way. He was wearing a Bing Crosby kind of cheerful orange and yellow short-sleeved golf shirt (where did he get these shirts?), which gave him the look of someone on vacation.

"Gosh, your job sucks," he added after a moment, watching her pen hover. "You can check yes. Go ahead. For the purposes of the study. Go on. What next? Is this study about my feelings, about my emotional response to the possibility, about my *relationship* with Huntington's, or is it more for tracking everyone in this cohort long term to see who gets sick after all?"

"Both. But you're not really supposed to know that."

"That's what I thought."

"Okay, next question. Did the doctor answer all your questions satisfactorily?"

"Sure, yes."

"Which one?"

"Which one what?"

"Which doctor did you see?"

"Is that the next question?"

"No, I'm just asking."

"Sarah Sunshine, who despite her name

79

was kind of serious and gloomy."

"There's a Benjamin Bunney at the Child Study Center."

"Amazing. What's your next question for me?"

"Do you understand that Huntington's disease is a fatal, autosomal-dominant neurological illness that usually strikes in midlife, causing involuntary movements, severe emotional disturbance, and cognitive decline?"

"That would be a yes. Who wrote these questions, the Marquis de Sade?"

"It gets worse. Now I am supposed to tell you that because it is an autosomal-dominant disorder, each child of a parent with Huntington's disease has a fifty percent risk of inheriting the illness."

"Tell me something new."

"I wish I could. They're working on it. There's going to be a blood test soon."

"Which you'll want me to take."

"Which I hope you will want to take."

"Same diff."

"Not really." Rebecca paused. They eyed each other. "May I go back to the questions?"

"Sure."

"The next one is, Do you have children?"

"Don't you think I would have mentioned

it by now?"

"It's the next question. I'm putting down 'no.' Okay, next. If your answer was no, has your meeting today at which you learned your test results changed your decision about having children in the future?"

"No."

Her pen was poised again. "No?"

"No. I had already decided not to have children a long time ago, before this. Turns out I was right."

She looked up at him then, tears filling her eyes. "I didn't know that. You didn't tell me that. I'm sorry," she whispered. "You shouldn't be here. I shouldn't have made you do this."

"Do the thinking about it or do the study? Or have you be the person to ask me these questions?"

"Oh, both. All three. All of it. You shouldn't be here."

"No. You were right," he said. "I needed to do it. I had been living in fear. Denying the reality while wallowing in it at the same time. It's important. So now I know. Now I know that I don't know. That nobody knows. Which is what I kind of already knew, you know? Seriously."

They sat there together in silence in the little office at the Yale Medical School, just down the hall from the room that housed a horrific collection of deformed fetuses in jars that she had thought to show him, but now wouldn't.

"So, do you want children?" he asked, breaking the silence.

"I don't know. Why? We should finish these. I'm supposed to ask you the questions."

"It's important. The most important thing, really, because I don't ever want to disappoint you."

They didn't talk with their friends about the possibility of Huntington's. It was George's choice, because of the way he had felt in his adolescence that knowledge of his family history set him apart, affected the way people acted. One girl told him flat out that she couldn't see him, because her mother said his family had a disease. An English teacher offered a kind of rapaciously invasive sympathy, as if every kindly inquiry for his mother's condition entitled her to some nugget of private medical information in return. Even more enlightened people than that could be careless with their assumptions about so many things, he had found. It was freeing to meet people who hadn't known him growing up and weren't obsessed with his possible Huntington's cooties every time they saw him trip on a crack in the sidewalk. So the Huntington's possibility was nobody's business.

In 1993, when the Huntington's disease gene had been isolated, it became even clearer just how the deadly booby trap on chromosome four was to blame. Every human being carries two copies of the gene for Huntington's, a segment of DNA that contains a repeating sequence of nucleotides called CAG (cytosine, adenine, and guanine, names Rebecca gave to the three ugly goldfish she won for a dart-game prize at a carnival out in Bethany, where she and George had gone for the afternoon after a trip to George's favorite used bookstore, really tough goldfish who managed to survive for more than a year despite her indifferent care). The number of repeats makes all the difference. People who will develop Huntington's have in at least one of their two Huntington's genes more than forty CAG repeats, an error that geneticists call a genetic stutter. Those with thirty or fewer CAG repeats within the gene will not get Huntington's.

With the test available, there seemed to be no good reason not to have the answer at last. George was tested in the last week of

May. Rebecca went with him for the blood draw. It was a beautiful Thursday afternoon, so exquisite that even gritty New Haven seemed romantic and filled with promise.

The test results came quickly in the middle of the following week, when George was back in New York. His CAG repeat range was thirty-six, in that dreadful range called "indeterminate." He might get Huntington's, and he might not. He might be a carrier, and he might not. He had agreed to find out his fate with a certainty. And now here he was, stranded in the no-man's-land in which he had always dwelled. He would get sick, or he would die without having developed Huntington's, even though he would always feel stalked by it every day of his life.

Over the years, Rebecca had come to feel that some of their friends with children, and they had many, both in New York and in New Haven, were threatened by their apparently voluntary childlessness — as if children were the obligatory glue necessary to hold a couple together after a certain number of years — and in their unlamented failure to bind themselves with babies, they were breaking some unwritten rule. They were simply two very well-matched people who each thrived on being seriously alone when they weren't together, as Rebecca had explained so many times to her friends, some of whom just didn't get it and probably harbored secret certainties that they each had lovers on the side, or that one of them was actually gay, or both of those things.

Rebecca spent many weekends in New York, and George spent a night or two in New Haven in the alternating terms during which he taught a composition seminar at the Yale School of Music. At other times, weeks could pass when they were apart, though they spoke almost every day. Rebecca and George gave each other more space and privacy than most people would admit to wanting or needing. How they lived suited them both perfectly, most of the time, although it wasn't suiting Rebecca at all perfectly at this precise moment.

Rebecca did very much wish for George's presence at this moment so she could tell him the news about her grandmother. Not a stroke or any other event, she had been told very carefully, just a general failure heralded by a rapid shutting down of her kidneys. It was no surprise; Esther Gottesfeld was one hundred and six.

■ ■ ■ ■

"Should I come right now?" Rebecca had asked Clara, the incredibly kind nursing supervisor at the home, with whom she spoke every week. She visited her grandmother every few weeks, though on a couple of recent visits she had found Esther sleeping so peacefully, like a little child, that she hadn't wanted to wake her. Of course it would be Clara who would call her now. They had each of them privately imagined this moment for a long time. Clara had been promoted a few times over the years and no longer changed beds or handled all the sad needs of incontinent patients, but she had been in charge of doling out Esther's medications ever since Rebecca was doing her postdoc, and the staff all knew that Esther was Clara's special pet. Clara assured Rebecca that she didn't think anything would change overnight.

"Miz Gottesfeld is sleeping most of her days now, but you know that's been true since the summer. If you rouse her, she'll still answer you polite enough," Clara said. "You know her way. But she's harder to rouse. Her sleeping is getting deeper and deeper, and she hardly wanted to eat a thing any day this past week, not even her favorites. And she's hardly drinking a thing. You know we won't force her, like we discussed, but if she's not drinking, she's going to go downhill real fast. Her kidneys are all but failed now, and that's going to take her down low pretty quick."

"Did you offer her rice pudding?" Rebecca asked, trying for a moment to make this call into one of the hundreds of insignificant past chats with Clara about her grandmother's daily details, a kind of call they would not have again and both missed already.

"She took a bite and said it had no taste, that it was tray? What's that tray word they all use here? She said it had no flavor without you soak the raisins first, and she would give me her special recipe to tell them down in the kitchen," Clara said with an appreciative laugh.

"Trayfe. Not kosher, unclean."

"Well, she knows we have that rabbi in here all the time for the kitchen. It's a clean kitchen."

"She's just giving you a hard time, Clara."

"Don't I know her by now? But something has changed. It's just her time. I've got a strong feeling about that. I can't say for sure, you know that. I do believe that if you come by first thing in the morning, that's when she has some little bit of strength if it's been a good night, and you wake her, then she'll be very glad you're here, that's when she'll talk to you, and you'll see the change for yourself. She hardly speaks to us most of the time now, unless we really force her to say something. It's just her time's come, that's all. She's going inside herself, and she's just all tired out now, God bless her."

Rebecca had promised Clara she would be there in the morning, speaking in her calm, steady way, switching into the professional reserves she had begun to acquire that first summer with the Huntington's study, the reserves she called upon when it was her obligation to tell a patient, or the parents of a child, or a whole assembled family of two or three generations, about the meaning of the hideous scientific data on her desk, printed out on paper stacked neatly in bland file folders, data that proved that the fetus or the patient or the family members before her (who would soon be snatching tissues from the several boxes artfully deployed on various surfaces around her small office, all the while trying to comprehend that their lives had just changed forever) had really terrible luck, the very worst sort of luck, the bad luck when your genetic dice have come up snake eyes.

The worst of all were the pregnant ones. Turner's, trisomy 18, Klinefelter's. No, the worst were the babies and small children. Tay-Sachs. Cystic fibrosis. Sickle-cell. Niemann-Pick. But the diseases, like Huntington's, that revealed themselves in middle age were horrible in their own ways. There had been a Huntington's case just the day before — a bank vice president in his forties from Guilford, the father of two young children of six and nine. They would have to be tested, when the parents were ready. His wife had cried so hard she had become incoherent, but he had remained dry-eyed while asking methodically for all the statistical data Rebecca could offer concerning their children. There are so many kinds of bad news, and Rebecca's job was to be the bearer of all of it.

She thanked Clara for calling and for taking such good care of Esther, and as she hung up the phone, a repressed sob caught her by surprise, painful and unexpected, a bubble in her chest. She cried briefly before blowing her nose into one of the ever-handy tissues, and then she had tried to phone George.

Now she was trying him for the last time before leaving a message she really hoped he would listen to, that she was on her way into the city. She would go home, pack a few things, and then go to Union Station for the New York–bound train. The first pure notes of the unfinished I Am Not Taking Your Call Right Now Waltz played, and Rebecca listened all the way through, hearing something she had never heard before, a melancholy undercurrent that surely had been there all along.

THREE

George had listened to his messages and was expecting Rebecca when she arrived at his door. He was hovering and impatient by the time he heard her familiar sounds in the hall, and before she could fit her key into the lock, he had the door open. Their hug was almost a collision.

"I had an ear out for your footsteps," he said into her hair after a moment. "You have very distinctive footsteps. You walk in duple rhythm, you know." He drummed the rhythm lightly on her shoulder with one hand to demonstrate.

"Doesn't everyone? Oh god, I'm so glad to see you," she said against his shirt. He was wearing one of his big, crazy Hawaiian print shirts over chinos, with cheap sneakers he bought out of the bins on Fourteenth Street, which made him look like a giant toddler much of the time. George was well over six feet tall, yet he moved with the unconscious gait of a child. This shirt was one she particularly liked, with red and white monkeys and bananas.

"I'm sorry I was 404 all day. I had a great day, actually, very productive, but I feel bad that you wanted to talk to me when you couldn't. You should implant a microchip or something. A LoJack. I am so sorry. I hate the way I am not a grown-up, if it added to your upsetness." He hugged her tightly for a moment and then resumed his syncopation on her back, now double-timing it, adding a complicated counter-rhythm with the other hand between the wings of her shoulder blades, suddenly genuinely fascinated with new possibilities, new inventions. "Beck, you know the wonderful 'Walking the Dog' sequence in *Shall We Dance*?" She nodded as she felt his big hands segue into the pattern of that familiar musical interlude.

He swayed a little, almost dancing with her, as he hummed the opening — "Hmm hm hm hm hmp-hmp" — and then interrupted himself. "You know Gershwin scored that using only six instruments?"

"You tell me that about once a month. We're not *both* senile. You're obsessed. Something about how he wrote it to mock big orchestral flourishes, right? Do I win the car? Or the trip to Hawaii? Or just your voice on my answering machine? But do we have to talk about this right now? May I come in, instead of having this truly fascinating if somewhat familiar conversation in your doorway, where there is a bit of a draft, which doesn't seem to bother you but makes me wonder if someone left the door to the roof open again? Maybe busboys up there on a smoking break, like last month? And do you want to say where you were more specifically? And may I tell you about Esther?" Rebecca asked, disengaging gracefully in order to drag her overnight bag in from the hallway and kick the door shut behind them.

George's loft was the entire top floor of a late-nineteenth-century building that had a mix of apartments and professional spaces in the five floors beneath him. The recalcitrant elevator always alarmed her, so Rebecca was a little breathless from having taken the stairs. The rich, garlicky aroma that had followed her up the stairs emanated from the Italian restaurant on the ground floor. She was hungry, though not enough to want to eat there. It was an old Village fixture, mentioned in memoirs of various Beat poets and New York School painters, but it was no longer very good (if it ever really had been — there was a time when red-checked tablecloths, candles stuck into Chianti bottles, and insouciant waiters with accents were all a restaurant needed to be considered the real thing).

Dubious hygiene standards in the kitchen attracted so many mice that, although George had been sufficiently amused and inspired by the nocturnal sounds of the building's scurrying inhabitants to write a charming little *Scherzo for Mighty Mice* several years back — which had since gained a huge following among music teachers of young children — after too many unamusing rodent-American encounters under his own kitchen sink and on his pantry shelves, George had finally conceded that Rebecca was right, he needed a cat. He had wanted to call the slender orange tiger they picked out at the shelter Milhaud, but Rebecca thought it a laughably pretentious name, despite points for the onomatopoeic element, and after George had rejected Helix the Cat for being completely stupid and pretentious, inexcusable even if Rebecca did work in genetics, they had settled on Joe Green, which suited the dapper little cat perfectly.

"So I spent the day in an amazing laboratory over at NYU," George said, "and I have to tell you about it for about six reasons, one of which will interest you especially. But Beck, first tell me what's up with Esther. After I got your message, I called there while I was waiting for you, thinking I might find you, but all Clara told me was that she was sleeping."

"She's failing. Her time's up," Rebecca said briefly, fighting sudden tears all over again (an intense crying episode on the train had alarmed the businessman next to her; she thought he had gotten off at Westport, but spotting him in the exiting throng when they arrived at Grand Central Station made her realize that he had simply changed seats in Westport to get away from her). She dropped into the corner of the big blue sofa where Joe Green was already stretched out along the top of the cushions. She plucked him from his perfect repose and snuggled him onto her chest, kicking off her shoes and lying back against the end cushion with her legs stretched out. She found the sweet spot under the cat's jaw and worked it until he began to purr. (Joe Green was a reluctant purrer, so it always felt like a major achievement when he succumbed.)

"She's not exactly dying at this minute, but Clara thinks the time is now, and I guess she would know. She's seen it before."

George sat down across from her at the

other end of the sofa and put his feet up, intertwining his legs with hers. "Kind of inevitable, I guess," he said. "Lucky Joe Green."

"I've been imagining this moment with Esther for the last twenty years, at least," Rebecca said. "The last thirty years. Maybe all my life. Joe Green is my hero, aren't you, Mister Verdi Mousekiller?" She rubbed her nose against his smug little triangular face. He blinked at her and then butted his head up under her chin, which brought on a wave of tenderness that welled up from somewhere deep in her chest. She felt tears rising. "So that's the story," she said, her voice breaking a little. George's steady gaze brought the tears up and over, spilling out now.

"I went by there just now before coming here, and she was sleeping," Rebecca added, trying to steady herself with the practical facts the way she always did. "I sat with her for a while, but I didn't want to wake her. So I told them I would be back first thing in the morning, by seven, something like that, and that I'd spend, oh, probably the whole day there, see what it feels like, see what happens. It could be the whole weekend, who knows. They promised they would call me here if there were any changes in the night."

"Changes?"

"If they think she's about to die. If her breathing pattern changes into Cheyne-Stokes breathing or anything like that. They'll check on her a lot. I told them I was just a few minutes away."

"I can go with you," George offered.

"If something happens tonight, that would be great. But you really don't have to be there at dawn with me. If you want to come by a little later in the morning, like, whatever works for you, nine-ish, that would be great. I don't know what your day is supposed to be."

"How are you doing?" George asked, taking both of her socked feet in his hands. Rebecca favored stripes. Today's socks were fuzzy, blue and green, which picked up the green in her sweater. He raised them up to his face and kissed each foot ceremoniously. "Are you okay? I love your little square feet. And your feet always smell so sweet! Where do such sweet little square feet come from?"

"Feet run in my family," Rebecca said wryly.

"Ha."

"And noses. I guess I'm okay. I'm sad."

"She's had an amazing and incredibly

long life," George said unnecessarily.

"I know, I know. It's just that once she got so old, it seemed as though she would just keep living indefinitely. She probably thought she would too."

"Maybe she's ready."

"Oh, I'm sure she's ready. I think she's surprised that she's still here. I'm the one who's not ready," said Rebecca.

"I know. But you really are. You know that. You want her to have a good death," he said gently, still holding her feet.

"It's true, I do."

They sat in silence for a while, just gazing at each other, the silence as natural to both of them as it was uncommon in most other people. Joe Green jumped off Rebecca and hit the floor with sudden urgency, as if he had just recalled a prior engagement. Bits of his fur lingered in the air behind him, and Rebecca wiped some stray hairs off her damp face with her sleeve. They both watched as the cat sat abruptly and washed intently for a moment before flinging himself away down the length of the loft toward whatever attracted him next.

"He really knows how to live in the moment," Rebecca said.

"So, Beck, listen. At dinner, I have to tell you about this genetics lab at NYU, where I was today. They're doing this incredible research with stem cells, and I have a lot of new stuff. I could go in about ten directions, just from what they showed me over there today."

"I want to hear about it. In a bit. Right now I just need —"

"What?"

"Just this. Nothing. Everything. Just sitting here with you doing nothing."

"I'm glad you're here."

"I'm glad I'm here too, George. I'm glad you're glad."

"And I'm glad that you're glad that I'm glad. Ain't we got gladness —" He drummed a paradiddle on the arm of the couch, finishing with a flourish at an invisible cymbal. "Dinner out, sweetie? I assumed you would be as starved as I am, and there's not much here. I didn't want to go out again once I got your message —"

"Anywhere but downstairs, please." Sometimes Rebecca loved just looking at George's face. She knew every line, every hollow, every crease. She especially loved the blissed-out look of intense pleasure that made his jaw go slack when he listened to music, including the music in his head that nobody else could hear. He scowled at her now with a look of mock disappointment.

"Coward. Where's your sense of danger? Where's your willingness to risk the unknown?"

"Yeah, well, Joe Green told me they were out of the mouse soufflé tonight. And he said the fettuccine *rodenti* wasn't al dente. I always trust Joe Green's advice. So does Moira Hodgson."

"Who doesn't?" He gazed at her fondly across the expanse of sofa. "You know, I love your voice, even when it's got a Brahmsian sadness. It has a wonderful timbre."

"Oh, please. A Brahmsian sadness? Is that a good thing or a bad thing?"

"No, really, I think your natural register is in G. I've told you that."

"Right. It's true, you have told me that, but now you're verging on the self-parodic, which means your blood sugar is probably way too low. Did you eat today? I'm starved. Let's go eat a really good dinner somewhere decent."

"Sounds like a plan."

"I hate people who say that."

"But you'll always make an exception, won't you, Rebecca?"

"I also hate people who always think there is an exception that proves the rule."

"You hate those people as much as people who say 'win-win'?"

"I despise those people. You're right. That's worse. I despise those people as much as you despise Nelson Riddle."

"Death penalty for all offenders."

"Absolutely. Sushi? There's that place just down the block on Eighth Street."

"You'll eat dodgy raw fish on a Monday, and you won't take your chances downstairs?"

"Anywhere but downstairs, please. I mean it."

"Your profound desire not to eat there trumps my eternal optimism."

"Advantage, Brahmsian sadness."

FOUR

Transcription of Esther Gottesfeld interview #3, conducted by Ruth Zion, West Village Jewish Home, New York City, July 11, 2000. Ruth Zion transcription, July 15, 2000

[question] Morris Jacobs? You begin there? For what? Why do you want to know about him? Jacobs was a nothing, a nobody.

[question] A contractor, yes, that is right. My sister and I, we worked for him at the Triangle. You know as much about all this old history as I do, apparently. [note for the record: this is demonstrably untrue but nevertheless flattering. rz] Just another one trying to get ahead and make some money like everyone in the garment business in those days, trying to make himself into something from nothing. He was our boss, and then he worked for the big bosses, that's right. That's how they did it. A lot of bosses all in a row and that way nobody at the top was responsible for anything at the bottom because they didn't know. They didn't care to know. Nothing changes in this world.

[question] Jacobs? He was a thief. He would change the time to get extra minutes of work from all the girls.

[question] He would set the hands of the clock back. Or just stop the hands until someone would make a complaint and then he would just shrug. He did it very often, yes, but he wasn't the only one to think of that kind of stealing. He was a man without a conscience who would take from anyone what he could get. I told you already when we were having tea, before you turned on your machine so you catch my voice, about how he would act like he couldn't do sums to give us the right money for adding up all the slips — we had these slips, they showed how much work we did in a week. Believe me, you don't want to waste time thinking about this little man, this nobody. I heard he died in a fire in his apartment a long time ago now.

103

[question] You could say there was some irony about it. That doesn't interest me so much. It was when I was working for the union, you know I was in the office of the Women's Trade Union League for those years after I closed my store when the neighborhood changed, we talked about that already on the telephone when you called that first time, you think I don't remember? Maybe I remember better than you. Williamsburg was a decent place to be for all those years on Stagg Street and then it was not so nice after that, and all my customers were gone and anyway it was too much work, with such long hours, and the stealing, it was bad, and I was robbed two times, so that was how I got the news, in the union office, there was a commotion about the irony of course, that he should live from one fire and then die in another, and then there was some little newspaper article with some wrong facts, these articles, they always make mistakes. [note: See *Long Island Express*, late edition, February 3, 1956, "Triangle Fire Survivor Succumbs to Blaze"]

[question] Oh, nothing important. I don't remember what was wrong, just that there were mistakes, like in every newspaper article. [humorous aside by interviewer, not relevant for transcription] He was living by himself in Long Beach, near the boardwalk somebody told me. Or I knew that from somewhere. Something caught fire from his stove, I think that was it. But about this, you already know. You know more than I do. I am not interested but you, you are interested.

[question] He had no family? If you say so. I don't care about that. A lot of the people I knew from that time at the Triangle, they retired there and Lido Beach, too, which was right next to Long Beach, but all little houses, not the nice big apartment buildings, these buildings were just like in the city, they had them at Long Beach, so it was like being in the city plus you got the ocean to look at. But he didn't have so many friends from those people. Not anyone I knew. I heard he got sick and wasn't right in the head, but I don't know about that. Why do we speak of him so much?

[question] I went out there a few times from the city on the Long Island Railroad. It was nice to walk on the boardwalk and see the ocean. What? Yes, in the hot weather. The sand was nice and cold on your toes under the boardwalk, that's what I remember, and then too hot to walk on out in the sunshine. You had to have tickets to go on the sand from the board-walk. From living there my friends had tickets and could give me one, for a guest.

[question] Yes, I had some friends there so I went, I just said that already, you have a problem remembering? From the Triangle, yes, there was Selma Breitenweiser, and Fannie Adler, she sewed the labels and inspected the finished goods, and there was that nice Teddy Kaplan, he had the glass eye, he was one of the cutters from the eighth floor, and Dora Levy too, she lived there but had to use a walker, poor thing so she couldn't go out very much, and it was not possible for her to walk in the sand. Katie Lewarski, she would make the collars very fast, she made good money, she was in that building in the same hallway as Dora. Always with a book, that one, on our lunch breaks she would be reading when the rest of us were gossiping.

[question] No, I never seen Morris Jacobs there. We go back to him again? I don't remember which was his building.

[question] I don't know what kind of illness, but he had trouble walking, and I heard he couldn't get out from the fire on his stove, and someone said to me once he had something wrong with him in his brain before he died. But I don't know about it. Maybe you'll find that out from somewhere else. Why are you so interested in him? A shmendrick. What's to remember, what's to discuss? You know what is a shmendrick? [reply] No, that is a schlemiel. A shmendrick is a little runt of a man. A bigger loser than a schlemiel. You know what they say? The schlemiel pees in the shower. The shmendrick gets out of the shower to pee [*sic*].

[question] I suppose I saw him when the trial was going on, I don't remember so much specifically. So many people were at the trial, to testify or just to watch. I don't really remember seeing him any day after the day of the fire. He got out with not a scratch. Do you want to know my memories or not?

[question] Did I see when he testified, you are asking was I there? I don't remember.

He did whatever the bosses say to him to do. He says the door was never locked. I say I saw him unlock it in front of me, I saw this with my own eyes, so I know it was unlocked after that. Why would he unlock an unlocked door? And who would lock it again? I lived. He lived. In the commotion it's easy to make a mistake of who you saw and when it was, and what was locked and what wasn't locked. Maybe he thought I was some other girl. Maybe he got confused like everyone did.

[question] So maybe I saw him testify, if you say I was there then maybe I was, but now I forget. You are asking an old lady to remember something not so important from a long time ago. Enough about Morris Jacobs. Everybody should just forget him.

[question] Why you ask me that? Did somebody say something to you? I never told anybody he bothered me. Maybe he bothered some of the other girls, and I don't know about that, but I never said to anyone he bothered me. Why are you asking this? What did you hear? Lots of the bosses, they took advantage of the girls. It happened all the time. You heard about it.

You had to be tough. It wasn't good, what a lot of the girls put up with to get ahead. And now we don't speak about that little shmendrick anymore. He is dead, and I would spit on it, if I go by his grave.

[question] There was nobody who helped me with my answers for the trial except the prosecutor. Oh, you are asking about Mr. Rubin? [note: Assistant District Attorney J. Robert Rubin] Yes, he talked with me to make me calm about what I had to say in front of everyone in the courtroom. The goyish one, what was it, Botnick? [Assistant District Attorney Charles S. Bostwick] Mr. Bostwick, okay, so that's his name, you know this, but you keep asking me to tell you what you know already, better than I know it, no, I only met him in the courtroom. Mr. Rubin was the one friendly with me before, the one who talks to me about what I should say and how I should act. Just be myself, is what he always says. Good advice! Now you change the subject and you go back to my testifying, but I still won't remember every minute of it. Have you ever sat in a courtroom for a trial? The air is so stale like they never open a window, so much time is wasted, everybody goes to sleep after a while. You think it is exciting when you know about a trial, but to be there, you find out, it is mostly just a lot of nothing and talking about the rules about what everybody isn't supposed to say.

[question] I am sure Mr. Rubin and Mr. Bostwick were disappointed by the verdict, but that was the decision for the jury, and it was the jury let those two gonifs [Max Blanck and Isaac Harris] get away like that with no blame. They were men, that jury, it was only salesmen and people like that, they probably thought we were stupid when we talk with our accents and we say English that wasn't so perfect, and all of them were sympathetic with the bosses, you could see it on their faces every day of the trial. And that judge, too.

[question] Nobody came to me from Mr. Harris. I don't know where you heard that. Who would say that to you? For money? If they gave me big money would I be living so modest? Why would I take money from those two? To tell a lie for them? [comment from interviewer] To say a door was unlocked when the door was locked? It would be blood money. I know the door was unlocked because I passed

110

through that door and that is why I am alive. Look at me. I am sitting here. How did I get through the door if it was locked? When I went through that door, it wasn't locked. I know that was the wrong answer for so many people who wanted me to say it the other way, but that would have been a lie for me to say.

[question] I am not going to answer such an insult. Stop with that. Would you ask your own grandmother such a question? Your own grandmother would slap your face for such a question. You look like a smart girl but your questions show you're not so smart like you think you are.

[question] Was I disappointed? The verdict? Do I regret? You mean personally? Ask a straight question and then I understand it. Nothing could bring back anyone from the dead. The trial gave attention to the fire and maybe that was the most important thing. Twelve girls just from my street, we buried. Essex Street, that's right. So many girls died, for what?

[question] I don't know how many children there were on that day, but usually there were little girls in the corner, maybe two or three, we called it the nursery, Rose Gottlieb, she was in charge of the little girls, giving them what to do, and sometimes she brought them some extra rolls to eat from the bakery where her brother worked, so why wouldn't they be there that day like all the other days, and it was a Saturday, so the little girls must have been there. Rose was a nice girl. She came from a farm, she was Polish, and she didn't like the city so much. But she was glad she didn't have to be with the chickens anymore like on the farm she came from. She had to wring their necks, she told me, so they can sell them in the market, and she had to do it or her father would beat her.

[question] How could the bosses be ignorant? Did they think fairies came in the night and trimmed the threads and sewed the labels? Of course they saw the children. Mr. Harris was always walking around and poking into everything. Nobody thought they were secret except when the inspectors came and then everyone pretended while the little girls hid in the scrap barrels with scraps covering them up.

[question] I didn't see any of the little girls on the sidewalk after. Maybe they burned up. I don't know what happened to them. They disappeared, I agree with you. You find out about them, you tell me.

[question] I already answered that. Now we go back? Nobody told me what to say except Mr. Rubin, he went over my story with me so I shouldn't be nervous, and then it turned out that I wasn't nervous enough, the way I told my story. They got me all confused. I don't want to keep discussing this.

[question] No, I already told you last time I didn't go back to work like before, because of my baby. My son, Isaac. The unions, they gave me some help, and the Red Cross had a special fund, also from other people, there were all these funds, there were charities, there was a special fund from the United Hebrew Trades, and there was Local 25 of the Dressmakers Union, they all did so much for people like me after the fire. Some of the girls had such burns, they suffered more than I did. I know it doesn't seem like I was lucky, but I was. I could keep alive. I didn't get such bad burns like some of the other girls. I could have my little grocery store, they helped me move to Brooklyn after the baby came, and they helped me to get it going, with a loan for buying the goods, and I could put food on the table for the baby. We always had enough. We didn't have more than enough, but we had enough.

[question] You know all about this from when we were already discussing it before, the last two times we discuss this already, why do you ask an old lady the same questions again? I think your memory is in worse shape than mine! [humorous comment from interviewer] Like I told you before, Isaac, he was a difficult baby, maybe being in the fire wasn't good for him already before he was even born. The colic was so bad, I was up every night with him. It was a bad time. A hard time. No baby should be born into so much sorrow. Maybe he got a shock from being in the fire even though he wasn't born yet.

[question] Yes, that is what people say, the new life is something good, something to enjoy, a new life to have after somebody dies. I always wanted to make the best of my life, it's true, but it wasn't so easy, having anything like joy, in those years right after the fire. So much was lost. You just have to live day to day and do what you can to get ahead. Sam was a very good man, you are right. I hope you put in a lot about Sam, even though you're always so interested in women this and women that. He was a hero. So good to my sister. He was a real mensch and I do not use that word carelessly.

[question] No, I don't speak about him so much. It tears my heart. Some things are private all your life. Not for talking about.

[question] Sam had no people left. He read in the *Forward* about his village, Skala, that was in Galicia, how the Cossacks came for all the men, and how there was burning, so it was good he got out before all that happened and so many Jews were killed. You think you can trust your neighbors and everything is peaceful but when the chance comes, neighbors turn on neighbors, because always there is this hatred for the Jews. I never met any of his people.

[question] Isaac wasn't so much like Sam, no. Who can say what makes a child, where the nature of a child comes. I am no expert on babies and children but everyone knows you can say that saying about how the apple doesn't fall far from the tree, but even so, every now and then an apple rolls away down a hill and surprises people.

[question] What for would I name my baby after that man? That is a crazy question you are asking. No, no, no. My baby was named for my mother's father, from when I was a little girl, his name was Yitzak, so I call the baby after him only with an American name. Yitzak Weissman was his name, I remember him when I was a little girl, he was an old man already, and we would get in his lap, my sister and me, and he would give us sometimes a little bit of sugar from his tea, he would keep this sugar all in one big lump, a cone of sugar, he kept it in a wooden box on the table, and he had this special knife for to cut it, and he would take some off for his tea, just a little bit, and put it in his mouth, to drink the tea through. We loved that sugar. He was a very religious man, a very good man, and so I think to name my baby to honor him. What are you, crazy, to suggest I would soil my baby's name to honor that gonif, that shirtwaist king he called himself?

[question] Isaac's death was an accident. You asked me that before also, do you think I have no memory and will give you another answer today just because you brought me poppy-seed cake? Which is by the way too dry and not so good. [note re inconsistency: the poppy-seed cake in question, purchased at a kosher bakery on Second Avenue, was made according to a traditional recipe, and was of the same type Esther Gottesfeld had praised on the occasion of the previous interviews in April and September of 1999. The bakery denies any change in the recipe in the intervening time. rz] I don't know what you are looking for. This has nothing to do with history. The car had something wrong with the brakes, they said. And Isaac was maybe not so good a driver, even though everyone in the world thinks of himself he is a great driver, and nobody ever admits being a lousy driver, but maybe he was, I got to say, anyway he got himself into an accident the month before already. No mother wants to live to bury her child, I can tell you. It was a shock. A terrible thing. His wife, Rebecca's mother,

117

she was a decent person, not Jewish, but a decent person anyway. It was terrible also for Rebecca, to lose both her parents like that, her mother and her father, and she's only eight years old. My own mother, you know about, I told you already about how she died when I was a little girl so long ago, and I never did see my father again after we came to America, but I know he is alive for those years. And he knows I am living in America, and that was something for him, even with the shock of hearing about my sister and the fire.

[question] Yes, I wrote to him that he had a grandson, so he knew about it. He wrote me back with sadness about Pauline and disappointment that I am not married to the father of my baby, and now it is too late to get married, so I have brought shame to the family, and also he had sadness about how I couldn't send him money anymore.

[question] My papa? He was just an ordinary tailor, not so high up in the town, and not so good a businessman either. It was my mother who had the brains for business. I never saw my brothers again. My sister and I, we were sending them every month some money to come but after I stopped sending money they didn't come and I never see them. I always hoped they would come. The baby, little Abie. I always waited to see him at my door. But they didn't come. They must all be dead by now. I never heard.

[question] Why didn't my papa come to America? He had got a new wife by then, the girl who was working for him, that was no surprise, I remember her from the town, a homely thing with a squint, but big bosoms she got, and she was very hardworking, and anyway, he was too old to start all over again. In America you got to be willing to make something new of yourself. He didn't have the temperament for that. My mother — she would have loved America. Why he didn't send any of the boys to me, I don't know. Maybe they were afraid after what happened to my sister. I wrote to him to ask for that, but he didn't say yes or no.

[question] That is an ignorant question you ask. Nobody would go back to what was there. Hardly anyone ever did, not like the Italian girls who dreamed of going back and marrying and having their families where they came from. We were so lucky to get away from the czar and all the terrible things going on there, they would come into the village and just take people, you have no idea — nobody had a dream of going back. With a little baby, nobody would go back on that terrible ship to return to that life. In America, you got a lot of chances. There were no chances left, back home. It was finished, all used up, for people like me.

[question] Yes, I was alone without my sister, and it was hard, but there was help, the United Hebrew Trades union helped me, and Local 25 of the Ladies Waist and Dressmakers Union, like I told you already, now we are repeating, you like that? You're like that lawyer, Mr. Steuer, asking for the same story again. I was a member already, and they helped me, and then I got my grocery store, and sometimes you just go on with what you know how to do every day. You only know what you did was the best you could do when you look back. You got to have a positive attitude.

[question] Just because I never marry again, you think I am a wallflower? A lot of men took an interest over the years, I am not so lonely as you think, always I had very good legs, and I kept my figure, and I dressed nice. There was always someone to take me out, if I wanted to go out. But I am not going to give you gossip and tittle-tattle about what is private to me.

[question] Maybe if you live longer you will know why some of your questions don't make sense. Not everyone lives according to the way you live, did you ever think about that? You look like a smart girl but maybe you spend too much time with books and not enough time just enjoying.

[question] Yes, we laid them by in the same cemetery with my Sam, and my sister is there also. The Workmen's Circle, a very crowded part of the cemetery, all filled up.

[question] No, I don't go there, why would I go there? What sort of person goes to cemeteries all the time? I'm too old to go to a cemetery in Brooklyn just to see the names on the stones and to feel sorry all over again. I'll go there when they put me in the ground where I have a place already, next to my sister. [description by interviewer of current deplorable conditions at the Workmen's Circle cemetery] So good for you, you went there to see it. Did you feel like it was an accomplishment? [comments from interviewer] It is a sad place, yes, what else would it be? So there are weeds? Who is there left to watch out for the dead? Let the weeds grow, why not? They got to have a place, too. So why do you tell me Selma Pickel's grandson was there when you went there to snoop around? I don't know him. Why would I know him? I knew her a little bit to say hello, from the union, that was a long time ago, but I didn't know she was there until you say it to me just now. Everybody has died and they put them someplace in the ground. I don't make a significance.

[question] Yes, you are right, it is a wonderful thing that at least I had my grandchild, my Rebecca. You say this like it is a new idea but we go over it already every time you come to bother me with the questions. Is that why you come here again? You already know she wasn't in the car that day with them, why do you ask me again? So I can say it again? It is good we had each other, yes. So?

[question] You want this for your tape

recording, even though we discuss it over and over? Ach. So I say it again for you and then we are done. Thank God for that, yes, she was asleep with me so they went out after we had lunch, it was a Sunday, when they would visit me, and I said I would watch her so they should go out and enjoy the afternoon. I don't think there is any more to the story of that day, you have heard it by now from me more than this time.

[question] How many times do I say to you there is no connection [between the Triangle Waist Company fire and the death of Isaac Gottesfeld and his wife, Barbara, in a car accident of uncertain origin on March 24, 1961], and you shouldn't keep asking me such a stupid question to make a connection that doesn't exist? How could you imagine something so foolish? What difference does it make that it was the day after the anniversary of the fire? You make nonsense out of my life just to make a cockamamy pattern. I am not going to answer more of your questions. No, no. Please turn off your tape recorder. I am very tired now and there is nothing more to say. No. *Farlawzt meer alain!*

[note: Esther Gottesfeld terminated the interview at this juncture, before all of the prepared questions had been posed, which is deeply regrettable considering the valuable information she possesses, especially given how remarkably intact her faculties remain as of this writing, in July of 2000, at age 105. rz]

[note: Despite numerous attempts to schedule another interview in order to complete the questions, Esther Gottesfeld was not able to comply with the request before her death earlier this year, perhaps owing to her declining health and advanced age, and so there remain significant gaps in the material. Attempts will be made to interview her granddaughter in the hope that she can add to the record, although she has expressed initial reluctance to cooperate. rz, October 2001]

FIVE

**GEORGE BOTKIN '73
AND THE QUEST FOR NEW MUSIC**
Yale Daily News Literary Supplement,
**Spring 1999
Interview by Blake Shapiro '00**

When George Botkin walked into Linsley-Chittendon Hall for the first time in the fall of 1969, a freshman trying to find his English 120 section, he was struck by the pitch of the building. What's that you say, you didn't know buildings had pitches, and we don't mean the roof? Welcome to George Botkin's world. Linsley-Chit is an F-natural building. Next time you have a moment, take a music major with you to check it out. He's right. The *YDN* Litmag talked with Botkin one afternoon when he was on campus teaching his popular music-composition seminar this term, and we went down into Linsley-Chit's resonant bowels so the MacArthur-winning composer could demonstrate the pitch of the building with a tuning fork he just happened to have on hand.

Botkin in his own words:

When I was an undergraduate here, I always loved to walk into Stoeckel Hall after I had been in the Kline Biology Tower for a lab, because through the doors of the practice rooms you can hear everything — movements of thousands of years of music written by human beings who have lived and died, and any of this music, at any moment, is being played or sung by music students of varying aptitude. I would wander in the halls and listen, and there would always be someone playing with joy, or with fury, or hesitantly and awkwardly, and some students always play every note on the page, while others always improvise, they can't help themselves. These days, those are Willie Ruff's students — they get in trouble if they don't improvise. I would always listen for that too, the really inventive improvising you can hear through a door. And it often made me think that if I could walk inside a living cell, then I might hear something just like that, the amino-acid sequences being played out one by one, a note for each, and the cell would be performed according to the genetic score, so sometimes it would be played with absolute precision, but other times there would be mistakes, or variations. And some of those changes would be good ideas, maybe great ideas, and some would be bad ideas, or really catastrophic, destructive mistakes.

The work I was doing in my labs, such as it was, made me think a lot about composition, and how the composer is always confronted by choice within the context of structure. Nature has that same set of rules, and sometimes nature can be stunningly inventive, while other times nature really screws up. I was trying to explain this to one of my biology professors who knew something about music, and he pointed out to me that you could say that every generation of cells in every living organism is playing the genetic score of its species, or if not the score, then at least following the charts the way a jazz band follows the charts. This was such a simple thought, and such an amazing thought. When you consider it, you realize that the history of music goes back, what, maybe a thousand years, or even a lot longer than that, all the way back to prehistory, if you consider that the first music was composed for the human voice. But meanwhile the genetic code has been playing its own music for who can say how long, maybe close to four billion years.

Some of the ideas in my music draw on this vaster history, as well as on the more recent vocabulary and form of human music, though it sounds pretentious to talk about it this way. Composition is about making choices and organizing your musical themes. You write them; you move them around. You develop your themes. It's all about the themes. You listen to what sounds right, what sounds wrong. There has to be structure of some kind, I believe, or it sounds bad, it just sounds like nothing. We all know that kind of fake music. It doesn't take you anywhere — it just wanders pointlessly and it irritates you and you don't even know why. We seek meaning in our music, at every level of consciousness, just as we do in our sentences, in our paintings. Why wouldn't we?

Proteins and the genes that encode them have structure. Proteins, if you are willing to think about them this way, are composed of phrases that are organized into themes. A protein sequence can be easily converted into a musical sequence. So what? Amino-acid sequences have complexity and patterning that can be used to inspire musical combinations that have aesthetic value, is what. That doesn't mean that every amino acid can hit the charts, or even that any amino acid can just be translated into its musical analog according to a system and you're done, it's a hit number in a Broadway show. Here's one way to look at what I might do. Say there are twenty amino acids in proteins — right there that's two pitches shy of three octaves in a diatonic scale. Seven pitches make the scale, and the sequence repeats, if you continue, just up the octave — then the eighth becomes the first, and the sequence begins again. In nature, you find structures and sequences like this everywhere you look. But as is true with any conventional music, anything you write, whatever it is, is altered radically when you change the tempo or the instrumentation. You can sing "Summertime" as a lullabye or a march. So that's a starting point, a jumping-off point. It still has to be aesthetically pleasing and inventive music, or you have nothing, just a system and a formula and a curiosity, an artifact of your process. A lot of people are making these sounds today, and some people might call it music, but I don't call that music.

Six

Rebecca arrived at the West Village Jewish Home a few minutes after seven the following morning. It was a perfect early September day, the sky a piercing blue, the air fresh and summery. It was a day filled with sunlight and promise. Rebecca regretted that this was probably the last of it she would see except for the little slice of sky visible from the window in her grandmother's room. She stopped on the corner for a double latte to take up with her, regretting the cliché that it was and, she supposed, the cliché that she was for craving it. But she knew the coffee at the Jewish Home was horrible — sort of amber and weirdly transparent, not to mention so entirely decaffeinated that George had a theory that it actually sucked the residual caffeine from out of your bloodstream and you ended up with a caffeine deficiency if you drank it.

Rebecca drew in a deep breath of

scrubbed morning air before going inside the home. The staff greeted her warmly. She found her grandmother sleeping.

Sipping her coffee, Rebecca regarded her grandmother's slight form in the hospital bed, which was cranked up halfway to a sitting position. Barely five feet tall in her prime, Esther Gottesfeld had become tinier and tinier in recent years, until now she was a miniature woman, child-size but lacking the sturdiness of a child. She wore a white nightdress with a pale blue quilted bed jacket over it, though the room felt too warm to Rebecca in her thin cotton shirt and jeans. Someone had brushed Esther's wispy hair in the wrong direction (she had always parted her hair on the left, claiming that a left part showed a sense of humor) and fastened it with a hairpin on one side. Her head hardly made a dent in the middle of the pillow. Her face seemed closed in on itself. The long, jagged burn on her neck that ran up to the edge of her jaw, an angry red welt that still attracted stares in Rebecca's childhood, though by then it had been a fact of Esther's life for nearly fifty years, had faded in recent time to a more delicate pale mauve.

Esther had stopped wearing dentures the day after her hundredth birthday — "the

131

hell with them!" she had said with finality, throwing them to the floor. Nobody had dared disagree with the decision. As her nose and chin had grown toward each other in her finely wrinkled face, she had come to resemble the frightening dried-apple doll on a broom that some union friend of her grandmother's had given Rebecca when she was a child. She had never known what she was supposed to do with it. It wasn't a doll you wanted to play with. It didn't go with her other dolls. It was not cuddly, this witch in a calico babushka astride a twiggy broomstick, her spindly legs of twine with ugly wooden shoes dangling at the ends, and Rebecca had hung it from the latch on her bedroom window, keeping it well apart from her other dolls and stuffed animals. The way Esther now resembled that witch gave Rebecca an uncanny feeling of déjà vu. Whatever had become of that doll? She wished she had it now. No, she didn't. In repose, Esther's face wore an expression of puzzlement, as if she were trying to work something out.

Rebecca gazed around the familiar room. Although her grandmother had inhabited this room for several years, it was uncluttered and sparely furnished, unlike most of the other rooms on the floor, in which were stuffed lifetime accumulations of knick-knacks and family artifacts and too much furniture — heavy, dark pieces that had for years filled houses and apartments, now much too big for these small rooms. The little television set was on, but the sound was off. There were three framed photographs on her grandmother's dresser: Rebecca's college graduation portrait — that hair! — next to a very old photograph of Esther with Rebecca's father, Isaac, when he must have been about ten, a very serious little ten-year-old boy standing beside his seated widowed mother, posed in a photographer's studio in Union Square beside an incongruous potted palm. Esther's long dark hair was loose for the portrait, covering almost the entire left side of her face, hiding her burn. In a smaller, tarnished oval frame, apart from the other two photographs, was a formal studio portrait, their rosy cheeks hand-tinted as was the fashion, of the two Auerbach sisters, Pauline and Esther, dressed alike in white, high-collared shirtwaists, with ballooning sleeves and tailored waists, above dark skirts, like two Jewish Gibson girls, as Esther always said — the only photograph of the two sisters together that Rebecca had ever seen, taken just a month before the fire.

"She's playing possum," Clara said from the doorway. "She was awake not five minutes before you got here." Clara strode into the room. She was from North Carolina originally, and her speech refused to acknowledge the latter half of her life spent in New York City. She approached the bed and spoke loudly, taking Esther's hand in hers.

"Miz Gottesfeld, you don't want to be sleeping while Rebecca is here to see you, do you?" Esther's eyes didn't open but Rebecca and Clara both saw the corner of her mouth twitch into a small smile. "Can you open your eyes for me, sweetheart?" Clara asked, a little more softly. She winked at Rebecca.

"I let you call me sweetheart only because I like you," came the faint notes of the voice from the bed, eyes still closed. "But don't make a habit."

"There you go." Clara chuckled. "Now you open your eyes and have a nice visit with your granddaughter, Miz Gottesfeld. She's sitting right in the chair here beside you."

The eyes fluttered open and Esther looked around blankly for a moment until she recognized Rebecca. She moved her hand very slightly toward Rebecca and smiled, closing her eyes again.

"I need to rest my eyes, but I know you're here," she whispered. "Just sit by me and I will keep knowing you are here."

Rebecca had been sitting beside her grandmother's bed for almost two hours, just watching her sleep, listening to her breathing, which kept stopping and starting, with longer and longer pauses. Rebecca realized that she had become light-headed at one point because she was unconsciously holding her breath each time Esther's breathing stopped, and the intervals were growing so much longer. Rebecca idly considered turning the television sound up, but decided that she preferred the silence and the sound of Esther's breathing. She wished she had thought to bring some music along. Esther liked Prokofiev, Rimsky-Korsakov, Tchaikovsky. (She had a natural affinity for the wild Russians, George had pointed out years before.) But Esther wouldn't let her leave a CD player in the room, saying that she listened only when Rebecca or George were there anyway so if they wanted to play her some music that would be nice if they brought it along but she didn't want a CD player of her own, it would just be a waste, a confusion, someone could break it or steal it. She had been giving away her things for several years, refusing to accept gifts, stripping down to bare essentials; it was her plan that by the time she died there would be almost nothing left of her worldly possessions that wouldn't fit in a suitcase.

The regular nurse's aide had come by to check on them and take Esther's vital signs, and then Clara had come to urge Rebecca to stretch her legs, go to the bathroom, get a drink of water, while she stayed with Esther. Now Rebecca had settled back in the visitor's chair, pushed right up against the bed so she could hold her grandmother's little blue-veined hand with its familiar leathery burn mark running up her wrist into her sleeve.

Rebecca studied the hand she held, so gnarled and breakable, the yellowed nails ridged and hornlike, the skin now oddly mottled and dark. The hand that had baked so many noodle puddings and sponge cakes, chopped so many beets for borscht, sewed so many millions of stitches.

Esther Gottesfeld had been famous for most of her life because she hadn't died on a certain day when she was sixteen years old. It was an old story she had told many times, to Rebecca and to the strangers who always came by to ask about it, who always wanted to hear it again and again. She was now the last person alive who could tell the story that people wanted to hear one more time, and one more time.

She and her younger sister Pauline had been sent to America with ten dollars and a small trunk of precious bedding and clothing between them, the clothes on their backs (three outfits all at once on each of them), and the name and Bronx address of a cousin of their mother's on a scrap of paper. The year was 1909. Esther was fifteen, Pauline just fourteen. The Auerbach sisters. They spoke only Yiddish, the language of their shtetl on the edge of Pinsk. Their mother was dead from an influenza epidemic that had also killed their little baby sister, whose name was Rachel, Esther always told people, who dutifully wrote it down, though it was not the part of the story that interested them. Their father, Binyamin, a tailor, had their three younger brothers to look after (Mose, Shmuel, and little Abie, the visitors would be informed carefully so they could write that down also), and the sisters both had good needle skills taught to them by their father, and they had good health, so he sent them to take their chances for a better life.

The cousin in the Bronx was not a real cousin after all, he was family not by blood but by marriage and apparently not a very happy one at that, and he had not been at all interested in helping them, which was a real how-do-you-do for two little girls just off a boat, but they were smart girls and they had each other, so they made a plan. After he chased them away down the street, after all the asking they had done to find his door, which had seemed, before he answered their knock, like the end of their terrible journey, they managed to locate a place to spend the first night, with a lady on his street who saw what happened and invited them inside to catch their breath and she made them tea, and she had seemed nice but it turned out she charged them too much, they found out later, so how nice was that? But that's how people are.

And they went back to his stoop the next day and waited for him, telling everyone who came along, and so many people spoke Yiddish in this street, that they were his little cousins from the old country who had come over with nothing and he was so kind to them, offering to give them so much help, and when he came home and they were sitting there, before he could chase them away again, everyone on the street was telling him they were impressed by his kindness and generosity to these little cousins, traits he was not generally known for at all, and with all this praise he was shamed into helping them just a little bit, but it was important, a start, just what they needed to make a beginning. He helped them find a place to stay, and he helped them find work.

So this cousin who was not a cousin, who would care to know his name? Esther would say scornfully, and then add that his name was Max Goldstein, who could forget such a schlemiel who had to be shamed into offering a helping hand to two girls from his own people? First he got them a little rented room, not so nice, but at least he paid for the first week out of his pocket. Then he took them to the pig market on Hester Street — that was what they called it, the *chazir mark* — where the garment contractors went to find new girls to work, so they found that same day their first jobs in a sweatshop on the Lower East Side, where they sewed jacket linings all day long, every day of the week, in a crowded tenement apartment on Orchard Street.

First that sweatshop for a month, and then another one, this time with dresses, and another, jacket linings again, America was the land of a million jackets and they all had linings, and Pauline and Esther always stayed together at the pig market to find work for two, and they got work this way for the first year.

It was so exciting to be in America they didn't mind the long hours and tedious work for such small money. They did mind being cheated all the time by the contractors, but they learned their way and tried to find good bosses and sweatshops with a little bit of light and a little bit of air to make the work easier. They shared a rented room on Essex Street, a nicer room than the first one from the cousin who wasn't really a cousin, in a tenement building filled with girls like them, some other sisters were sharing too, from all over Russia and Poland and the Ukraine and the Austro-Hungarian Empire, so they could talk Yiddish and feel at home.

But they both learned English very quickly, which you had to do if you wanted to get ahead and not stay a greenhorn. The Italian girls also had to learn English fast. Sometimes in one of the little sweatshops on Orchard Street they would be working next to Italian girls who didn't know any English yet and they had no language in common, but still, they understood each other.

After that first year, they had a step up when they found better jobs in a garment factory making shirtwaists, and they could make a little more money to send home to their papa for the boys. There were hundreds of girls all together at tables in these factories but it was a better way to work, at the machines all lined up in open spaces with high ceilings, than all squashed together in somebody's dark parlor with a screaming baby sick with a fever half the time and dirty clothes and laundry and cooking and people all working on top of one another. And by then the Auerbach sisters had become skilled sleeve setters, a valuable ability, because this was a job not everyone could do quickly without too many mistakes, and they found even better jobs in a better garment factory, the biggest waist company in New York. The biggest waist company in America. The biggest waist company in the world.

"How are we doing?" George asked softly from the doorway.

"Okay. Well, not so okay," Rebecca whispered, gesturing for him to come over by the bed where Esther lay breathing shallowly. She hadn't opened her eyes for a long while. "I really think this is it," Rebecca whispered. George's shirt of yellow and red taxicabs was incongruously festive in the dim room. The little television on the table in the corner flickered soundlessly, showing images of ugly rotating zircon jewelry. Earlier it had been knives, and before that, coins. Who bought these things? Rebecca had repeatedly offered Esther a bigger television set than this one, but Esther had said what did she need that for, she didn't watch so much anyway, there was nothing worth watching so much that she needed to see it big. Rebecca ordinarily hated home-shopping mindlessness, and she had no knowledge that Esther watched it either. Probably one of the nursing aides had kept Esther company in the night and had turned it on.

"May I?" George asked as he switched it off without waiting for her reply. Rebecca got up from her perch in the chair beside the bed and stretched. She hugged George briefly, and then he sat in the chair Rebecca had just vacated. With George here, the air in the room suddenly seemed stale, and she opened the window and peered out to see the little portion of blue sky visible from Esther's window on the inner courtyard of the Jewish Home.

George moved from the chair to sit carefully on the foot of the bed, where Esther's tiny legs didn't reach, and Rebecca sat on the side of the bed and took her grandmother's cold hand in hers. They both watched Esther's labored breathing for a while, and then George took Rebecca's free hand and held it tightly. She held his hand tightly too. She had to be careful not to reflexively squeeze her grandmother's little hand too tightly with the other.

"I think time stands still in this room," George said after another long while had passed.

"The hands on my watch are actually going backward, I think," Rebecca agreed.

Esther turned her head from side to side restlessly on the pillow.

"Esther, look, George is here," Rebecca said, squeezing the tiny hand that now gripped hers.

Esther opened her eyes briefly and searched the room blankly until she found Rebecca, and then she looked again until she saw George.

"That's nice," she said weakly, and closed her eyes. "I don't want to be such a bother, but it's nice you're here to sit by me." The skin of her neck and jaw looked like parchment stretched thin over ancient bones, the burn scar standing out in ropy relief. As if they had agreed in advance to do this, each of them reached out with a free hand to hold one of Esther's thin blanket-covered shins, as if to hold her in place, to keep her from floating away.

Clara came by, checked Esther's pulse briefly. She checked the catheter bag, which Rebecca saw for the first time, as it had been hidden under the edge of her grand-mother's bedclothes. The negligible contents were very dark. Clara made notes on Esther's chart and then stood by the bed watching them for a few minutes. She looked closely at Esther, whose eyes were closed, her mouth a hard line. When Rebecca looked up again, Clara had gone silently out of the room.

"At least they were together at the end," Esther murmured restlessly, her eyes closed. "They had each other. I know my sister would understand. It was so terrible. Every-one had to make a choice, everyone had to choose so quick. There was no time. The heat was so terrible, the screaming was so bad. It was so terrible, all of it, it was like hell, like hell on earth."

George looked at Rebecca, an eyebrow raised.

"Esther," Rebecca said gently, touching her grandmother's cheek. "What are you saying?"

"Esther, that's right, she was the smarter one, and the prettier one too, but Pauline, she was tough, she was a tiger," Esther mumbled thickly. She was panting, as if running. "Sometimes tough is what matters, it's more important than smart or pretty, you have to be tough."

"You're smart and pretty *and* tough, Esther," George said. "You're a great lady and you've lived a long and good life and you should just relax now." He leaned over and kissed her on the forehead and she smiled faintly, her eyelids fluttering open for a moment. "I'm just going out for a quick walk, and I'll be back in a few minutes."

"That's fine," she said weakly.

"Want anything? I just need some air, I'm going to run around the block, probably." Rebecca shook her head and he ducked out the door. The room was quiet, the only sound the bedside clock's suddenly audible tick.

"Don't go, I'm coming to you, wait, *vart, vart far meer,*" Esther mumbled, her last words slurred. Esther lifted both her hands off the bed for a moment and then dropped them back as if they were too heavy. *"Vart far meer — farlawzt meer nisht alain een der velt."* She moaned slightly and shifted restlessly under the covers. *"Dorch der fire ich kum tsu deer . . ."* She turned her head from side to side on the pillow and moaned.

"Are you in pain?" Rebecca asked. "What's wrong? Can I do anything for you? What do you need? Should I get someone?"

Esther's hands clawed at something unseen, and Rebecca took them in her own. *"Es ist azoy nisht schlect,"* Esther mumbled. *"Vart . . . vart . . . farlawzt meer nisht alain . . . Ich veel gayen mit deer."*

Rebecca climbed onto the bed and held her then, lying down beside her, tucking herself alongside the insubstantial body, whispering, "I'm here with you, you're not alone, I'm here, I'm with you," putting her head down against her grandmother's thin little chest, the impressive solid bosom of Rebecca's childhood having long ago dwindled away with everything else that had made her grandmother so sturdy and powerful for so many years. She put her arms around the tiny form and rocked her and tried to hum a wordless childhood lullaby to her, one that Esther used to sing to her when she was sick with a fever.

"Vart far meer . . ." Esther muttered. One hand crept out across her covers in search

of something and Rebecca reached around to gather it up in one of her own, and Esther relaxed finally, her hand gripping Rebecca's tightly. She moaned softly each time she exhaled, but there were no more words, and Rebecca sang gently into the wisps of hair that brushed her mouth.

When George came back ten minutes later, he lay down on the other side of the narrow bed with them and joined Rebecca, humming a melody that looped and curled around her lullaby, and they held the little body between them and told her they were all together, that she wasn't alone, that she was with them and would always be with them, and they sang songs to her, songs they both knew, songs Esther had sung to Rebecca, songs George made up on the spot, songs Rebecca learned instantly as she heard herself singing them, songs about everything and nothing, union songs, campfire songs, sad songs about love and loss and together forever and lost ships on a stormy sea. They sang to Esther for all the hours that remained of the last day of her life, which flickered and held and flickered again and finally the life went out of Esther Gottesfeld when the pale afternoon sun was casting its fading light. It was more than ninety years since the day she didn't die, but you can only survive a disaster for so long, and ninety years is a very long time.

■ ■ ■ ■

PART TWO

■ ■ ■ ■

SEVEN

Transcription of Esther Gottesfeld interview #2, conducted by Ruth Zion, West Village Jewish Home, New York City, September 25, 1999. Ruth Zion transcription, October 10, 1999

[question] What do you think an ordinary day at the Triangle was like? We were all together, working hard, but in a way, it was a joy, I know today you wouldn't think so, but from where we all came, even if we worked and worked, there was never enough of anything to get along, and life was hard. In America, even though we worked so hard all the time, it felt like freedom to us. And we were all together, the working girls, and even though you couldn't talk so much, you felt like you were all together. It was the feeling of the union, even without the union. That's what we had.

[question] The noise was very big, all the time. But you know, I felt safe inside all that noise, it was like a big machine, and to be one of the workers, well, let me tell you, we were all little parts of that big machine. At the end of the day, when the motors were turned off, it was so strange, the quiet. I didn't like it so much. There was something I loved about the noise. It kept me company and made the work go by fast. I could always make songs in my head to go with the noise.

[question] At the Triangle, there was no singing allowed, except sometimes just at the end of the day when maybe it didn't matter so much to the bosses. A lot of the bosses wouldn't let you talk. Not a word, unless you had to ask about the work or say to someone give me your scissors. Some of the factories were extra strict like that. I heard at Bloom and Millman there was this one boss who watched you like a hawk every minute and you couldn't even put your eyes across the room, always your eyes had to stay just on your own work. I couldn't accept that, so my sister and I never went there even when it could be good work for us there, before the Triangle.

[question] Some places there was a lot of singing, sometimes in the little sweatshops everybody sings, even if they don't know the language, I remember one time my sister taught this Italian girl we worked with, when we were sewing the linings in men's overcoats, this was a little sweatshop on Orchard Street.

[question] It was August of 1909, that first summer was so hot. That was such a hot work we had to do, with these heavy coats on our laps, there was no air to breathe, but we would sing, you would just sweat so much your whole dress would be wet on your back, it really was a sweatshop! To pass the time, we would sing sometimes, and this Italian girl who was there, she was a little doll, such a tiny little thing, Rosa, from Sicily, she learned all the Yiddish songs from when we were little girls that my sister taught to her, even though she didn't know what any of the words meant. We thought it was so funny when she would sing along with us in her sweet voice about the thief who fell in the well and drowned and nobody cared, even the rabbi didn't care.

[question] It seemed like freedom to us, I

know we weren't getting so much money, but you can't judge from how it is now, you have to judge from where we came from, how it seemed to us then. We were happy, you can't tell me now we weren't happy when I know we were, even with the long days and the work. That was one of my arguments with the unions, they were always telling the girls what they didn't have and how they should ask for more or have a strike, but they didn't always understand that for most of the girls, what we had, it felt like a lot, it felt like being a success, to be in America and have a good job and work every day with all the other girls like we did.

[question] I didn't get headaches so much. I know a lot of girls suffered with their eyes because of the work. My sister had bad eyes, sometimes she had to squint over her work when the light was poor, and that gave her the headaches. I was lucky, with sharp eyes. I didn't need glasses. I never needed glasses to read or look at something close up, like to thread a needle, until I was fifty and I got tired of holding it out, a book or a newspaper, to be far away from me so I could see. My sister ruined her eyes sewing, that's what they told her, but she was vain, so she didn't like to wear the glasses they gave her, she would take them off where anyone could see her, she thought it made her look old and plain, like a schoolteacher.

[question] The language some of the men used was very vulgar. A lot of the girls came from these little villages, these shtetlach, where girls and boys were always kept apart, the boys were in the cheder all day long while the girls were at home doing the work for the family. And now we come to America and we're all mixed up together, nothing is separate, sometimes even with the same toilets to use, and it was shocking how the men would speak so coarse and vulgar, like they don't know any better but you know, most of those men, they would never talk like that at home, before they came to America. So for them maybe it was part of being an American big shot, to talk about sex all the time. Maybe some of them were lonely for their families, I don't know.

[question] It made me very uncomfortable but what can you do? I had brothers, I wasn't so surprised as some of the other girls maybe. I wasn't born yesterday, even then. And I was tough. My sister and I just stopped our ears and kept our heads down. If they saw you didn't like it, they would just do it more, so we decided we would never show our feelings, but my sister, sometimes she would blush very red, and then one of the cutters or the boss saying the dirty things would see how red she got, and that would make him satisfied and then he would just say more, or say it louder right beside us.

[question] What does it matter now? Yes, I knew about some girls who got bothered by the men. I just told you already about my sister, why do you ask again about my sister? Usually just a pinch on the bottom, or they touch you on your bosoms when you go by. Nothing that would kill you. She was tough.

[question] You heard about girls who slept with the bosses but they kept it a secret from the others, nobody would be proud of that. Why are you asking about all of this? What does it have to do with the fire?

[question] Girls always tried to protect themselves from the worst of those kind of men, never go alone with him in some corner of the factory, or on the stairs, be careful you don't get in a situation. You had to be careful. I don't want to keep discussing this so much. What else do you want to know about?

[question] I met Sam Gottesfeld, my fiancé, he was the father of my son, at the Triangle, yes. We were going to get married. He worked there maybe six months ahead of me and my sister. He was there already a year and a half, that's right. He was a machinist, with a lot of skills. They needed the machinists to keep everything running. His hands were always black with the oil on them, he couldn't even get them clean on Sundays, under his nails it was always black even though he was a very clean man, always with a clean shirt, because he would go from one machine to the next machine, all the time, all through the day. He was a gentleman. That was how we met him, he was always fixing our machines, making adjustments when the belt would break or come loose, or something needed to be changed, or you broke a needle. My sister had a machine with a cockeyed wheel when we began and he had to keep fixing it so many times she told him he was making it cockeyed just so he could come over to her again.

[question] Yes, then he and I began to go for walks on our day off, that was how we became engaged. I don't want to discuss this so much, it isn't important to the story of the fire anyway.

[question] We had Sunday off because we were pieceworkers. Some of the week workers had to go on Sundays too. There was this sign in the elevator in the Triangle, it said YOU DON'T COME TO WORK SUNDAY, YOU DON'T COME TO WORK MONDAY. But we were above that, except sometimes Sam went in on Sundays, when they needed him, and he could make good money doing that. The elevator men, they made good money that way, doing extra days.

[question] I don't remember how much they gave him.

[question] I am sure he told me about his money once we were engaged. We would be making plans for the future and telling each other everything like any engaged couple. We talked about the future and we made our plans. We were kids. But I don't remember now so much. I am an old lady now.

[question] He had four hundred and twelve dollars in a cigar box under his bed, from his room, he had a room on Allen Street, they gave me that after the fire. The landlady saved it from anyone stealing and she gave me the cigar box. It was all he had, but some clothes.

[question] I don't keep the cigar box anymore. It was just a cigar box. What would you get from seeing it?

[question] I don't know about primary sources, but I can tell you, it had in it the money, the four hundred and twelve dollars, and also inside that cigar box — okay, you interrupt and I tell you, my fiancé didn't smoke cigars, but he had worked in a cigar factory, so maybe that is where the box came from, I don't remember the brand on it. What was I saying about? Oh, yes, inside this box there was also the letter from his mother's sister to tell him his mother died of her sickness, that was just before my sister and I met Sam, and also in there was the engagement photograph he kept with him to look at in his room, they spent good money on that just to celebrate.

[question] It was Sam who spent the money so foolish, just for a photograph of the two of us. What did I say? My sister, she egged him on and she went with us to that photographer on Union Square and I make a mistake, you confuse me and get me tired and mixed up. Forgive an old lady who gets mixed up sometimes. You know how I live so long? I have a good attitude, and I always try to be looking for the good side of things. That's how I keep going every day. You should try it, don't always have your head stuck in the past. The past is past. Why think about it so much?

[question] That was all there was that he had for personal possessions in his room that anybody gave to me. Somebody could take his clothing, what he had there, I don't know. You are a regular ragpicker, wanting to know about this, wanting to know about that. I am away for so many weeks after the fire, I only get the box when I am back in the city.

[question] I don't know anything about how he kept his things, he shared the room with one of the cutters who died also in the fire, Ellis Grossman, so he didn't have too much personal that was there, sharing just a little room. Maybe that landlady put the photograph and the letter in with the money into the cigar box to keep it all safe because she already rented out the room while I'm still in the hospital, and then I don't see her until I get back from the country where they sent me after that for a month.

[question] No, I was never in Sam's room, I never seen it.

[question] I don't keep it [the engagement photograph] here, it's put away special.

[question] That is private information and I am not going to discuss how Sam and I had our private times together. There are ways. There are places you go. You ever go up on the roof of a building, where the stairs come out in a little house? But I am not going to discuss about that. I told you already it's private information, about Sam and me.

[question] I went to the country to rest, it was a very nice offer from these people who had a big country estate, to have some of the girls from the fire come and rest. They had delicious food.

[question] Their name was Loeb. [note: the philanthropist Solomon Loeb, with his wife Betty, who was an early supporter of Lillian Wald's Henry Street Settlement, opened their home in Hartsdale, New York, for the rest and recuperation of fifteen survivors of the Triangle fire, from March 30 to April 30. rz] Very nice people. They had a lot of money, but they didn't show off so much, they were very modest people. German Jews, a lot of them act like they're superior, like they're the only kind of good Jews. They act like the Jews from Russia are an embarrassment to them, like they don't want to have connections with us or it will rub off, and those are the ones who think they're so special they look down on us and call us kikes, and they act like they think common people like me all come from Galician horse thieves and pickpockets, and we're not special like the Ashkenazi, but these were very nice people. He looked like a rabbi. She was a homely little thing, and she didn't speak any Yiddish. Some of us who had some English, we could explain what she was saying for the girls who didn't have such good English yet, so she could talk with them, if we helped. And he spoke some Yiddish with us, a bisl, when she wasn't there, like he's guilty to talk Yiddish with us and maybe she wouldn't like it so much.

[question] It was the first time I was in the countryside since I came to America. The air was very fresh. All the trees make it fresh. You never heard a train go by your window, you never heard anything but birds in the morning, no noisy streets, or people shouting down from their windows, or the noises of the carts on the pavement, I never heard such birds, chirping and cheeping, and carrying on, they woke me up sometimes the first few mornings when I would wake up and I don't remember where I am. I had some nightmares when I was there, but I wasn't the only one with nightmares, every girl there got a shock, that was why we were there — the ones that got a shock too, not just burns or broken bones. But didn't everybody who was there that day of the fire, didn't everyone get a shock? You know those birds can be very loud, especially if you're not so used to that type of noise. It was a very deluxe experience for us girls, coming from such modest backgrounds, to go there and sleep in nice feather beds with nice warm blankets and feather pillows like royalty got, and everything was done for us, with three cooked meals served to us like we were fancy guests. It was a good rest I needed.

[question] I don't know how my ribs got broken in the commotion. I never knew that, but it doesn't matter. What difference does it make now? I lived. Maybe with the pushing by the Washington Place door that opened the wrong way, I am sure you will want to ask me about that. That's what everybody always asks about.

[question] I was just knowing that I was having a baby then. Just before the fire I am thinking this must be happening to me, because of the way I am feeling every morning. Have you ever had a baby? [reply from interviewer] So you don't know what it is like. I felt sick some of those days when I was there out in the country in the beginning. They took care of me, with a doctor who told them to give me eggs and meat every day, and there was so much milk, as much as you wanted to drink. All the girls gained weight. Some of the girls, they were so young they could still grow and they got a little taller and their clothes didn't fit good anymore, from all the good food and fresh air, so they got nice new clothes. I was given a very nice dress that would fit me over the baby. I felt the baby kick while I was there. That first time, I thought I had bad digestion. I didn't know anything, nobody ever told me.

[question] I don't want to talk about Sam knowing about the baby. That's private information. We were going to be married right away. Everyone knew we were engaged. There was that cake we never had a bite to taste, because of the fire.

[question] I was in mourning for my sister also. This is a bad time in my life I don't want to think about so much. It was a very bad time. We're done for now. Leave me, please. Thank you for the poppy-seed cake you brought to me but that is all I have to say.

[note: Esther Gottesfeld became emotional

and terminated the interview at this point, although she did agree to a future interview when this researcher hopes to discover further relevant information concerning the trial and some of the discrepancies in her testimony. rz]

EIGHT

AP wire, September 19, New York — The last living survivor of the Triangle Shirtwaist Factory fire died earlier this month on September 7 in New York City at the age of 106. Esther Aeurbach Gottesfeld, who was seventeen at the time of the notorious fire on March 25, 1911, worked on the ninth floor of the sweatshop and survived the fire that took the lives of 146 garment workers, most of them women, by finding her way through the flames up to the roof of the building. Her twin sister Pauline died in the fire, as did her fiancé Samuel Gottesfeld, the father of her then unborn child, Isaac, thought to be the youngest survivor of the fire, who was born six months after the fire and who predeceased her in 1961. (Esther Auerbach took the name Gottesfeld in 1911.) A resident of the West Village Jewish Home for many years, Ms. Gottesfeld was known to be an invaluable resource for scholars and historians of the fire, which is considered by many historians to have been the inspiration for improved worker safety regulations as well as changes in the New York City fire code. Her granddaughter, Rebecca Gottesfeld of New Haven, survives her. Funeral services were private.

Rebecca was carrying what her grandmother always called a lazy person's load, so as not to have to go back downstairs and out to the street to the car again, and she had several heavy plastic grocery bags strung along her left arm, cutting into her wrist a little through her jacket sleeve. She tried to insert her key in the lock with her other hand, which held a bundle of accumulated mail from the entrance hall, when she heard her telephone ring. She was rushing to open the door in time to pick up the phone before it stopped. It might, after all, be George. The keys dropped on the doormat, and Rebecca swore. She put the grocery bags down in the hallway, and some lemons rolled out of one of the bags. She shifted her briefcase into her other hand and retrieved the keys. The phone had stopped ringing.

She turned the key and pushed the door open, then gathered up the lemons and the grocery bags, along with her briefcase, and shoved everything into the apartment. As she closed the door, the phone began ringing again, which meant the caller hadn't waited to leave voice mail, which increased the likelihood that it was George. Rebecca grabbed the phone off its base while carrying the groceries into the kitchen and shrugging out of her jacket, which she draped on one of the kitchen chairs.

"You got me just coming in, sweetie, dropping everything everywhere," she said. "I'm glad you called right back —"

"Is this Rebecca Gottesfeld?"

"Sorry? Who's calling, please?"

"Is this the Rebecca Gottesfeld who is the granddaughter of the late Esther Gottesfeld?"

"Yes, speaking. Who is this?" Rebecca dropped to the couch and put her feet up on the coffee table, with the bundle of mail in her lap, which she began to flip through idly.

"Oh, hello, Rebecca. We haven't met, but my name is Ruth Zion, and I knew your grandmother. I am so sorry for your loss. I saw the obituary in the newspaper today, and I had no idea that she passed away, until now. Of course no wonder — so much has happened. You have my sincere condolences. What a difficult time this must be for you. You are the only Rebecca Gottesfeld in New Haven so I took my chances, and it turns out that I was right in my assumption that I had located you, though the obituary did contain an error, so for all I knew you didn't live in New Haven at all."

"No, you found me. But who *are* you?"

"As I just said, my name is Ruth Zion, and I am a scholar of feminist studies. I was quite privileged to have known your grandmother so well. She was a remarkable woman. It's a pity the obituary wasn't more prominent."

"She wouldn't have cared."

"Surely your grandmother would have wanted the record to be accurate in its depiction of her sister and herself? They were not twins."

"You're right. She was the older sister."

"Your grandmother's sister Pauline was two years younger, was she not? That was my impression from all of my research to date."

"Not even two years. They were just fourteen months apart. An Irish girl they knew told them they were Irish twins. My grandmother always celebrated her sister's birthday."

"Oh, that is valuable information. Those birthdays were on what days?"

"Esther's birthday was October twentieth and Pauline's birthday was December twelfth. But why do you want to know? Why am I telling you this? Who are you?"

"Ah. Thank you very much. Let me just make a note here. Thank you. Just a moment, so. Oh, this pen is running out of ink. There. I must tell you I am disappointed that I had no way of knowing about your grandmother's passing away, or I would have paid my condolences in a more timely fashion. Nobody informed me. I only just now saw the obituary, or I would have wanted to attend —"

"It wasn't reported until now, for obvious reasons, I guess, with everything that's happened. I was surprised by the wire story today, in fact. You're the first person to call about it. We didn't really have a service. Just a private service at the grave. I had wanted to do a little service at the synagogue on Charles Street near the home, where Esther used to go, for the people from the home, but then with everything going on, we just couldn't do it."

"What a pity."

"And there's really only me, and one other person. All her friends died a long time ago. Anyway, how did you know her?"

"Let me explain to you how I came to

know Esther, if I may, Rebecca. I believe you and I are contemporaries, in fact. I am a historian, actually, and I called upon her on numerous occasions in the past few years —"

"Where, at the home, you mean?"

"Yes, at the West Village Jewish Home. That is indeed where she resided at the time when I first made her acquaintance, and where I saw her on numerous occasions. Do you know, when I saw her last summer, in July, I felt it. I knew I would not see her again. Sometimes I just feel these premonitions."

"She was one hundred and six, after all. For the last twenty years or more, I thought every time I saw her might be the last time."

"Yes, of course, and it was a very fortunate thing for me, with my work, that she was so long-lived, I must say, or I would not have had such access to a primary source, which informed my work quite a bit. Very rich material. I myself live in Manhattan also, on East Thirty-fifth Street actually, which is not terribly far away, if you know your New York City geography."

"I grew up in New York. My grandmother raised me."

"Ah, yes, I know this, of course. Your own parents died so tragically, didn't they? My condolences to you on that, as well."

"It was a long time ago —"

"But I don't mean to be so gloomy! This is such a difficult time for all of us, isn't it? Fortunately for me, I am sufficiently north of the World Trade Center, though the smell in the air has been very strong, which I am acutely aware of. With my asthma, it makes me very sensitive, and the traffic is quite terrible, and it's all so tragic. The handmade signs all over the city are very moving, I find. Very moving. Tragic. I just don't look at them. We are all in shock, I suppose. The city needs to heal, that's what they say. You aren't mourning anyone, are you?"

"My grandmother died a few days before."

"Oh, of course, yes, I know. I meant to ask if you sustained any personal losses, but of course, what was I thinking, you were in mourning already, before September eleventh. What a funny little coincidence, that your grandmother should die just before the tragedy that could have triggered some valuable memories of her own tragic experience. How unfortunate. But ironic. Very ironic. I should add a footnote about that. Wait, let me just make a note. Why is it that you can't find a good pen when you're on the telephone? I myself have had no direct personal loss, though my doorman had a cousin who worked in that restaurant on the top floor, Windows on the World, and they're still searching for him, a busboy who was apparently not a legal resident, so there is no paperwork for him, which makes it very difficult for his family, and they cannot collect any benefits."

"There are probably more of those cases than we'll ever know about."

"True, true, life in the Big Apple. And it was ever thus. But you are safely in New Haven, of course. Anyway, who among us hasn't been affected in some way? We live in a difficult time. What were we discussing? Oh, yes. I usually walked downtown to see Esther, unless it was raining, and then I took the bus. The tape recorder I used wasn't very heavy —"

"You recorded my grandmother?"

"I recorded her on three occasions, and we conversed at length on two other occasions, telephonically. When I conducted my interviews with your late grandmother at the home —"

"Interviews about the Triangle fire."

"Yes, of course, what else? Her recollections, faulty as they were, and highly problematic, too, are a valuable primary source for scholarship among individuals such as myself, working in the field."

"The field? A whole field about the Triangle factory fire?"

"Oh, of course. I appear to be making erroneous assumptions that you have familiarity with my work when you apparently do not. Forgive me. I assumed that you would have familiarity with my work and my inquiries about your grandmother's experience, which was so very unique. But I wonder, perhaps you might know my book anyway, although I believe your own profession is a very different one, which involves genetic counseling and research at Yale University, does it not? So prestigious. I am sure, in its own way, it is equally important work. Your grandmother told me all about you, of course, so I feel as though we have almost met —"

"Your name isn't familiar to me, so if my grandmother mentioned you it might have been a while ago, and lots of people have come to interview her, so anyway, what's your book?"

"*Gendered Space in the Workplace, Past, Present and Future.* I imagine that she may have spoken of it to you at the time of publication. Perhaps you saw the very good review in the *Post-Feminist Studies Quarterly*? The quibbles were unjustified, I thought, but you know critics. It came out five years ago from Manatee Press. I devote an entire chapter to the Triangle fire. That fire was a seminal event —"

"Whatever that means, and are you sure you want to use that word?"

"Seminal? But it was, you see. It was a seminal event in the history of gendered space. I inscribed a copy personally to your grandmother, I am sure you have seen it on her shelf —"

"Not really. She usually gave away her books. She pretty much stopped reading a few years ago. She liked seeing the *Forward* when a copy came her way, but she never wanted to pay for a subscription of her own, and other than that she really didn't read very much of anything these last few years."

"Do you mean to say it was not among her personal effects at the time of her passing? I am extremely disappointed to hear that. I had assumed —"

"Really. I'm sorry, but I'm sure I don't have your book. And I don't think I have ever seen it. Anyway, what can I do for you right now?"

"Oh dear. I am trying to absorb this information and adjust my sense of the situation. Hmm. I don't suppose you have retained the distinctive seashell that was placed on her bedside table the last time I called on Esther, in July? That was the occasion on which I brought that seashell to her as a souvenir of my trip to Jacksonville, Florida, for a conference last June, just before our visit. I will never forget that last occasion with your grandmother, when, as I told you, I just knew."

"A seashell? I don't know. Maybe. Did you find it on the beach or something? What did it look like?"

"No, I purchased it at the Jacksonville airport gift shop, because I wanted to bestow upon Esther a token of my esteem to celebrate the success of the paper I had just presented at the conference, plus I did not actually ever go to a beach during my time in Florida. The conference was the annual meeting of the Herstorical Society."

"Historical Society of what?"

"*Her*storical. You know, history, *her*story, her story —"

"Oh."

"I assure you, it's a very good organization, and I can get you information on the next conference, which I believe will take place in Akron, Ohio, next June. You might find it very interesting, although your own work is so different, I am sure, although perhaps you are equally concerned with gender, in your own way. My paper took up the shirtwaist as a representational gesture of early-twentieth-century female expression of desire to be attired with the freedom of male garb. The title of my paper was "Desire and Attire: The Shirtwaist Reconsidered." It received a great deal of attention, if I do say so. The seashell was a chambered nautilus, I believe; it was a not inexpensive gift, though not the largest size in the shop. I was in the mood to make a generous gesture because without your grandmother my paper would not have been the success that it was."

"Oh, wait, sure. A chambered nautilus. A pink curvy thing that sort of looked like an elephant ear?"

"I thought it referenced Georgia O'Keeffe in a very intriguing way, if I do say so, which was why I selected this particular sort of shell. You are familiar, I presume, with the very unique and important contribution that Georgia O'Keeffe has made to the oeuvre of women's art in the twentieth century?"

"I understand your fascination, and I'm sure you admire Frida Kahlo, too, and, I'm guessing here, Judy Chicago, but I don't know what ever made you think my grandmother had any interest in Georgia O'Keeffe references."

"You are very knowledgeable about feminist art history."

"Not really. In any case, I gave it to one of the nurse's aides at the home. She was very kind to my grandmother."

"Ah."

"Is that a problem? Is that why you called me? Do you need it back? Did it have some significance I missed? It was chipped. I almost threw it away."

"No, no, I had just hoped that some documentation of my connection with Esther Gottesfeld would be represented in the archive inventory, for historians, for the record, for posterity. How unfortunate that it got chipped. I assure you it was a perfect specimen when I presented it to your grandmother. Had it been chipped it would have been discounted. The staff in those places can be quite careless when there is no family member present, in my experience."

"Those people were great to my grandmother every day she was there. But what historical record, or I suppose you mean the *her*storical one, do you have in mind?"

"The archive to which you have naturally made deposits of significant material from the estate concerning your grandmother's role in history, if I am not presuming, for the historic record. I would like to ascertain

179

the identity of the institution you have selected, for my own knowledge."

"I don't know what to tell you. Ruth, right? Ruth. Listen, there isn't anything to ascertain. There just isn't an archive for my grandmother's personal things, which at this point in her life were pretty few. I'm sure you know about the Kheel archive up at Cornell, and the Triangle holdings in the various New York libraries, and the ILGWU files, but there really isn't any kind of plan for adding stuff from my grandmother now. She didn't exactly have an archive or a bunch of personal papers or anything. I mean, I still have to get into her safe-deposit box at the bank, once I complete the paperwork, which is taking forever, with everything in New York so crazy and awful at the moment as it is, and who knows when I'll get the copies of the death certificate, and there's no urgency about it. It's just a small safe-deposit box, so I doubt that there will be very much in there in the way of archives, so to speak. So is that it? Is there anything else? You caught me just as I came in from work and I'm really beat and I've got —"

"Oh, where are my manners! I do apologize. Shall I phone you another day?"

"No, go ahead, if there's something —"

"Yes. There is something. You knew it too!

You could tell! Your grandmother was absolutely right about you! She said you were a very perceptive person, Rebecca, if I may call you Rebecca, and she was absolutely right."

"Okay —"

"I would like to speak frankly with you, if I may."

"I kind of assumed that was what you were already doing."

"Ha ha. Yes, of course. Very humorous. Of course. That was very witty. Rebecca, I have reason to believe — well, how shall I say this? I hesitate to bring this up to you, but you might as well hear it now, from the horse's mouth. It must be said. I have reason to believe that your grandmother was not entirely truthful."

"Is anyone?"

"I myself try to be truthful. You sound like a truthful person, as well. And I am usually a very good judge of these things. I mean to say that I believe that Esther very specifically concealed certain information about the events of the fire."

"Oh my god, that's old news, Ruth. It's the second gunman on the grassy knoll of Triangle fire theories. That guy, whatshisname, in the sixties, Lou Lipman? I'm sure you know who I mean —"

"I am intimately connected to the work of Lou Lipman, let me assure you. In fact, I can reveal to you in utmost confidence that I have special access —"

"Okay, whatever, so you know what I mean. The point is, he tried to make a connection between her testimony at the trial and the locked door, and the discrepancies with the Jacobs testimony, and the acquittals, and then there were the insurance payoffs, to paint the whole thing as a conspiracy, et cetera, et cetera. What more can be said about it at this point? Her testimony in the end was probably more useful to Blanck and Harris than to the families of the dead, it's true, and it's really unfortunate. She was always pretty sad and regretful about that. But I'm sure you know all about this. They had a brilliant lawyer —"

"Max Steuer."

"There you go — you know about this. He got her to repeat herself on the stand —"

"Twice, actually."

"Okay, twice. He tricked her into using the same words over and over, and she thought that was what she was supposed to do, for accuracy, so her testimony ended up seeming to be rehearsed, which it kind of was, in a naive way, and the jury concluded that such rehearsed testimony must be false, which it really wasn't, though she probably got a lot of little things wrong. People do."

"Have you ever seen a transcript of that testimony, Rebecca?"

"No, I haven't."

"I have one. I would like to show it to you, if I may, to get your response. Possibly you will agree with my theory if you read the transcript. And I have had access to the Lipman papers, thanks to the kindness of his son Jonathan, who has been very helpful to me, so I have his interview notes, and therefore exclusive access to material he did not feel he could include in his book, back then."

"I don't know what the point is here. Whatever Lipman left out of his book, or what was said at the trial — nothing can change now. You can't retry the case. Nineteen eleven is a long time ago!"

"I am taking the liberty after we speak of mailing you the transcripts of my three recorded interviews with Esther and the relevant pages of the trial transcript concerning your grandmother's testimony. Perhaps when you are more informed —"

"I don't know why you think I need to be more informed on a dead subject that

interests you a lot more than it interests me
—"

"But I have a list —"

"I'm sure you do! I'm sure other people have lists as well! May I finish? I'm sure my grandmother made mistakes. I wouldn't disagree with someone who can prove that. If I read the transcript, maybe I'll see the mistakes. If I hear your tapes, I'm sure I will hear mistakes. I might agree with every damn thing on your list. It was a huge tragedy. But so what? Who knows why we believe things that aren't really quite true? Human memory is fallible. Rashomon and all that. There's nothing more to say about it now. Especially now, with a much bigger tragedy affecting everyone."

"As a scholar and as a woman, I cannot agree with you at all. A great deal more not only can be said about the Triangle fire, Rebecca, but will be said about it, in my forthcoming book."

"You have a new book?"

"*Out of the Frying Pan: Women and Children Last* has finally come unto fruition upon the completion of quite the ambitious undertaking, let me assure you. I am very much an expert whereof I speak. It will be published next spring."

"Surely not Manatee Press again? Tell me,

how could someone with your credentials want your intellectual fruition to be published by an imprint with the word 'man' in the title?"

"Oh! Ha ha ha. That was very humorous. You have a very sophisticated sense of humor, Rebecca. I am sure, however, that you, with your Yale University affiliation, recognize that Manatee is one of the leading postfeminist presses today."

"No, I've never heard of it until you said the name earlier in the conversation. Look — is there something specific you want to ask me or tell me?"

"I am presently revising my manuscript in light of your grandmother's death, and yes, as a matter of fact it is indeed coming out with Manatee, and you should be grateful that I am taking the trouble of informing you now, as this book is going to stir up a great deal of renewed interest in Esther Gottesfeld, her prevarications, and the role she may have played, so I thought I should do you the courtesy —"

"The moment you heard she was dead? This is great news for you, isn't it, Ruth? She lived long enough for you to pick her brains, and now she has conveniently died. You can't libel the dead, so you can say whatever you please in your little book, right? Isn't that right?"

"My little book, as you put it, is eight hundred and twelve manuscript pages, and that is without the footnotes, acknowledgments, dedication, epigraph, or index. Clearly you are very upset by your loss. I misjudged the timing for my condolence call to you, for which I apologize. You are in an understandably sensitive mood. I can hear that."

"Calling up a stranger to tell her you think her beloved grandmother who has just died was some kind of liar, and now you're planning to stir the shit, is that your idea of a condolence call?"

"I will take that as a rhetorical question, just as I will overlook your unfortunate use of vulgar language, because I recognize that you are becoming very emotional, regrettably, owing to your grief. I am still planning on including you in my acknowledgments."

"No, don't assume it was rhetorical. It was a real question. What the hell do you want from me? Why are you really calling?"

"There is no need to get huffy and rude with me, Rebecca. I was merely informing you of the imminent publication of my book."

"That's it? That's why you called?"

"Well, as I said, I have a list, some very important questions for you as I finish the last corrections on my manuscript as well as some final summarizing thoughts in the last section of the text, not to mention trying to respond to all my editor's queries on the manuscript. You wouldn't believe the number of Post-it notes! I believe that once you familiarize yourself with the transcripts I am mailing to your home, now that I am certain that you are the right Rebecca Gottesfeld — the Willow Street address is correct? — you will understand my concerns more sympathetically."

"Even if I wanted to, how could I possibly answer your questions? I wasn't there."

"You were the closest person in Esther's life. I am assuming you are the sole heir to her estate? She told you about things in her life. Surely, even when you were a little girl, you heard details of her experience in the fire to which outsiders may not have been privy. You have undoubtedly seen or may now possess certain priceless artifacts that may seem valueless to you, but the significance of which would be clear to me. I give you the example of the precious chambered nautilus I gifted to your grandmother when last we met, which you didn't see as having the meaning it had for her and for me."

"For you, we know."

"Yes, well, my point is that what may seem like common knowledge to you could in fact be a unique piece of unrecorded data. And I have not ascertained the existence of anyone else closer, and she never married or seemed to have any significant gentleman callers, at least not so far as I can determine from any record —"

"Like that's your business."

"I am always seeking secondary sources, as any scholar does."

"So I'm what you would call a secondary source."

"A valuable one, indeed."

"First of all, there is no estate. She had almost nothing in her possession, so we aren't going to probate court or anything like that."

"But you are her designated heir?"

"She wrote a simple will years ago, after my parents died, so yes, I am, not that it's any business of yours. But there is no estate."

"I doubt that very much."

"What do you mean? Just what exactly are you looking for?"

"My questions are these, and I will just read them off to you in the hope that you may be willing, though I do understand your reluctance to tarnish your dear grandmother's memory, to shed some light on these crucial details, as I really do want to make my book as thorough and accurate as it can possibly be."

"I'm listening. But I have to tell you, I'm really not in the mood for much more of this, plus I doubt that I know anything that would help you."

"Thank you. I am sure you know a great deal more than you realize. You are reminding me very much of your grandmother, incidentally. One. Where is the money? Your grandmother was almost definitely paid twenty thousand dollars for her testimony by Blanck and Harris, or their agents. I have three reliable secondary sources for this. Believe me, years of my life have gone into pursuing this single detail. It's going to blow the lid off Triangle studies. But I have not been able to trace it after she received the payment in early 1912, after the trial. She appeared to live modestly all her life, as did her son, your late father, as do you, so far as I can tell, though your fiancé, if that is what you call him, your composer friend, is very comfortable, with all of his prestige and success. Perhaps the answer lies in this safe-deposit box you have mentioned, so it goes without saying that I am very interested in that. What bank is it in? If you let me know the contents of this safe-deposit box when you open it, which will be soon, I hope — this could answer my most important question."

"I really can't believe you are asking this. I'm not going to talk about anything like that with you."

"Think about it. It's very important. Two. Did your grandmother speak to you of the children? I am virtually certain that there were, over time, numerous children present on the ninth floor of the Triangle, and so there is no reason to believe that there were no children present on the day of the fire, yet they show up in neither the names of the living nor the names of the dead. I believe children must have died in that fire, but their presence in the Triangle factory was covered up."

"She did, actually —"

"Good. We will go back to that. It is also very important. Please hold that thought. Three. Was your grandmother sexually abused at the Triangle Waist Company, or did she speak of others who worked there who may have suffered from sexual harassment or sexual abuse? Was Pauline ever sexually abused? That interests me particularly."

"She never said anything about things like that. What are you *talking* about?"

"Yes, well, I am in possession of a great deal of important information on this subject. Perhaps if you agree to meet with me for a formal interview, then I can explain to you the nature of my research."

"Does something make you think my great-aunt Pauline was sexually abused, or are you just fishing?"

"I have a great deal of interesting information on this subject, I assure you, from some very reliable sources. I take it very seriously. We will have to discuss this more thoroughly, I can see. Four. Why did your grandmother's story have so many little discrepancies? I have listened to all of my tapes, and I have pored over transcripts of her other interviews, which I would like to send to you so that you may peruse them as well, so I have taken the liberty of making photocopies for just this purpose. I find that her story has discrepancies of detail that go beyond ordinary human fallibility, and so I conclude there is more to the story than the manifest content. I have in point of fact, sorry as I am to say this to you, concluded that certain parts of her account of her escape from the fire are knowingly false. The conflicts are evident to me. The events as she describes them could not possibly have occurred."

"I think we've been over this already. There is really nothing I could tell you —"

"You might change your mind when you read through all the material I will send to you. So these are the four essential questions on which I seek to shed further illumination, and I do have some others, but I gather you may not be receptive to dwelling on all this right now, which would be understandable, of course, though it is a matter of some urgency with regard to my publication schedule."

"You gather that, do you? You suspect that I might not be receptive to dwelling on all this right now? How on earth did that thought ever occur to you? What primary source provided this amazing insight? Or was it a secondary source? Hats off to you, Ruth Zion, for your unerring sense of the subtleties of human nature that so many other people without your keen historian's eye might well overlook!"

"There is no call for hostility, Rebecca. I am being very civil with you. Very cordial. My work is important, I assure you. That is why I am recording this conversation with you right now, in addition to taking detailed notes. This is the way I work, so that I can transcribe all my interviews and be sure of the accuracy of anything I decide to use. I assume I have permission to record this conversation? I meant to confirm this with you earlier, my apologies, but it was a bit confusing when we began, what with my condolences and the need to confirm your identity."

"Are you serious? This phone call is taped? Oh, well, then, I'm totally thrilled and flattered to be recorded for your vast archive of scholarship, for posterity. As Esther used to say, that eats the cake!"

"Your grandmother was not this sarcastic, but I do not think you are very much like her in as many ways as I first supposed."

"You're the expert on Esther Gottesfeld, apparently, so I am sure you know far more about her character than I possibly could."

"Surely you are speaking in sarcastic tones with me because of your sorrow and loss, so I will not take umbrage. But I must say, your attitude is not a productive one. I am very disappointed. I had hoped we could establish some common ground. Some rapport as feminists. Woman to woman. I really do want to dialogue with you. Don't you think your grandmother would have wanted that?"

"Do you really feel qualified to say what

my grandmother would have wanted? You know what? I think you are remarkably perceptive, Ruth Zion, *her*storian extraordinaire. My attitude is *definitely* not a productive one. I am *definitely* being sarcastic. Woman to woman — please just leave me the hell alone. Do *not* call me ever again. I mean it."

"Why don't I call you back to set up a meeting after you have perused the materials I am mailing you — Rebecca? Hello?"

NINE

"You don't have to come with me, George. Seriously. Whatever it is, it's small enough to fit in the smallest size safe-deposit box they have, so it can't be very heavy. Even if she had a solid-gold ingot in there, I should be able to manage, since only one would fit in that box, and that would be only, what, twenty-seven pounds."

"I love the way you know things like that. Anyway, I don't doubt your physical strength," George said.

They were in the coffee shop on the corner of Twelfth Street and Sixth Avenue, with the Sunday *New York Times* and the rubbery western omelettes that Rebecca always required on the Sunday morning after Thanksgiving, which they had spent on their own, perversely eating spaghetti, despite no shortage of invitations from various friends and acquaintances. It would have been different at Scott and Aaron's, since they were practically family, but they had taken Mya to spend time with her Cincinnati grandparents. Neither George nor Rebecca had especially wanted to join some other family's traditional celebration as token lonely people with no Thanksgiving to go to, no matter how generous and openhearted it might have made their hosts feel, and anyway, both had an absolute horror of football on television.

They had always spent Thanksgivings with Esther, every year taking her out for a traditional Thanksgiving meal in a restaurant. This contradicted precisely how "traditional" the meal could possibly be, George would usually point out, a moment that Rebecca would then point out was part of their tradition. Meanwhile, Esther would be ignoring this conversation entirely while scanning the menu for creamed pearl onions, for which she had such a fondness that nothing else about any particular Thanksgiving meal registered one way or the other with her, just so long as there were creamed pearl onions on the menu.

Esther may not have especially cared about where she had Thanksgiving dinner at this late stage of her life, but she had always fussed over her own Thanksgiving feasts throughout Rebecca's childhood, taking pride in her production in the little kitchen on Bleecker Street of all the tradiional dishes for this truly American holiday that was for everyone, like the Fourth of July was for everyone, not like Christmas or Easter, which were reserved for the Christians even if they acted like the whole country was welcome to be involved. Making a Thanksgiving dinner for themselves was one of the ways the Auerbach sisters had tried to be Americans so long ago in their tiny room on Essex Street. Twice they had made a boiled chicken and something approximating a mince pie on the gas ring in their room, in the two years they had together as greenhorns working so hard, having so much fun, making themselves into regular Americans.

When, throughout her childhood, Rebecca helped Esther with the mince pie every year, Esther would always give her a little ball of dough with which to roll out a baby pie of her own, and as Rebecca crimped the top crust over a spoonful of mince, Esther would usually sigh the same sigh and tell her again that hers was just like those little Thanksgiving pies that her sister had made for them in the sink, with raisins soaked in wine and bits of stale bread in a plain dough that was very tough because they couldn't use lard, which was trayfe, and who had money for butter when they had spent it all on the scrawny chicken? Rebecca believed her little pies provided a requisite symbolism, like Elijah's glass of wine on the seder table, an offering for the absent guest. In her adult life, whenever she baked a pie, which was infrequent, although her apple pie was especially competent (the secret ingredient was a shot of Jack Daniels over the apples), she always made an extra little one, and she would give a thought to Pauline's improvised mince dumplings on Essex Street so long ago. Only these days George would usually eat what he called her fractal pie in two bites before it was cool.

George reached across the booth and felt one of her biceps appreciatively, grunting, "Mmm. Strong woman, able to lift gold ingot. I like strong woman. Strong woman bring home secret family gold ingot."

"Interesting fantasy. More likely her top secret borscht and noodle kugel recipes, and oh, I don't know, old insurance papers."

"How was her kugel?"

"It weighed you down for the week. Sometimes it was in my school lunch. Along with the thermoses of goulash and the tins of sardines that marked me as a freak next to those peanut butter and jelly sandwiches everyone else had. There was this girl, Arlene, who always had grape jelly sandwiches on white bread. I thought they looked like wounds, but I was desperately jealous of her odor-free lunch. Nobody wanted to sit near me on those goulash and sardine days."

"Let's hope there is no goulash in the safe-deposit box."

"More likely, I'll find appliance warranties. Maybe my father's secret strategies for a business model based on replacing old rusted carburetors with other old rusted carburetors."

"Is that what he did?"

"I told you about that. Have you ever heard of the vast empire of stores, with locations coast to coast, Gottesfeld Auto Parts?"

"No."

"That's why. Are you feeling me up?"

"I am definitely feeling you up. I just didn't know if you would want me along for the fun of it, or the sadness of it, or the whatever of it. So do you think she had secrets?" He traced the line of her arm with one finger, grazing the sleeve of her sweater, from elbow to wrist and back again.

"Everyone has secrets, George." Rebecca idly stacked up the little tubs of Smucker's strawberry jam that had been served with their toast.

"Stashed in the Emigrant Savings Bank. You know what I mean — secrets about the fire, her testimony at the trial —"

"If she did, I doubt there will be a list of annotated explanations. Maybe she did. Now you're reminding me of that irritating Ruth Zion person. As threatened, she wrote me last week, and I haven't opened the envelope yet. A big padded mailer. I forgot it in New Haven, right on the table by the door. I had meant to bring it with me so I could look at it on the train, but obviously I have a mental block about her, plus I dread to think what's in there." Rebecca squinted at one of the jam packets and read out the ingredients. "Yum, fructose, just like the old country. You know Esther used to put jam in her tea sometimes? There were always seeds in the bottom of her cup. The reused tea bag thing was bad enough, on a saucer in the fridge, ick, but the reused jammy tea bags were really foul."

Evelyn, the waitress who always wore ample smears of blue eye shadow, even for the early breakfast shift, filled their coffee cups yet again, the way she always did for George, whom she called Honey, and rarely did when Rebecca (whom she called Sweetheart only when George was there too) ate there alone with a book or newspaper.

"So you really don't want me to go with you? I have to admit I'm curious."

"No need. It's in deepest Brooklyn, somewhere on Myrtle Avenue, and from there I'll probably go straight to my train."

On the train, once they were under way, Rebecca pulled out the contents of her stained Balducci's canvas tote onto her lap and thumbed through the envelopes and folders that had been jammed into her grandmother's safe-deposit box. She had been made to wait so long at the bank before signing in and dealing with the paperwork, having produced the requisite death certificate and estate papers, wanting not only to open the box to retrieve the contents but also to cancel the box rental, that by the time it was all done, she had just shoved everything from the box into the tote without taking the time to examine anything. Otherwise she would have missed her New Haven train. The bank employee, a dignified black woman with impossibly long, airbrushed fingernails, had smiled politely at her, but Rebecca felt that she had probably been secretly appalled at the cavalier dumping of the box contents by yet another dead person's relative, eager to scoop the loot.

It was all pretty much exactly what she had anticipated. Canceled insurance policies, ILGWU membership documents, Women's Trade Union League documents, a gold WTUL pin for Esther's twenty-five years of membership, Workmen's Circle documents, including the deed to the cemetery plot that would have made life simpler back in September if Rebecca had had it in hand at the time. In the end they had succeeded in burying her grandmother in the grave she had reserved for herself there, between her sister and Sam Gottesfeld, one row away from Rebecca's mother and father, whose graves were obtained with the intervention of the union back in 1961, on the grounds that Isaac Gottesfeld was a Triangle fire survivor guaranteed a burial plot by the Workmen's Circle. The day they buried Esther, George had commented to Rebecca later that night that the sight of her parents' headstones one row away had made him think about how when you go to a crowded movie theater, the group can't all sit together.

Here was a tiny screwdriver, perhaps two inches long, with a tiny red wooden handle on which was printed GOTTESFELD AUTO SUPPLY. In a cracked leather eyeglass case, there was a flimsy pair of silver wire spectacles with thick, cloudy lenses. Rebecca held them up to her face and tried to look through them at the passing landscape, but the effect was a complete blur that made her dizzy. Who was the last person to look through these lenses? She folded them tenderly and slid them back into the leather case. There were three coins wrapped in a scrap of newsprint, stuck together by something brownish and gummy. When Rebecca unwrapped and separated them, she found an Indian-head penny from 1907, an unfamiliar coin from 1910 with a female head on one side and a V on the other, which she realized must be a nickel, and a small, thin silver coin which she at first took to be a dime, until closer inspection revealed that it was a foreign coin from 1909, with a numeral 10 on one side over some Cyrillic letters that might signify kopecks.

The real prize seemed to be the tarnished nickel pocket watch that was wrapped in creased brown paper and tied with a ribbon on which the words "Grossberger Bakery" repeated in green script. Gingerly, Rebecca had unrolled the bundle, not knowing what to expect, and at first she didn't understand the significance of the object in her hand, but then she did. As she held Sam's watch, almost the way one would cradle a wounded baby bird, she could feel something loose sliding around inside the case. When she prized open the smooth metal lid that concealed the face, she saw that the watch crystal was badly shattered, with pieces of the glass missing. The hands stood at seven minutes past five. There were no markings on the watch case, which was attached at the loop over the winding stem to a worn, braided black cord.

Here was her own birth certificate, Esther's naturalization papers from 1912, a canceled mortgage document for an address in Brooklyn (which Rebecca realized must be the little house where her father grew up, once the grocery store was prosperous enough so they didn't have to live in the back anymore, though Esther had moved from there to the house in Flatbush where she had lived when Rebecca was little). Here was the marriage license for Isaac Gottesfeld and Barbara Edwards, paper-clipped to a short newspaper article Rebecca had never seen before, a two-paragraph description of the car accident on Flatbush Avenue that had killed her mother and father the year she turned eight. The paper clip had left a rust stain on the clipping and on the marriage license, which was a negative image printed on shiny paper, folded into quarters that were almost completely torn along two of the worn fold creases. Barbara Edwards, age thirty-one, had married Isaac Gottesfeld, age thirty-eight, on July 22, 1950, at Borough Hall in Brooklyn. Rebecca recognized neither the addresses they gave nor the signature of the witness. A friend? She supposed it might have been a stranger they found loitering in Borough Hall, or a clerk. Rosemary Gianelli, who lived at 63 Joralemon Street. Rebecca wondered where she was now, if she would recall having witnessed this wedding. How had Barbara and Isaac spent their three years alone together before Rebecca's birth? She knew so much less about them than she knew about her grandmother.

Barbara's parents, Rebecca's grandparents, lived in Grosse Pointe, Michigan, and were only somewhat more devastated by their only child's death than they had apparently been by her decision to marry an impecunious Jew. Perhaps for them it had seemed like a logical sequence of incidents, the inevitable outcome of events once she started on this unfortunate path. They had sent Rebecca small, impersonal ("WASPy," explained Esther) birthday gifts until she went to college in Vermont, which was paid for by a Hodgson family trust established by Rebecca's long-dead great-grandfather, who had made his money in railroads and real estate. Grandmother Edwards had made it clear to Rebecca that the college tuition payments, which they were legally bound to offer, would be the extent and limit of her Edwards family legacy. In order to get the tuition money, she had been made to sign an agreement relinquishing further claims to numerous family trusts, which had been notarized by the secretary at the Workmen's Circle office, where Esther worked part-time, after the Women's Trade Union League was closed.

"They treat you like this because their blood is so thin, people like your mother's family," Esther had fumed, while the secretary, an elderly kvetch who had worked in the fur trade, got out her special official embosser. "They're going to die rich with everything comfortable, and they got to send their lawyers with papers to protect their money from their greedy Jewish granddaughter. Shame on them."

Roger and Grace Edwards lived their final years on the outskirts of Grosse Pointe in an assisted-living facility with its own golf course. Rebecca had hardly ever thought about them, and she assumed they had hardly ever thought about her, except when they sent her their annual printed Christmas card, on which Grandmother Edwards always conscientiously crossed out the "Merry Christmas" and wrote in "Season's Greetings" as her way of showing awareness of their only granddaughter's regrettable heritage. They were essentially strangers. When Rebecca was in graduate school, word came from their attorney's office that they had died, first Grace and then Roger, only a month apart. The letter was accompanied by photocopies of the documentation to remind her that she was not entitled to any inheritance.

Isaac had tried to make a go of it in the auto parts business after the grocery store closed, and Rebecca remembered that Esther had spoken a few times about a feud between Isaac and his former partner in the business, Benny Adler, saying that each of them had swindled the other in some way that tied up her father's meager estate for most of Rebecca's childhood. In the end, the estate was finally settled the year she entered Stuyvesant High School, and Rebecca inherited nothing. The taxes owed on a garage on Ten Eyck Street had wiped out the modest legacy left over from the bitter litigation and legal fees expended in pointless pursuit through the legal system of the hapless Benny Adler. Esther had placed too much faith in the judgment and legal acumen of Sol Kramer, a slightly shifty union lawyer who handled the matter as a favor to her for very low fees. ("You pay peanuts, you get a monkey," Esther had concluded when the whole sorry matter was done.) But now Rebecca had something tangible from the auto parts business after all — the screwdriver.

Thinking about her parents now, holding these papers in her lap as the train raced toward Connecticut, Rebecca thought about the way a fire in 1911 had changed everything in her family. If Sam had survived that fire, so much might have been different. And Pauline would have had a life, would have been a sister to Esther all these years. She would probably have married and had her own family. There would be aunts and uncles, cousins. There were so many phantom people who might have been.

Sam would have died by now, of course, but Esther and Pauline would have stuck together through thick and thin. But then, if not for the car accident, Rebecca's own father might be an old man of ninety, perhaps still going strong, considering Esther's astonishing longevity. Rebecca might still have a mother — many of her friends had living mothers in their eighties. Rebecca sighed and closed her eyes for a moment, letting the train rock her, trying fruitlessly to imagine her mother as an old lady. She missed Esther.

She could hardly remember her parents at all. Other people have full recall of their early childhoods, but her early memories were few, more like snapshots of some random specific moments than like the hours of home movies everyone else seemed to have in their heads. A night-light in the form of a slowly revolving circus tent, with clowns tumbling all the way around, and her parents coming in to kiss her while she feigned sleep. The cherry and almond smell of her mother's Jergens lotion. Sometimes Rebecca put Jergens on her arm and then smelled it, just to keep that faint connection. There was a night when she heard them laughing in a secret, different way, when they had come in from having been out for dinner, all dressed up. Playing in a sandbox, with other children around her, digging her feet into the cold sand. A neighbor's dog lapping at her face while she sat helplessly strapped into her stroller, her mother preoccupied in a conversation with the neighbor. A birthday party with three candles on a cake, her mother helping her blow them out. Riding in the backseat of a car on the way to visit her grandmother, feeling an upsurge of love for the backs of their heads.

Rebecca's strongest memory of her father, who spent long workdays away from home and was rarely present for meals, was not a happy one. They were at the beach with Esther, whose union friends with ocean apartments always gave them guest tickets for access across the boardwalk to this stretch of sand. Esther, in her ancient navy one-piece with white polka dots, had been set up on a folding chair under an umbrella, next to the Styrofoam picnic cooler, while they spread towels on either side of her. Rebecca had been taken into the water by her father, and after some initial splashing, he had picked her up and swung her onto his hip against his wet skin as they waded out into the receding tide.

"Do you want to go out?" he had asked. Yes, she had replied, apprehensive about the surging waves that repeatedly pushed against his legs and challenged his balance, but he had only walked farther into the sea. "Oh, you want to go in, you mean?" he had asked then, and she nodded, too scared to speak as the water had lapped at her shins tucked inside his arm. But he laughed then, and walked them deeper, taking step after step, teasing her as she squealed in rising terror while the water smacked against her waist, saying, "But you said you wanted to go *in,* into the water." No, she pleaded, I mean I want to go *out.* "Oh, you want to go *out* to sea!" he had cried, walking them deeper yet.

A therapist in New Haven, hearing this story, had asked Rebecca to say more about her family, to say whatever came to mind, and what had come to mind startled them both. She believed that her father wouldn't have died in the car accident along with her mother, that they would both be alive today if it were not for the Triangle fire. But Esther herself would have died years ago had she not been so busy surviving the fire so effectively.

"How does that work?" the therapist, Roberta Waxman, had asked respectfully in her gentle voice, leaning closer to Rebecca over her Eames ottoman in her quiet and tasteful office on Bradley Street. "Say that again please? I want to be clear. If it weren't for the fire in 1911, your parents would be alive, they wouldn't have died in the car crash that occurred when you were eight years old, but your grandmother who raised you, meanwhile, the one who is now one hundred and three, she wouldn't still be alive? She wouldn't have needed to keep living the way she has if they hadn't died? So the fire caused the accident, and the accident made your grandmother live to be one hundred and three?" And of course Rebecca, scientist that she was, had no logical explanation for this construction, nor could she even understand where those thoughts she didn't know she possessed had come from.

The businessman seated beside Rebecca was peering with obvious interest at the documents in her lap. She gave him a long, deliberate stare. Without acknowledging her, he turned his gaze back to the spreadsheets on his laptop, pretending, as people do, that he had been lost in reverie, gazing only into the middle distance, and hadn't really been looking at her personal papers at all. Was it really such bizarre behavior that she was examining these things now, on the train, instead of waiting for the privacy of her own apartment? The acrylic-nail woman at the bank would probably have expected her to do just this. A thin sealed envelope lay between two documents in the bundle on her lap, and Rebecca opened it carefully. There was an unfamiliar photo of a man who was presumably Sam Gottesfeld and — which was it, Esther or Pauline? — posed formally in a studio beside a potted palm, with frozen, unsmiling faces. She was seated. Sam, his curly hair center-parted and brilliantined into submission for the picture, stood partly behind the chair, slightly turned, with one hand resting possessively on her shoulder. He could have been Italian. With his broad features and almost hooded eyes, he looked very unlike her own father. Esther had always said Isaac took after the Auerbach men. Rebecca flipped the picture over and saw in faint, unfamiliar penciled script, "engaged, February 1911," which meant, of course, this had to be her grandmother, though she had thought at first that she was looking at Pauline, the younger, slightly taller sister in the framed photo Esther had always kept on her dresser throughout Rebecca's life. Now Rebecca had it on her own bedroom dresser. They had looked so alike, according to Esther, that many people really did believe they were twins, and sometimes they pretended that they were, just for fun.

Rebecca turned the picture over to study it again. Of course it had to be Esther, his fiancée. Esther looked older than her years in the tailored shirtwaist with its mutton-leg sleeves. Something like a large, ornamented pin in the shape of a figure eight glinted on her bosom. Rebecca studied the flowing, layered skirt, trying to imagine what was involved in getting dressed in all that every day — what it took to be regular Jewish Gibson girls.

Rebecca realized that Esther would have already been pregnant with Isaac at the time of this portrait, although perhaps she hadn't yet known it herself. She searched Esther's face closely for some sign of this, but found her gaze opaque and distant, very different from the lively and receptive Esther she had known all of her life and now missed so painfully every day. She held the portrait at arm's length to see it for what it was when it was taken, rather than for what it had become, a tragic document of an aborted future that would never be. Everything would change for them in a quarter of an hour on a Saturday afternoon, just weeks after this photograph was taken. This had to be the only photograph of them together. Rebecca wondered why she hadn't ever seen it before now, why her grandmother had kept something so precious, the closest thing to a marriage document she would ever have, in the safe-deposit box, hidden from view. Well, maybe for Esther this *was* like a marriage document, the only marriage document she would ever possess, a precious artifact to be preserved, like a birth certificate. Rebecca studied the faces of her grandparents again, looking for traces of her father's melancholy features in Sam's face. Maybe something around the mouth. By the time Rebecca was born, her father was twice as old as his own father would ever be. The cliché that came to mind was true — Sam and Esther were both so young. They had their health.

There is something more sticking inside the envelope that had contained the engagement portrait. Rebecca fishes it out gingerly. It's a small slip of paper, torn along one side. It's hardly anything, just a slip of brittle paper printed with the words:

Day: _____

Name: _____

No. Pieces: _____

There is very faint pencil writing on the dotted lines, but because of where the slip is torn, Rebecca can only make out part of the writing all the way down. "Mar—" is on the first line, "P. Auerb—" is on the second, and "25—" is on the third line. At

215

the bottom, in a different hand, in a darker grease pencil or crayon, is printed "Jaco—." Whatever this slip of paper signifies, it is important enough for Esther to save it all these years with her engagement photograph. Rebecca tucks it, with the photo, back into the envelope with care.

What else? Sales contracts for cars long gone. A union lapel pin. A Brooklyn Public Library card for Isaac. A class photo of Isaac's from Brooklyn PS 3, with all the boys in jackets and ties. Rebecca notes with interest that there are five blacks in the class. Were they called colored then, or Negroes? Isaac's diploma from Boy's High School. A report card of Isaac's, also from Boy's High. A certificate of appreciation from ORT, folded inside a cardboard folder, with gratitude for Esther's meaningful years of service. A 1972 letter from Teddy Kollek, mayor of Jerusalem, inviting Esther to go to Jerusalem as his guest. Rebecca recalls no such trip ever taking place. In fact, Esther never left the country, so far as she knows. A letter dated March 31, 1911, from Mayor William J. Gaynor of New York City, addressed to Miss Esther Auerbach, c/o Mr. and Mrs. Solomon Loeb, Hartsdale, New York, offering her his sincerest condolences on the loss of her sister and her fiancé, whose "heroic deeds and brave demeanor shall be remembered in the city of New York for decades to come." Several of Rebecca's elementary school report cards, stapled together. A postcard of Bear Mountain that Rebecca suddenly remembers, the moment she sees it, having chosen it and mailed it to her grandmother from Girl Scout camp her first summer away. A 1956 news clipping from the *Long Island Express,* in a small unmarked envelope of its own, with the headline triangle FIRE SURVIVOR SUCCUMBS TO SUSPICIOUS BLAZE, reporting on the death of Morris Jacobs. A 1990 note card from Rose Friedman, postmarked California, saying, "It was good to see you at the ceremony. It's hard to believe we were both so young, now that we're both so old. *Nisht schlect!*" One more worn brown envelope remains in Rebecca's lap, along with a confetti of brittle paper crumbs shed by all the papers she has been unfolding and refolding.

The train is pulling into Bridgeport. The nosy businessman has closed his laptop and tucked it into his briefcase, which he now snaps shut on his lap with weary precision. He tosses his *Wall Street Journal* on the floor under the seat in front of them before standing up. His suit jacket is folded fussily in the overhead rack, and he reaches over Rebecca for it carefully so as not to drop things from the pockets. Rebecca waits for him to leave before opening this final envelope, which is sealed closed with tape newer than the envelope, which has many folds and creases from previous use.

Surprisingly, the words "FOR MY GRANDDAUGHTER REBECCA" are printed in her grandmother's familiar hand on this envelope. Through the train window Rebecca can see the businessman on the platform, flailing a little as he punches his arms into the sleeves of his jacket, first one, and then the other, his briefcase clamped between his feet. The train starts moving again. She tilts the envelope, and out slides a bundle of seven brittle savings passbooks from the Emigrant Savings Bank, tied with kitchen string, stacked in chronological order, several of them encased in brittle plastic sleeves. They are each in the name of Esther Auerbach Gottesfeld. All but the most recent one have been canceled, and the balance of each has apparently been carried forward into the next. The oldest four passbooks have handwritten entries; the first deposit is recorded in an almost incomprehensible spidery copperplate, for $20,000, on January 3, 1912. The current passbook has a pale blue cover. The first entry, dated 1986, is for $183,637.17. It has been up-dated ten times, once a year. The last entry is in 1996. As with the other passbooks, there are no subsequent deposits shown after the starting balance. This money has simply been gathering interest from 1912 to now. The most recent balance, on October 28, 1996, is $201,567.34.

TEN

People of the State of New York v. Isaac Harris and Max Blanck
Trial Testimony, Friday, December 22, 1911, Day 15

District Attorney Bostwick: Please state your name for the record.

Witness: My name is Esther Gottesfeld.

Defense Attorney Steuer: Objection. The witness is giving a false name.

Judge Crain: Witness will provide her legal name for the record.

Witness: My name is Esther Auerbach Gottesfeld. My fiancé was Sam Gottesfeld and I got his little baby and everyone knows he died —

Steuer: Objection! Witness is testifying outside the scope of the question.

Crain: Please limit your testimony to direct answers of the questions you are being asked, Miss Auerbach.

Witness: Everyone calls me Mrs. Gottesfeld. That's how I go.

Steuer: Your Honor, under the circumstances, the defense has no objection to humoring the witness with regard to this matter of nomenclature.

Witness: Now you don't mind so much?

Crain: Please wait for a question, Mrs. Gottesfeld.

Bostwick: Please state your place of birth, Mrs. Gottesfeld.

Witness: I am Belarusian, now is Russia, from Pinsk. With my sister.

Bostwick: Please tell the court when you came to America, limiting your testimony only to your own experience.

Witness: I am here since January 12, 1909. That's the day we arrive on Ellis Island. We don't get to set foot off Ellis Island until January 13, but Ellis Island is America already, so we don't mind, that's the day we celebrate to arrive in America. I learn English pretty good since then.

Bostwick: Your English is very good, but I will remind you that we have a Yiddish interpreter here if you feel that you cannot express your answers clearly in English.

Witness: Mr. Steuer, he also speaks good

Yiddish. And Mr. Rubin. You, I don't think so.

Bostwick: These proceedings are in English, however. So please speak up if you find yourself unable to express your thoughts clearly in English, and we will summon the Yiddish interpreter. Now, please state your profession for the record.

Witness: I sew. Now, I am home with my baby, but before that I was a sleeve setter at the Triangle Waist Company. I worked there with my sister, she died from the fire.

Steuer: Your Honor.

Crain: Mr. Bostwick, please remind your witness to limit her answers.

Bostwick: How long did you work at the Triangle Waist Company?

Witness: I work there with my sister since the end of April in 1910, so almost a year we were working there is my answer to your question.

Bostwick: Where did you work at the Triangle Waist Company?

Witness: I worked on the ninth floor, with my sister, we sat next to each other, where the machines were all the new ones, the Singers. Not like on eight, where they had also those Willcox machines, not so good in my opinion. Maybe if you are not so skilled you don't know the difference.

Bostwick: Can you tell us where on the ninth floor your Singer sewing machine was situated?

Witness: I was in the middle of the second row of tables, with my sister, it was near a pillar. I faced away from the window behind me. That's how we all sat, in those rows.

Bostwick: Please describe for us in your own words the events of March 25 of this year.

Witness: The day of the fire.

Bostwick: Yes, the day of the fire. Please describe only your own experience, not what happened to anyone else, if you don't mind.

Witness: This is what happened. I am working at my machine, with only a few minutes left before the end of the day.

Bostwick: Do you recall the time when you first knew about the fire?

Witness: Just before the workday is finished, we are there, so it was fifteen minutes before five in the afternoon. Somebody rang the bell so some girls were leaving but some of us were taking just a minute more to finish up. I remember so clearly I can still see it, that I had only two left sleeves to finish in my work — my sister

Pauline, I got to mention her here, Your Honor, she did the right sleeves and I did the left sleeves. It was the end of the week and we just got our pay packets, from our boss Mr. Jacobs, and I took them both, for my sister too, and I tucked them into my stocking, so she could keep working for those minutes to finish what she got to finish for the week.

Bostwick: Go on.

Witness: So I hear at that moment a big noise behind me, while I am still bending down with my stocking for the money, like nothing I ever hear in my life before, so I think, Is it an explosion? So I turn around, and everyone is turning around, and what do we see? Flames! The flames are coming up the window from underneath. And the windows, they're breaking from the fire, so many got out from the eighth floor, all the bosses and the people in that office, on the tenth floor, they got out, but we are on the ninth floor —

Steuer: Objection!

Crain: Witness will limit her testimony to her own experience, please.

Witness: So there is this big explosion like I already said. And now I see these flames and the girls all around me started to shout and scream, my sister also, and everyone goes in a commotion, and the flames, they get bigger at the window and then they come inside with us, coming along the wall and across the floor, it's like water flowing, I've never seen anything like that, and everyone is frightened and suddenly it's pandemonium. Now the flames go all around, every which way, and it gets hot like a furnace. Everyone screams, but nobody moves, everybody is like a statue for just that second, maybe this is my imagination but that's what it seemed like to me, everyone is frozen like a statue, and then there is a rush of all the girls, everybody trying to go out, but there is in the way all the machinery, on the tables, and there are girls trying to crawl under but you can't go under, and everybody is pushing and there were girls climbing across the tables, but some of them, their long skirts got bunched and they got caught in the machines.

Bostwick: Please continue.

Witness: It was like a madhouse. Everyone was screaming and pushing and calling and some girls were praying and nobody could hear what anyone else was calling out. Then Mr. Grannick, one of the older garment cutters, he stood up on a chair and tried to call out something but nobody could see him except if you were close because of the smoke. There was so much smoke, and people were screaming and coughing and choking and nobody could hear what he was saying with the noise — he was one of the ones who got out — and I saw a girl with her hair on fire, and then another one was running by with her clothes all burning up. It was all a shock.

Bostwick: Do you want a drink of water?

Witness: No, I go on now and tell the rest. There were these two Italian sisters, they just stood there screaming but not moving, which doesn't help anyone, and they were in my way, they were choking and their faces were all red, so I go past them, and they're not moving, and I never saw them again. Then I see there are too many girls at that door —

Bostwick: Which door is this?

Witness: The Washington Place door. Nobody could go out that way; it was a terrible thing, but nobody's fault, because the door, it opened in, didn't we all know that already. They inspected us going out that door every day, they had a guard to look into our bags and even poke us to see if we had anything hidden in our garments, they always had to make sure we weren't stealing any of the goods.

Bostwick: Did you try to open this door?

Witness: All those girls were pushing and pushing together, it was just so terrible I can't really describe it, with the smell of everything burning, hair and clothing and the black smoke everywhere, to make everyone choke, and they were all pushing at once. That smell of burning flesh, like cooking meat only so terrible, once you smell it you will never forget it. Some girls are burning and I heard the girls in the front who didn't get burned maybe even got squeezed to death from the pushing but nobody could open that door.

Steuer: Objection.

Crain: The jury will disregard the witness's remarks about what she has heard rumors about but did not experience personally on the day in question.

Bostwick: Please tell us what you did next, Mrs. Gottesfeld.

Witness: I had this idea about the other door — it was for the bosses only to use on the weekend, when the freight elevator, it wasn't in use, these stairs were not for the girls, they told us, so it was a rule, and at the Triangle you got to follow all the rules or they get rid of you and there is always someone who wants to take your place — it was by the back side of the building, the Greene Street side, instead of the Washington Place side, they would go on these other stairs, they were by the freight elevators to walk up to the tenth floor, that's where the offices were. So I go across the room, but I had to run right into the flames to get across. And this is where I lost my sister, because I was holding her hand and then I let go, and she didn't follow me, she must have been afraid of the flames, so —

Steuer: Objection. Witness is testifying outside her own experience.

Crain: Please describe only what happened to you, Mrs. Gottesfeld. Your own experience.

Witness: So then I see Mr. Jacobs, the one who just paid me —

Bostwick: This is Morris Jacobs?

Witness: Yes, Morris Jacobs, and he's got a waist wrapped around his face like a mask, so he can breathe with all the smoke around us, and when I see him go to this other door I mentioned, and he has a key from inside his pocket, and I see him unlock the door, and he goes in the door but then he closes it behind him.

Bostwick: Please go on.

Witness: I need a moment to collect. I am very emotional because of my sister I can't

228

talk about.

Crain: We'll reconvene in one hour.

[Recess]

Bostwick: Now, Mrs. Gottesfeld, please tell us what happened after you saw Mr. Jacobs go through the door. I will remind the jury that this is the Morris Jacobs whose testimony was heard on Tuesday of this week.

Witness: I follow Mr. Jacobs, like I said. I try to open the door he just passed through, but something is making it stay closed. I think to myself why is it sticking like this, but then I push so hard on it I could feel it open a little and I realize that Mr. Jacobs is trying to close the door and maybe, I don't know why, lock it behind him, maybe he is in a panic and he has some idea he can control the fire from going in the stairs, and I don't know why he would do this —

Bostwick: Please just describe your own experience.

Witness: So I push as hard as I can and then the door, it flies open, and I go through, I fall down, but then I get up, and there is nobody there, and I see so much flames and smoke that I think, Well, you can't go down the stairs, but maybe you can go up the stairs, so I go up the stairs, even if it doesn't make sense, because I think how did they get out from the offices, maybe the roof, and it's empty, they have all saved themselves already, from the pressing and the shipping tables there is nobody left.

Bostwick: Were there other people around you? Did other girls try to follow you through this door?

Witness: I don't know. I don't remember. I don't think anyone was right behind me, but it was all confusion and the smoke was so black and everyone was coughing and screaming and crying. And it's all in a moment.

Bostwick: Are you aware that numerous other witnesses have testified trying the door to this stairwell but finding it locked, and nobody can recall seeing you or Mr. Jacobs at this door on the Greene Street side? Why do you suppose nobody else was able to escape the fire the way you escaped the fire?

Witness: You ask me not to talk about other people and only say my own experience. Now you ask me to say what happened to other people I didn't even see. What do you want I should say? I am trying just to tell my own story, like you said before when I talked about my sister.

Crain: Order, order. Witness makes a good point for the defense. Please continue to limit your testimony to descriptions of your own experience, Mrs. Gottesfeld.

Witness: I seen a ladder going up to a hole in the ceiling so that was it. I go up the ladder, I see daylight like I never thought I would see again, and then, like a miracle, I am on the roof, and there are firemen up there. They order me I have to crawl across another ladder, this one goes over a big gap to another building on the Waverly Place side, and somehow I do this, with my eyes closed, because I am afraid of falling down in the space between the buildings. It's like a nightmare, but I do it. So I go over, and people help me stand up, and then I just walked down ten flights of stairs like everything in the world is ordinary again, just for those minutes it takes me to go down the ten flights. So then I am on the street, and I see all the bodies —

Steuer: Objection.

Bostwick: Thank you, Mrs. Gottesfeld, that's all we need to hear about at this time.

Crain: Court is in recess until two o'clock. *[Recess]*

Steuer: How old is your baby, Mrs. Gottesfeld?

Witness: He is three months.

Steuer: Is he a healthy baby?

Witness: He eats good, but colic he got.

Steuer: My condolences to you for the death of your baby's father. It is fortunate indeed that in your delicate condition you were able to survive this tragic occurrence and have your baby without complications. Now, Mrs. Gottesfeld, will you tell us, in your own words, what happened on March 25 of this year, at the Triangle Waist Company, beginning at approximately 4:45 that afternoon?

Witness: You want I should say my whole story again?

Steuer: Can you remember it? Are you able to tell your whole story with accuracy?

Witness: Of course I can.

Steuer: Please do so.

Witness: All over again?

Steuer: You claim that your memory is accurate.

Witness: If you want. This is what happened. I am working at my machine, with only a few minutes left before the end of the day. I had just two left sleeves to finish in my work. We had just got our pay packets, from Mr. Jacobs, so I am tucking them both in my stocking, and just at that same moment I hear a big noise behind me, like nothing I ever hear before, so I think, an explosion? And what do we see everywhere? Flames! The windows are breaking from the heat of the fire and everyone is screaming, and the flames are coming inside, and everywhere, they come along the wall and they come across the floor. And now it gets hot like a furnace. Everyone screams, but nobody moves, everybody is like a statue. And suddenly after that all the girls are trying to go out, everybody is pushing and the girls are climbing across the tables, and crawling, and their skirts are getting caught in the machines, and people are going on fire.

Steuer: Didn't you say the flames were like water flowing?

Witness: Yes, it is just like water flowing, the way those flames are creeping along.

Steuer: Did you see Mr. Grannick?

Witness: Mr. Grannick, he gets up on a chair, but nobody can hear what he is telling us, with the noise and confusion. And then I see a girl with her hair on fire, and everyone is choking and coughing, and then another one goes by running with her clothes all burning up. And I see these Italian sisters just screaming and praying, so I push past them, and then I see too many girls at the Washington Place door.

Steuer: Tell us about this door, please. Were you familiar with this door?

Witness: Everyone knew the way this door went, because they inspected us every day as we go out that door. The guard, he looked into our bags to make sure we weren't stealing any of the goods.

Steuer: So you knew from experience that this door opened in, but in the panic and disorder everyone was pushing the wrong way on this unlocked door?

Bostwick: Objection. Attorney Steuer is testifying, Your Honor.

Steuer: Did you know from experience that this door opened in?

Witness: Yes.

Steuer: In your experience, was this door ever locked during the workday?

Witness: No.

Steuer: Why didn't someone open this door, then?

Witness: There was so much panic and everyone was pushing. Nobody could open the door. All those girls were pushing and pushing together, it was just so terrible, with the smell of everything burning, hair and clothing and the black smoke everywhere, and everyone was coughing and crying, and they were all pushing at once. There was the terrible smell of burning hair, and the smell of burning flesh, once you smell it, you will know it forever, like cooking meat only so terrible.

Steuer: Would it have been possible to open the door if there hadn't been so much confusion?

Witness: I don't know.

Steuer: On a regular day, would it have been possible for anyone to open that door?

Witness: I guess so.

Steuer: Was that door usually locked at closing time?

Witness: No, it was the door we all have to go through, one by one, like I keep saying.

Steuer: So you never knew the door to be locked?

Witness: That was the door we go out, how could it be locked? You ask the same thing a different way but it's the same thing.

Steuer: Thank you. Please continue. What did you do next after you saw all the girls crowding in such confusion and disorder that they couldn't open the Washington Place stairway door?

Witness: I had this idea about the other door — it was for the bosses only, not for the girls, on the weekends, it was a rule — but it was by the back side of the building, the Greene Street side. By the freight elevators, they could go up these stairs to the tenth floor, that's where the offices were. So I go right into the flames to get across. Maybe that was when I got my burn on my face and my hand, I don't remember. Mr. Jacobs has a waist wrapped around his face like a mask, so he makes it safe to breathe, he knows how to make himself safe, and I see him going to this other door, and he's got a key, and I see him unlock the door, and he goes in the door but then he closes it behind him.

Steuer: Did you see him take the key from his pocket or was it on a string hanging by the door?

Witness: I am pretty sure I seen him take the key from his pocket.

Steuer: Are you aware that four other people have testified that this key was kept on a string of material, hanging by the door, two of them testifying just this morning in this courtroom, sitting where you are sitting now, having sworn to tell the truth, just as you have sworn to tell the truth?

Bostwick: Objection.

Witness: I never seen any key on any string by that door, and that's the truth.

Steuer: Had you ever had any occasion to go through this stairway door in your ten months working at the Triangle Waist Company?

Witness: No.

Steuer: Had you ever tried to open this door in the past, to ascertain whether or not this door was kept locked or unlocked?

Witness: No, I just told you. I never go in that door.

Steuer: So for all you know this door was always unlocked?

Witness: For all I know. For all I know they got dancing girls for the bosses up there every day.

Crain: Order, order.

Steuer: Had you ever tried to fit the key on the string into the lock to this door before the day in question?

Bostwick: Objection. Mr. Steuer is badgering the witness with repetitive questions.

Crain: Mr. Steuer, you have established that the witness had no personal familiarity with the door in question. Please continue, Miss Auerbach.

Witness: I go by Mrs. Gottesfeld.

Crain: Mrs. Gottesfeld, I beg your pardon.

Witness: I followed Mr. Jacobs to that door. The Greene Street door for which I got no personal familiarity.

Crain: Order, order.

Witness: So when I go to open the door,

something is making it stay closed. I push and I push so hard that it opens a little, and I know Mr. Jacobs is on the other side closing the door, so I push as hard as I can and then the door flies open, because this door opens out, into the stairs, not like the other door, that goes in, like we said, and all of a sudden he must have let go and run away, and I fall right through the door and fall down. After that, I get up, and I don't see any girls behind me, and I don't know why not, I don't know why nobody else thinks of the Greene Street stairway to go out, and when I see the smoke and the flames, I know I can't go down the stairs after all, but I think maybe I can go up to the roof, because I think how did they get out from the offices up on the tenth floor where the bosses were, and I was right.

Steuer: What happened then?

Witness: I go up to the tenth floor where there is nobody left from the offices, all the people are gone from pressing and shipping, also, just the tables are there, with the goods lying all around, some even on the floor, and I seen this ladder to where there is daylight, which I never thought I would see again, and like a miracle, I am on the roof, and the firemen up there order me to crawl across a ladder they have, over a big gap to another building, so I close my eyes and I do it, even though I have fear to go down the crack in the buildings. And that's it. Some students help me stand up and I walk down the stairs of that other building out to the street. And I am not allowed to say what I saw after that.

Steuer: Didn't you say that going across on the ladder between the buildings was like a dream?

Witness: No, I said it was like a nightmare. That's what it was. A nightmare.

Steuer: Thank you very much, Mrs. Gottesfeld. Very good. Now, will you tell us again about your experience of the fire in the Triangle Waist Company?

Witness: What do you mean?

Steuer: Tell us everything you have just told us.

Witness: All over?

Steuer: If you can. In your own words of course. You are telling your story in your own words?

Witness: I got all my own words to tell this story. Even if my English isn't so excellent. You think I borrow somebody else's words? This is what happened. I am sewing at my machine, and there are just two left sleeves to finish and then I am done. Mr. Jacobs just gave us our pay packets for the week's work, so that's what I am doing, putting them into my stocking to be safe, when there is a big noise behind me, like nothing I ever hear before, some kind of explosion. And what do we see everywhere? Flames! And now there are windows coming apart from the fire, and everyone is screaming, and there are flames everywhere on the walls and they come across the floor, like water flowing, like a river of flames. And first everyone is quiet for one moment like a statue but then everyone is trying at once to go out, and the girls, they are climbing up on the tables to get out, and their skirts are getting caught in the machines, and everywhere is people going on fire and stuck and not able to get out. It was a madhouse.

Steuer: And then what happened?

Witness: Mr. Grannick, he's a cutter, like I told you before, he gets up on a chair to announce a plan maybe but nobody can hear, with the noise and confusion. And there are these Italian sisters just screaming and praying, so I push past them, I'm sorry, but I had to, I never seen them alive again after that, and I see all these girls with their hair on fire and their clothes on fire, and everyone is coughing and choking, and the smell is so terrible now, you can smell the burning hair and that smell of burning flesh I will never forget the rest of my life, and then I see all these girls at the Washington Place door. This door, it opened in, we all knew that, but with all the panic and pushing, nobody could open the door. Everyone was in a panic with the smell of everything burning, hair and clothing and the black smoke everywhere, and everyone is choking, and they were all pushing at once, all the girls. So then I got this thought about the other door on the Greene Street side, by the freight elevators, those elevators, they didn't run on Saturday and so maybe that is why nobody else thought to go that way. So I go right through the flames to get across to go there by that door, because I see Morris Jacobs with a waist wrapped around his face so he can breathe, and I follow him. I don't know why nobody else thinks of this but I don't remember any other girls behind me. He unlocks this door with a key, I don't know where he got the key, and he goes in the door, and then before he can close it tight from the other side I push in right after him.

Steuer: What happened then?

Witness: I push and I push so hard that door opens a little, even though Mr. Jacobs is on the other side, trying to close that door. But I am stronger trying to open it than he can hold it closed, or maybe he got scared of the fire and ran away, because the next thing, that door flies open, into the stairs, and I fall right down into the stairway. So I get up, and look down the stairs but it is all flames and smoke, so I know I can't go down the stairs, but I am thinking maybe everybody can go up to the roof this way, because I think that must be how they get out from the offices on the tenth floor.

Steuer: Did you go up to the tenth floor?

Witness: I go up there and nobody is left, and I look around where there are the pressers and the shipping tables, but then I go up this ladder to where there is daylight, and it's a miracle to see I am on the roof, with firemen all around, and a fireman says, "Oh, look at this, I thought that was it but here comes one more," and they tell me I have to go across a ladder they put across the big gap between the buildings. I have to do it or I won't live, so I close my eyes and I do it, and it's like a nightmare, but I do it, and then when I get to the other side there are students who help me stand up, so I can walk down the stairs of that other building, like a normal day, all the way down to the street, and then I go out. That's what happened.

Steuer: Thank you, Mrs. Gottesfeld. You certainly do know your testimony. That's all, Your Honor.

Crain: Mr. Bostwick?

Bostwick: Mrs. Gottesfeld, when we discussed your coming here today to testify in this trial, do you recall what I told you to say?

Witness: You didn't tell me to say nothing. You just said I should tell my story in my own words.

Bostwick: And have you done that?

Witness: I done it three times already so far!

Bostwick: Thank you, Mrs. Gottesfeld. The People have nothing more for this witness.

Crain: We are adjourned at this time until Monday morning at nine o'clock.

ELEVEN

George hadn't looked at the *Huntington's Concerto* in a very long time. He had started to write it, with all the grandeur and finesse he could find at the time, when he was an undergraduate, but the *Protein Rhapsodies* had diverted him and he had never gone back to it, though he had not forgotten it. Every time he dropped a glass or couldn't recall a word or tripped over a crack in the pavement, he remembered it. Rebecca didn't know about this piece. Given her hatred for the disturbing lymphosarcoma sonata, George had never mentioned it, though he thought she had a surprising lack of curiosity about his inexplicable failure over all these years to be inspired by Huntington's disease in some way for his music. There was no way out, as there seemed to George to be potential for bad karma if he took it up again and a kind of whistling in the dark bad karma if he let it remain tucked away. It remained a bundle of sloppy notations for an unfinished twelve-tone polyphonic mess.

He was, this cold and rainy December morning, not thinking at all about the Huntington's piece as he moved it aside while rifling an old file of idea pages, charts, jots, scratches, sketches, and completed compositions in search of the musical manuscript that contained all the notations for a sophomoric effort he had indulged in when he was, in fact, a sophomore in college. The project had been grandiose. It consisted of a series of crystal bowls sunk strategically into the sand along a calculated tide line on the beach at Hammonasset State Park, where he had gone for the day with an oboe player named Beth Gould, who drove her mother's old Volvo station wagon. Because of her wheels, George had been much nicer to her than he might have been otherwise, though she imagined their bond to be musical. (She never understood that any number of brief romances with various art students who worked in larger formats had been sparked by their attraction to her cargo capacity.) The bowls were of varying sizes so each would resonate and chime in different tones as the incoming tide filled them and jostled the marbles in the bottom of each one. He had found the bowls — mismatched finger bowls, somebody's forgotten heirlooms from another time — in a junk shop on Whalley Avenue. Where were those bowls now? Oh yes, he had given them to Beth Gould, wherever she was now; hers was not the household name in oboe virtuosity she had been so convinced was her destiny.

They had both gotten sunburned that day. They stopped for dinner at the Clam Castle on the way back to New Haven, and Beth had been sick in the parking lot afterward, and George never knew if it was from the fried clams or too much sun. (In fact, it was the combined effects of both those things, plus her dawning realization that George Botkin had no interest whatsoever in her thoughts about music or anything else.) They had spent hours on the beach that day. He had recorded the tones of the bowls filling, using a cassette player that was never the same after that because of the sand that got into the works, and he had then written the piece, scoring it for a jazzy vibes duet, transposing themes and certain melodic elements from that recording, embellishing along the way. Although *High Tide/New Moon* had a certain bravado and charm, it was a juvenile and self-indulgent effort, the kind of music that is far too pleased with itself conceptually.

He was looking for it because there was one simple little sequence that had stayed with him over the years, the one progression in the entire piece that he thought might have value and originality. Had he remembered it correctly? As George dug through the old sheets, setting aside all the Huntington's folders that had been on top of this pile, Joe Green chirruped on the sill where he sat on high alert, tail flashing. The three cats who lived in the top-floor apartment in the nice red brick co-op on the other side of Tenth Street were in view, sitting upright between pots of flowering geraniums in matching poses on their windowsill, the muted glow of lights in the apartment behind them making them into silhouettes.

"What's Joe Green looking at?" Rebecca wondered, emerging from the shower, wrapped in one towel, drying her hair with another.

"The girls, I think. Aren't they in position? That's usually what interests him out there, right, Joe Green?"

"There they are. Pretty. They look totally alike. They must be sisters from the same litter. Those markings on their chests are exactly the same. I wonder if their owner can tell them apart. Who belongs to them?"

"Why do we assume they're all girls?"

"I've told you. Look at them. They're calicos. Three colors. It would be a genetic rarity if they weren't girls. They have to be girls. Anyway, look at those delicate heart-shaped faces. They're girls. Boy cats have big cabbage heads."

"Joe Green has a perfect little head. Don't insult us boys."

"Sorry." Rebecca rewrapped her towel around herself and came over to where George was working by the window. "It's cold in here."

"I think she's a curator at the Met, or the Frick, one of those," George said. "She moved in about a year ago, I think."

"Who?"

"The woman who goes with the girls. You asked. I met her once at a block association meeting a few months ago. She wants to keep our block alternate side of the street parking. She advocated for more callery pear trees. Oh, and she's a Democrat. I stood on line with her to vote in the last Democratic primary. Her last name has to be A to H, because we were in the same line."

"Who is this?"

"You know who I mean. You met her once with me, on the street. Remember, she was splashing across the street in those big green galoshes that day it was raining insanely? And she said hello to us and something about the 'dirty weather,' and you asked me who she was and how did I know her?"

"Oh, yes, yes, our age-ish, maybe a little older?"

"Yeah — plain, but smart-looking, kind of serious — she looks like your basic West Village classic leftover Vassar art history major. She lives alone, at least I've never seen anyone else there, a cat lady with her cats. And she's a huge improvement over that creepy guy in the bathrobe with the strobe lights, for sure."

"She's the one I said looked like a therapist?"

"That's the one. Don't go telling her your innermost thoughts next time you see her buying fruit at Balducci's."

"I might."

"Ah!"

"What?" Rebecca bent over to see what George had pulled out.

"Don't! Your hair is dripping."

"Sorry."

"I was looking for something old, and I found it. You remember my telling you about the piece I wrote based on glass bowls and seawater and the tide?"

"Not really."

He took the folio pages over to the piano, and after a pause to polish his eyeglasses, something George did ritualistically whenever he sat down at the piano, he began to play.

"Pretty!"

"Too pretty. Pretty juvenile," George said, stopping.

"No, I like it, keep going."

"You like everything."

"I certainly do not."

He began at the beginning and played it through, with an exaggerated wristy flourish on the last little glissando. It was short. He played it through again. "See? Juvenile. Cheap thrills."

"Strange, how potent cheap music is," Rebecca said mockingly. She was rummaging through the old folders on George's desk. She read aloud from a sheet of graph paper on which George had long ago scribbled, "Polypeptide bonds of *Dicksonia culcita,* each frond of which naturally forms an individual Sierpinski's triangle, but as a plant, the entire structure of fronds forms a larger Sierpinski's triangle consisting of smaller Sierpinski's triangles."

"Oh, I'm glad you found that. I need that. Don't put that back in the folder, leave it out."

"George, honey, that's not a sentence in English. You realize that?"

"It doesn't matter. It's really intriguing to me."

"Because?"

"Because of what you just read. Because of the way nature does that."

"I thought that was why you liked the Fibonacci sequence, because of what nature did. Wasn't that the one with all the spirals and whirls and pinecones and seashells and perfect ratios and whatever?"

"Yeah, it is, but it's too obvious. And I kind of want to stay away from Fibonacci sequences because everyone who is anyone is writing a Fibonacci novel, or opening a Fibonacci restaurant, or laying a Fibonacci sidewalk, or weaving a sweat lodge from recycled industrial waste in a Fibonacci form, even as we speak. And bad music it is, even with all the pinecones and seashells and circles of Willis for decoration. Anyway, it ain't got nothin' on these amazing ferns. I got big plans for these ferns. They inspire me."

"Fern music?"

"That's it. Perfect for fern bars. I could

make a career." He tapped the imaginary ash off the imaginary cigar that went with this huckster's voice.

"Are there still fern bars? And what does the circle of Willis have to do with Fibonacci numbers?"

"Nothing at all. I just like saying the name, circle of Willis. I was testing to see if you understood what I was talking about."

"That's condescending."

"Sorry. I was just using words. You know me, I'm a word magpie. Epexegesis. Loculus. Gallimaufry. How do you know about the circle of Willis?"

"You're still being condescending. Patients with sickle-cell anemia can suffer arterial occlusive strokes, and the circle of Willis is often the site of the damage. You see it in the diagnostic Doppler."

"Well, that's a downer."

"You're not kidding. It's *really* a downer. The average age for these patients is five."

"Five what?" George was now scowling at the manuscript in front of him. "Hm?"

"These are children, George, they're very sick five-year-olds. Now *you're* not listening to *me.*"

"Sorry." He put down his pencil and turned back her way. "You do have a pretty horrible job, don't you?"

"I have to admit I am not missing it so much."

"You don't have to go back to it, you know."

"Yes, I do. It's what I do. What's the alternative, being kept by you?"

"You know, we are so lucky to be in the rare situation of not having to do too many unpleasant things for the money, and I would call it supported, not kept, though of course I do plan to keep you. I mean I plan for you to keep me. I want us to keep each other."

"I would have a hard time with that. I know you don't get it, but the money thing is hard for me. It's important. I have always supported myself. It's thrilling to be giving away Esther's money, but it really isn't a life-changing amount — Hold it, wait, what's this?" Rebecca had been rummaging deeper through George's old material.

"What?" The score in front of him had caught George's attention again, and he was examining it critically, making new pencil notations and talking to himself. "Can it be any more obvious? Oh shit, yes, it can," he muttered to himself under his breath.

"This. Oh my god." Rebecca dropped the folder in her hands, and the sheets of *Hun-*

tington's Concerto charts spilled onto the floor.

"What?" said George, engrossed, leaning in closer and frowning, then vigorously erasing all that he had just written, scattering erasure crumbs across the pages. "Crap. Crap crap crap. Who wrote this crapulosity? Hm?"

"A Huntington's piece? A concerto? Pay attention! How could you work on something like this without telling me? Especially after that lymphosarcoma disaster."

He swiveled on the bench to face her. "Oh, that, hey. No, no. It's very old, for one thing. Give it here." He took the empty folder and a few sheets she had started to pick up from her hand and laid it on the piano bench beside him. "Rebecca, listen to me. I haven't even seen it in years, and I am not working on it. For another thing, I haven't touched it since long before Stark got sick, and for a third thing, since we're on the subject, you have never asked me once in all these years why I haven't ever considered writing something connected to Huntington's. I don't know why you're so surprised that I would think of it." He got up from the piano and brushed his eraser crumbs into a neat pile, then knelt down to gather all the pages together.

"Promise you won't do it. Promise!" She pummeled him on his shoulder for emphasis.

"Won't do what? Ow. What are you so frantic about?" He sorted the sheets into their proper order and stood, holding the bundle of pages defensively.

"You won't work on this piece ever again, will you?"

"Hey, Rebecca, you make it sound like I have to promise you I won't get Huntington's. Do you think I could get Huntington's if I finish this piece? Which is, by the way, an ugly juvenile botch for all kinds of reasons not remotely connected to the disease. Not that I was planning to work on it, but you know, you're kind of pissing me off."

"Do you think you could?" Rebecca hugged her damp towel around herself. Her feet were cold, and her teeth were chattering suddenly. The heating system in the building was impossibly antiquated, and in order for there to be decent heat on the lower floors, the top floor was often roasting hot. When he was working, George often didn't notice this until sweat dripped off the end of his nose. Then, on even the coldest days, he would have to open a window an inch or two until the loft became chilly and one of them was bothered by the draft.

"Could what? You should get dressed. You're freezing. Look, I don't know. I'm sorry, I don't mean to snap. This is a bad subject. Doesn't it make me a narcissistic lunatic if I tell you sometimes I kind of imagine I could bring it on with my music?" He got up to close the window.

"Not really, if you take seriously even half the hocus-pocus the New Agey people ascribe to your musical powers," Rebecca said. She went over to him, shivering, and he put his arms around her. "If you take the positive effects as genuine, all those *Echinacea Serenade* healings so many people swear by —"

"Who swears by that? Nobody serious even thinks actual echinacea has anything but a placebo effect."

"Oh, that's not true. Sharon swears by it. Only everyone we know believes that listening to the CD helps clear up colds. You *know* this, George! So how can you deny the potential for the negatives if you admit the positives?"

"But I'm Mr. In-Between! Beck, sweetie, you're being much too reasonable and rational and scientific, except about echinacea, maybe. A little craziness makes it work, trust me." He pushed her damp hair out of her face. "You're so rational."

"Not really. All my rational and reasonable and scientific friends would laugh at me."

"Come on, haven't you ever wondered about Huntington's music? Why I never tried to write any, I mean? You know me! Why haven't you? That doesn't make sense, really."

"Oh, I've wondered," Rebecca said. "I remember wondering about this the week we met and you told me about Huntington's in your family. I was just afraid of it. I never dared bring it up. I *am* afraid of it. Aren't you? I see it every week, and I am always afraid of it. I'm not being rational at all. I just never wanted to think about it. I didn't want to let it in the room."

"Well, sweetie, it's here, it's always been here, it's been in the room forever, since long before we met, and it wasn't just up to you to bring it up, I know. You *know* how I wonder if I have it every time I drop something or cut myself shaving or forget a word."

"My father was always dropping things and cutting himself shaving."

"Really?"

"Yeah. He was a total klutz. Between him, with the bloody drips all over the bathroom when I was little, and then Esther, with her hands all red from making borscht, I grew up thinking that my family was actually red in tooth and claw, and not just their politics."

"Well, I could have told you about it or said something at some point. I did kind of hide the piece from you, okay? And I admit I was tempted a little, when I had the CAG testing done, but I never went back to the piece at that time. So look, I'm not going to work on it, you don't need to worry. Never. So relax. Okay? Done." He pulled her over to the sofa, and they sat huddled together and touching each other — the way couples waiting for their appointments with her often sat huddled together and touching each other, Rebecca noted.

"George, listen. Seriously. We definitely should have talked about this long before now. It's ridiculous that it never came up over all this time. I'm sorry if I made you feel that you couldn't talk to me about it, for whatever reason. You sound angry."

"I'm not angry at you."

"I'm not *angry* at you, or I'm not angry at *you*?"

"*I'm* not angry at you," George said, "but

that reminds me of someone who probably *is*. Isn't that Ruth person coming over later?"

"Damn it, yes, she is. I keep forgetting she's coming. Taking this month off, I thought I would get so much done, but instead I get stupider by the day, and now I can't even remember the days of the week. Or I didn't want to remember her, because she is such a huge pain. But I guess we've just established my excellent denial credentials."

"She's coming when?"

"Four."

"Okay, then. Before she gets here, I want to read through everything she sent you, and then I want to sit down with you and make a plan about what we want to show her, what we want to tell her, what we don't want to show or tell her, and what we want to find out from her."

"Good thinking. Thank you. Let's do it. My guess is, she'll be early, and she'll bring dry poppy-seed cake."

"Isn't poppy-seed cake supposed to be dry?"

"Esther would have explained to you the world of difference between dry and too dry. It's like the world of difference between enough and more than enough."

"Which will this be?"

"Too dry."

TWELVE

Transcription of Esther Gottesfeld interview #1, conducted by Ruth Zion, West Village Jewish Home, New York City, April 12, 1999. Ruth Zion transcription, April 25, 1999

[question] I was born in Belarus — everyone just says Russia, because the names are changing all the time — on October 20, in 1895. I came with my sister Pauline and we got to America on a boat that landed at Ellis Island on January 12, 1909. You want to know about my life before we got here? [explanation of scope of interview from interviewer] Okay, it's just that lots of people want to know the names of my family and I could tell you if you want, also about life in the shtetl and how it was in Pinsk before we came to America. But you got your plan, okay. It interests some people to hear, anyway, even if they don't

261

need the information.

[question] We got our jobs at the Triangle on the same day, because my sister and I make a promise to each other always we stay together and we work together, because we are all we got, each other, so we always stick together and take care of each other.

[question] My sister was a wonderful girl. She always looked out for me.

[question] I was the older. So I looked out for her also, like I said. We looked out for each other.

[question] We started at the Triangle almost a year before the fire, in April 1910, with the jobs we had the whole time there, we were sleeve setters, a tricky job you got to do it just right and you can't hide the mistakes the way you can hide some other kinds of mistakes you make, working so fast. You set the sleeve crooked, you ruin the piece. You can't make mistakes and you got to work fast. My sister Pauline, she did the right sleeves and I did the left sleeves and between us we could finish a lot of shirtwaists. Sometimes if everything went perfectly we could do twenty-four shirtwaists in an hour, three hundred shirtwaists on a good day, but that was only if the machines didn't break down and if the thread didn't break. You had to be careful you didn't put a needle through your finger. You know why that was bad? Nobody cares if it hurts or gets infected. It was bad because then you would bleed on the goods, and the bosses would make you pay for anything you ruined with your blood, even just a little dot of blood and the piece was ruined. So if you were bleeding you would tie a piece of scrap around your finger tight to keep working. You always got to keep your blood to yourself, which girls know anyway if you know what I mean, but it was hard because you got to work with your hands and they can get caught and you can have a sore place that keeps bleeding, especially in the winter if you get chilblains, that's what we used to call them, and that would hurt very much in your fingers and make them split and bleed too easy.

[question] I worked a little slower than my sister, so sometimes she would have more finished work in her pile. The way we did it, because she worked faster she would do her sleeve first and then I would take from her pile to do the left sleeve.

[question] Did I say my seams were better? When did I say that, I never met you before. [Remark quoted from oral history in *Remembering the Triangle Factory Fire Fifty Years Later,* commemorative booklet published by the ILGWU] Okay, so forty years ago I made a comment maybe I shouldn't say about my sewing being just a little better than my sister's. If you know so much, why do you come here with poppy-seed cake — maybe we can get some tea to dip it and it won't be so dry — to pester an old lady asking questions you already got all the answers for? You ask me questions just to hear me say the same things, for some kind of test? I am very old. Do you know what it is to be so old? You learn you don't care so much about a lot of things you used to think were important.

[question] We were pieceworkers, girls were hired by the boss who they worked for, not by the big shots. No, I hardly ever seen Mr. Blanck, until I work there a week already, then he came walking through and everyone got extra busy with the work and I didn't know why until a girl explained. I seen more of his face at the trial than I ever seen at the Triangle when I was working there every day. Mr. Harris, I see all the time, he is always walking around, snooping into everything, asking questions, checking the work, making everyone nervous. He made even the bosses nervous the way he was always checking into everything. The boss we worked for was Morris Jacobs, he's the one who hired us. He had all the girls in our row working for him, and another row besides. We get these slips to write how much we do every day, how many waists we finish, and those numbers are double-checked by Magda, the girl who takes them to the finishing area, this nice Hungarian girl who told me how much worse off she was in a necktie factory before she came to this job, and I think she got very badly burned in the fire. So we give him, Mr. Jacobs, all our slips at the end of the week, and then he pays us, but we always have to watch him, because he was a thief who would steal from the girls any way he could, he would count crooked and then act like he didn't notice the mistake, but if he is such a bad counter, why are all the mistakes in his favor and he never makes a mistake in our favor?

[question] You want to hear about the day of the fire. This is what happened. I am working at my machine, just before the workday is over with just a few minutes to go, and I know I have only two right sleeves to finish in my work — my sister Pauline did the left sleeves and I did the right sleeves. We just got our pay packets from Mr. Jacobs, and he gave me also my sister's, and I tucked them into my stocking, so she could keep working to finish what she can do for the week. And then all of a sudden there is a big noise behind me, while I am still bending down fixing my stocking with the money, like nothing I ever heard before, like a bomb has gone off, or some explosion. Next thing, there are flames coming up the window from underneath us, we didn't know that until after, and the heat is breaking the windows, they're breaking from the fire, that's the thing — everyone who could do it got out from the eighth floor, and up on the tenth floor over us they got a phone call and they know about the fire, but on the ninth floor, nobody tells us about the fire.

[question] Everybody is screaming and yelling all at once and the ones near the smoke, they have faces all red and so many girls started already coughing and choking. So all the girls all around me started to shout and scream, my sister also is screaming, and everyone goes in a commotion, and the flames are coming along the wall and across the floor, and all of a sudden it's like water flowing toward us but it's flames, like a river, and all around me is just pandemonium. Now the flames go all around, every which way, and it gets hot like a furnace. But for just a moment, maybe a second but it seems longer, it's like everybody is a statue, just frozen, but after, all the girls go in a rush, everybody trying to go out at the same instant.

[question] No, I don't remember anyone saying to me anything about a good way to go out. I heard about the fire escape and how that was a big disaster, and those photographs are so terrible, just so terrible, all twisted and useless like that. A lot of the girls were piling into the elevator, that was a very nice man who ran that elevator, the Italian, Joey Zito, he was friendly with Sam, he always said he would teach Sam fishing, and I know he saved a lot of girls. So now the girls, they're trying to climb across the tables, but some of them, their long skirts got bunched and they got caught in the machines and now it's a madhouse, and everywhere the girls are running and screaming and pushing and calling and some girls were praying. Nobody could hear what anyone else was calling out. Mr. Grannick, one of the older garment cutters, he stood up on a chair. He tried to call out something but nobody could even see him except if you were close, because of all the smoke and noise. Maybe he had a good idea of what to do, I know he got out some way, but nobody could understand him plus some of those girls didn't even speak English anyway. My sister is right with me and we are holding hands together and she is screaming but I am saying to her, Look, we have to find our own way out. There was so much smoke, and then I see a girl with her hair on fire, and I see Rose Gottlieb, she is crying and running this way and that way, and then another one goes running by me with her clothes all burning up, and she is screaming like an animal, not like a human at all, and there is snot all running down her face which is red like a beet, I still remember just what she looked like, poor thing.

[question] I don't know who she was but I think she couldn't have lived from that, from what I saw. Did I say yet about the Italian sisters? These sisters, I always noticed them because they were the same age as my sister and me, these girls just stood there screaming, and they're not moving, and they were blocking the way for everyone, so I go past them, I have to push them to get by, and I never saw them again. I still feel so bad about that, to tell you the truth. I don't like to think about this so much.

[question] I come to the doors now. All the girls are at the Washington Place doors, but nobody could go out that way. It was a terrible thing, I don't know if it was somebody's fault, because the door, it opened in, and we all knew that from every day. They inspected us going out that door every time we leave, they had a guard looking in our bags and checking us, even our clothes, to make sure we didn't have anything hidden in our garments. They were afraid we would steal the goods.

[question] I never took anything, and my sister she never took anything, but I knew some girls did. It wasn't worth the risk, because if they catch you, they fire you and I heard in some shops they have people, they pay some prostitutes is what I heard, but that could be just a rumor, I don't know, I never saw it with my own eyes, these tough girls would follow you, they said, after you got fired, and they would beat you up in the street to teach a lesson.

[question] At the door, girls were pushing, it was very terrible. There was this smell of everything burning, hair and clothing too, but the worst smell in the world — if you smell it once you never get over it in your whole life — is that smell like cooking meat, that smell of burning flesh. It makes you ashamed, to smell that, it is the worst thing in the world. I smelled that, and it is still in my nose. I will never forget that smell. So this black smoke was everywhere all at once, to make everyone choke. I heard the girls in the front maybe even got squeezed to death from the pushing because nobody could open that door, is that true, do you know? [informative comments] Ach, that is so terrible. So many girls died that day and each way to die was a terrible way. There were no good ways.

[question] So I had this idea about the other door, the one by the elevators on the Greene Street side. We weren't supposed to use it on a Saturday because those freight elevators didn't run on the weekends so we weren't supposed to use those stairs on the weekends. Maybe the bosses used those stairs to go up to ten, for the offices, but the girls weren't supposed to go by those stairs. So I go across that way, but I had to run right into the flames to get across. And this is where I lost my sister, because I was holding her hand and then I let it go, I don't know why, and she didn't follow me when I thought she was right there behind me, she must have been afraid of the flames, maybe she thought I was crazy to go into the flames to escape, but you had to do it, you had to go into the flames to get out.

[question] I don't know where was Sam because I don't stop and think this. He was somewhere on the floor, I found out later, he was always over by the windows to help the girls, the whole time when he could have saved himself, that's what he

271

did, a lot of people down on the street, they saw him.

[question] I don't know why he didn't find us. I don't know why I didn't look for him. Just call out to him to come to us, to go with us. I don't know why. I don't know why my sister went to him away from the chance to go out. I can't tell you the answers to these questions I have in my heart for all these years, don't you think I am asking myself these questions too? No, it's all right, I always got Kleenex right by me.

[question]. That's right, now is when I see Morris Jacobs, and he's got a waist wrapped around his face, so he looks like the robber that he is, and with all the smoke he can maybe breathe a little better, so I think, this is a smart man, and a very selfish man who keeps himself always comfortable, he can figure out how to save himself, so he is going to this other door, by the freight elevators for the stairway we aren't supposed to use on weekends when the freight elevators aren't running, and they only want us using the other stairway and the passenger elevator, and he has a key in his pocket, and I see him unlocking the door, and he goes in the door but then he closes it right behind him, as I am running toward the door as hard as I can go, which is, like I said, when I lose my sister's hand. I try to open the door he just passed through, but at first it won't open. I think to myself why is it sticking like this, but then I push so hard on it I could feel it open a little and do you know what? That little scheisskopf of a man, that Morris Jacobs is trying to close the door and lock it behind him, for what reason I don't know, except maybe he isn't thinking straight and it is a habit, or maybe he has an idea to control the fire from going in the stairs. So I push very hard one more time, and like something you would dream, that door flies open, and I go right through and fall down.

[question] Maybe that is how I hurt my ribs, you are right. I don't know. So then I get up, and I see nobody, but I see so much flames and smoke that I think, well, you can't go down the stairs, but maybe you can go up the stairs, so I go up the stairs, even if it doesn't make any sense to go up, because I think how did they get out from the offices, maybe the roof, and when I go up, it's empty, and I go by the pressing tables and there is nobody left.

[question] I was only there a moment, because then I see this ladder going up, so that was it. I go up the ladder, and like a miracle, I am on the roof, and there are firemen up there. One of the firemen says, "Look at this, here comes the last one." They order me very rough to crawl across another ladder, over a big gap to the next building on the Waverly Place side, and I crawl across with my eyes closed, because I am afraid of falling so much. It's like a nightmare. So I go over, and people help me stand up, and then I just walked down ten flights of stairs like everything in the world is ordinary again. So then I am on the street, and a policeman shouts at me to get away like I am just a busybody, because there are people jumping and I could be killed, and a girl comes down right near me just then, it was a shock, and such a horrible sound, that noise, you don't forget it once you hear it in your ears, and she is just lying there, so I go across the street. And everywhere people are looking up, so I look up, and the first thing I see is so terrible, the girls are just jumping, jumping, jumping from so high up. They are pouring out of the windows.

Some of the girls were still on fire after they landed, and when they were lying dead on the sidewalk, the firemen had to turn the hoses on them, to put out the fires. Everywhere you look is something bad you don't want to see. I see this one girl jump, and her skirt catches on the sign pole that sticks out from Blum, the fourth-floor business —

[question] What difference does it make? As a matter of fact they made trimmings and notions, but why you got to know that? Do you want to know what is important about this sign? This girl, she hangs there screaming, and she is burning up, and then her skirt burns away so it can't hold her, and she gets dropped down from the sign, right on the sidewalk underneath, and she is still burning, and the sound, that was so terrible when she fell, like a bag of wet laundry falling. And they turned the fire hose on her, to put her out. They had to do it. You could see the firemen's faces, they were so upset with themselves, they were helpless. I saw this fireman just crying like a baby. What could he do? Nothing. There was nothing he could do. They were there to save people and they could save nobody.

[question] Wait, I'll tell you, I'm not finished yet with my telling, if you want to hear. Let me tell it the way I tell it. So then I walked to the corner where I could see the sidewalk on the Washington Place side because I was looking everywhere for my sister, to find her body if she has fallen, and there were bodies everywhere, so I am trying to see their faces. I knew so many of them, so it was one shock after another to look into those faces, and I would be relieved it wasn't my sister but oh! it's Dora, or oh! it's Jenny. I saw this one girl who had a gimpy leg, she worked on eight, she was all burned but I knew her from her shoe she had made special with a block so she could walk normal. I went with her one time to get that shoe fixed by the man who had a shoe repair on the Bowery, and she explained to me if we flirt with him he would fix her shoe for nothing, so that's what we did. It was innocent. I saw some of the men who died too, who worked on the part of the eighth floor where they couldn't get out so easy, where the fire started. Some of the dead were burned all black like a cinder. I recognized them by their dress, or like that girl with the special shoe, she was Polish, but then some of the dead girls were perfect, no marks on them at all, they still looked so beautiful and young and full of life, except they were dead from the fall.

[question] I am about to say some more about the firemen. Their ladders didn't go high enough, you know all about that, it was in all the articles and books. They didn't go high enough so they were useless, why that was allowed I don't know, the buildings were going up to ten floors but the ladders they got are still only high enough for six floors, and the other thing that was useless, that was those big nets they had. I saw them holding this net like in a movie in the middle of Greene Street, and next I saw three girls jump together, so they go right through this foolish, cockamamy net that isn't strong, and those girls hit the pavement, they hit the pavement all at once, with so much force it flipped all the firemen right into the net on top of the dead girls.

[question] So now is when I see Sam for the first time since the fire broke out. I look up to see why is everyone pointing and shouting, and then I see him, I see Sam, my fiancé, in the window, and he was helping the girls. I was sitting on the curb because I was feeling like I might faint, and I can never forget sitting there with blood running past me, it went over my shoes, it was water from the fire hoses mixed with blood, and it was like a river of blood running past me, and I was so shocked I just sat there letting it run over my shoes, they were ruined, I think the hospital threw them away, and I couldn't even open my mouth anymore like I forgot how to talk English, and I was just watching everything, but I had a feeling like I don't even understand anything anymore. I see coins all over the street, money was lying everywhere, from the pockets it must be, it fell out when those girls were jumping. People must have snatched it up. What did it matter? Those girls didn't need it anymore.

[question] I don't know, did I see three girls or did I know from reading and being told about the three girls he helped before my sister. I don't know anymore, because it is hard to separate what I really remember after all these years. I feel like I saw it. There were three girls, and there was Sam helping each one to step up on the sill, one at a time, like getting into a carriage, and there was fire all around them, coming out of the window, and he was helping each one so gentle, so kind, that's what he was like, he would always have the nice words to make a plain girl feel pretty, and each girl, she would get calm when he gave her his hand to get her steady on the window ledge, and then he would let go each one of them, and each girl would just fall away, and then the next girl would get up in her place, and they were just falling out that window, with Sam helping them.

[question] I never thought to jump, I have to say. But I wasn't burning up. I think if you are burning up, you want to jump out into the fresh air, and draw another breath, and save yourself for another few seconds, so you can have one more breath of air. It just seems like human nature, if you have the choice. You take the chance, even if it isn't any kind of real chance, because you can. You jump and you hope.

[question] I am nearly done with telling you what happened, but I got to say about my sister and what happened next. Sam goes to help the next girl get up on the sill, the fourth girl, he gives her his hand and helps her get steady, and I see it is my sister, she is there with him in the window. He helps

279

her up, and then she waits for him and what does he do but he gets up onto the ledge next to her, and he put his hand on the side of the window, to get steady, and you can see the flames right behind him, coming out the window next to him, and then he takes her arms and he puts them around his neck, like he can save her like if they were swimming in the ocean, and he puts his arms around my sister and they kiss each other, and then they jump, the two people I have in the world, they jump out of the world.

[question] What do you ask? What do you think I felt? How could you ask such an ignorant question? I have just told you if you were listening. Maybe you listen again when you sit with your tape recorder and hear my voice after I am dead. Stop. You don't have to say something sweet to me, I know I won't live forever.

[question] What happened after that I don't remember so much. I woke up in the hospital where they took me from the street, and I am burned, and I am in pain from my ribs when I cough from the smoke I have breathed, and everything is being done for me to help me, and everyone is nice and gentle, and they tell me I am so lucky to be alive, that's what they all say to me, they say to me that Pauline is dead but I am so lucky, but I am all alone and that is what I know. I will have the baby and I need to stay alive for that, I have to do that, what choice do I have? It is too late for any choice. And I am all alone in the world. So this is what happened.

[question] I don't want to talk any more today. Leave me.

[note: Esther Gottesfeld was overcome with understandable emotion at this point and terminated the interview, although she did agree to future interviews. rz]

THIRTEEN

George didn't dare catch Rebecca's eye. He was nearly bursting with a laugh that had begun when Ruth Zion appeared at their door ten minutes ahead of schedule with a bakery box containing the inevitable poppy-seed cake. The potential for inappropriate mirth had continued to build through the business of welcoming her, hanging up her raincoat, making coffee, chatting randomly while the coffee dripped through, and watching her fuss as she laid out her note-books and folders and pencils and recording equipment on his work table (which had required the relocation of stacks of musical manuscripts and old copies of *Scientific American*). Now, with Ruth's tape recorder switched on, the microphone cocked importantly in the middle of the table, coffee served all around in the pretty Deruta mugs he and Rebecca had picked out a couple of years ago on their trip through the Veneto the summer his *Black Hole Concerto for Tuba in B flat* was premiered at Spoleto (the mugs were found the same day they saw some amazing Giotto frescoes and failed to eat some disconcerting donkey ravioli), George was still at high risk for a disgraceful and inexplicable guffaw if he even thought about looking in Rebecca's general direction. The first bite of poppy-seed cake had very nearly set him off, and it was an escaping bubble a moment later, just the one silent spasm of laughter, combined with the hilariously desiccated cake, that had caused him to inhale a lungful of crumbs and seeds, which brought on a protracted coughing fit, during which he turned red and a few tears ran down his face. Even then, even while gasping and choking and springing up to get a glass of water from the kitchen while waving away Ruth's alarmed question about whether or not she should switch off her tape recorder so as not to waste the tape, George had to maintain a vigilant avoidance of meeting Rebecca's amused gaze, for fear of a relapse.

"Is it too warm in here for you, Ruth?" Rebecca asked. "George likes it warmer or colder than a lot of normal people do. I'm always opening or closing the window in this apartment, so let me know."

"No, it's fine, I don't mind being a little warm, and it is probably necessary for me to avoid a draft, with my asthma," Ruth said. "Don't worry about it.

"Shall I start?" Ruth asked when George returned to the table somewhat more composed. Ruth reminded him of the anxious, unfulfilled women who chaired committees having to do with local symphonies or museums, the sorts of organizations that invited him to speak at their annual festivals, where his music was frequently performed. The sorts of women who loved anything having to do with "the arts." She had rewound her tape recorder and repositioned the microphone, and now she switched it back on.

"Let's," said Rebecca, who was sitting sideways in her chair at the head of the table, her body twisted in what George recognized as an unconscious and literal manifestation of her desire to avoid facing Ruth. He slid his foot under the table and searched for one of hers to touch it in solidarity, while still not meeting her eyes.

"Interview with Rebecca Gottesfeld, granddaughter of the late Esther Gottesfeld, at the home of George Botkin, 42 West Tenth Street, New York City, December 9, 2001. Also present is George Botkin. Shall I begin with my questions?" Ruth asked. "I have my list. Or shall we start with the things you said you wanted to show me? I am so sorry we got off on the wrong foot, and I do appreciate the vote of confidence you have expressed, and I know you won't regret your decision to cooperate with this important —"

"I'll start," Rebecca said. She opened the folder on the table in front of her and drew out the mysterious torn slip of paper that had been in the envelope along with the engagement photo. She and George had gone through everything from the safe-deposit box just an hour earlier, making a plan about what they would show Ruth and what they would hold back, considering all the variables. She put the slip on the bare wood in the center of the table beside the tape recorder.

"A credit slip! My goodness! Where did you get this?" Ruth exclaimed with far more genuine feeling than either Rebecca or George would have imagined her capable of having. At least she really was passionate about the material. She snatched it up eagerly.

"It was in with my grandmother's papers, so I assumed it was significant," Rebecca said, choosing her words with care. "Can you tell us what it means?"

"Oh my, yes! It is regrettable that it is torn, but yes indeed, here you have the date, the name of the machine operator, which we assume is Pauline Auerbach, the number of pieces — this would have been for the day's work, so you can see here, the number of pieces completed was in the two hundreds, which confirms that she was a fairly fast worker with experience, which we know, and here at the bottom you have the name of the contractor for whom she worked, which, according to all my sources, Esther being one of them, and this confirms it, was Morris Jacobs."

"Why would she have saved it?" George asked.

"That is a very good question," Ruth said, laying the slip in front of her with reverence and giving it a little pat. "Ordinarily, these slips were handed in at the end of the workweek in order for the workers to be paid by the contractors. That's why they're so scarce — once the pay was calculated, the contractors would ordinarily have disposed of all the credit slips. The ones we see are the blanks, the unused ones."

"Maybe this one had been thrown away by the contractor, and that's why it's torn," Rebecca said.

"Perhaps," Ruth agreed. "But I do wonder how it came into your grandmother's possession, and why she would have saved this particular torn slip. George has asked a very good question indeed."

"Could it be from the day of the fire?" Rebecca asked.

"Oh my!" Ruth picked up the bit of paper and scrutinized it again, as if hoping to see something more revealed in the few words. "Wouldn't that be something!"

"It does seem to have a March date," Rebecca observed. "If it was from the day of the fire, that would explain why Pauline still had it, and why my grandmother would have kept it."

"But they had just received their pay packets minutes before the fire broke out," Ruth said. "So she would have turned in all her credit slips, along with Esther's. I don't know why either of the Auerbach sisters would have had any credit slips in their possession at that juncture."

The three of them gazed solemnly at the little scrap of paper for a moment.

"May I photocopy this for my records?" Ruth asked. "I would like to compare it to the credit slips they have in the Kheel archive at Cornell, and perhaps learn something more from that. And there are some other scholars to whom I wish to show it. In March, at the Herstorical Society annual meeting, I am giving a PowerPoint presentation concerning —"

"Sure. We can do that later."

"Do you recognize the handwriting?" Ruth asked Rebecca. "You see, that is the sort of thing with which you can be so uniquely helpful."

"I'm not sure. It's just a few words, and it's torn."

"Do you know your great-aunt Pauline's writing? Are there any examples extant? Letters? Legal documents?"

"No, not really. I don't think I have ever seen her writing. Unless this is her writing. Don't you think it must be? It looks just like my grandmother's writing, but it's just a few words in pencil, so it's kind of hard to tell."

"Ah." Ruth sat back, disappointed. "One might assume this is Pauline Auerbach's handwriting, but we have no way to verify it without another definite sample."

"But Esther must have thought the slip was important. It obviously meant something to her or she wouldn't have saved it the way she did."

"True. Good point. Was this in the safe-deposit box you mentioned when we spoke?" Ruth asked a little too eagerly.

"Yes," Rebecca said shortly. "It was."

"Do you have anything else you want to show me that your grandmother put away? I have been so curious about that safe-deposit box! My goodness, this is a productive meeting already, and I haven't even asked a single one of my questions!"

Rebecca took out from the Balducci's tote bag the eyeglasses in their case and the coins, and Ruth leaned forward avidly.

"These are marvelous artifacts," Ruth said. She pored over the three coins, which she held in the palm of her hand. "The Roman numeral five is so interesting. What do you suppose this brown substance is on the coins, though?" She began to scrape at the nickel with her thumbnail. Ruth's nails were short and coated with beige polish.

"I wondered if it was blood, actually," Rebecca said. Ruth put the coins down. "There's nothing remarkable about them, except she had them saved," Rebecca added. "They're all from before the fire, 1910, 1909, I think the oldest one is 1907, the Indian-head penny. And one of them looks like a Russian kopeck, that little silver one — it's not a dime."

Ruth was now opening the glasses and holding them up at arm's length to see the magnification property. "Are these your grandmother's spectacles?"

"I don't really see how they could be," Rebecca said. "She never wore glasses with that kind of lens. That's a really strong prescription, and even at the end of her life she didn't need that much correction. Anyway, she didn't keep her old eyeglasses in the bank in a safe-deposit box, she kept them in drawers all over the apartment. She used to do this thing with her glasses that drove me crazy, as a matter of fact. Whenever she got a new prescription, she would fill it, put the frames with the new prescription away, and only then would she start using the previous pair of glasses she had put away with the last prescription the year before."

"Really?" George said. "So she was always one prescription behind?"

"Yes. She was always saving them. It never made any sense. But anyway, these here are really old frames, and I am certain I have never seen them before or I would remember them from when I was little, if they were Esther's."

"Did you ask her why she did it?" Ruth asked.

"I did. More than once. I'm telling you, it drove me nuts."

"What was her answer?"

"She said something I never understood about how it was so she could see the world a little blurry on purpose, that a lot of people go through their lives without being able to see clearly, and who did she think she was to see everything perfectly?"

"Pretty crazy. That makes no sense at all," George said. "Why get prescription lenses then? Why not just sit home and be blind?"

"I can't explain it," Rebecca said.

"How fascinating," Ruth murmured, taking notes all the while. She finished writing and picked up the eyeglasses thoughtfully, holding them in front of her face to peer through the thick, cloudy lenses, which from Rebecca's vantage point magnified her nose, her pores, and her faint mustache. "A deliberate subjugation, in her latter years, of her potential female power to perceive the truths in this man's world," she added.

"She never thought about it that way, I guarantee you," Rebecca said impatiently.

"Maybe she had seen enough," George said.

"Anyway, I'm telling you, I never saw her wear these frames or anything like them," Rebecca said. "She always wore those sort of pointy Joan Crawford glasses when I was little, and then more recently she got these gigantic square black eighties frames that she loved, so she just kept those going all this time. These look like genuine antiques, don't you think? They've got to be really old."

"Maybe they belonged to Pauline," Ruth said.

"That's what I wondered, actually," Rebecca said.

"She referenced her sister having bad eyesight in my interview with her on two occasions, and one of those was recorded, in my second documented interview with her in September of 1999," Ruth said, "with which I assume you have familiarized yourselves? She said her sister had been given eyeglasses because her vision had been ruined by working under deplorable conditions. She described Pauline's vanity, her not wanting to wear the glasses where men would see her and find her less sexually desirable or marriageable."

"That makes sense," George said. "I think you're right."

"In your transcript that's not quite the way Esther spins it, but I agree, these really could be Pauline's. George and I were just reading through those today, before you got here," Rebecca said. "But still, I also kind of wonder if they could be Sam's."

"Does the case indicate anything?" Ruth wondered.

"The case looks a lot newer than the glasses, and it comes from an optician in Long Beach, according to what it says inside the lid, so that's probably not a useful clue at all," said Rebecca.

"We have no evidence that Sam required eyeglasses, while we do know from the oral history record, as you just said, that Pauline had bad eyesight," Ruth pointed out. "And these look like a woman's style."

"I don't see how you can really tell, but okay, these are probably Pauline's." The three of them contemplated the eyeglasses that lay in the middle of the table.

"Why weren't they broken?" Rebecca said, interrupting the thickening silence. "If she was wearing them to sew when the fire broke out. If she took them off, they wouldn't be here now. They had to get out of the building somehow. Somebody carried them out at some point."

"Maybe these were her spares," Ruth offered.

"You think a working girl in that era could afford a second pair of eyeglasses?" Rebecca asked.

"No, I suppose a working *woman* probably couldn't," Ruth replied. "Maybe she wasn't wearing them when she, you know, passed away. Maybe they survived the fall. It's strange what fell intact from the World Trade Center, you know, my podiatrist told me that he knows someone in Jersey City, I believe he said it was his cousin, but I might be mistaken, who found a perfect tax return, not a mark on it, and this was for a well-known Wall Street figure. It was in a tree in his backyard, and he —"

Rebecca looked at George, who nodded. She reached into the front pocket of her jeans and pulled out Sam's watch by the cord, fumbled for a moment with her bitten thumbnail to find the thin slot that allowed her to pry open the cover, and placed it, open, on the table. George picked up the eyeglasses and studied them.

"I think this is the treasure, Ruth."

"What makes you think so?" Ruth asked with a little suspicion. "Why?"

"I'm guessing this could be Sam's watch. It's broken. The glass is cracked, and you can hear parts moving around inside, so something happened to it. And I think we know what. Look at the time."

Ruth peered at the watch, and then a look of incredulity swept over her face. "Do you think?" she breathed.

"Doesn't it make sense?" George said,

looking up from the eyeglasses briefly.

"May I?" Ruth asked, gesturing toward the pocket watch before picking it up and holding it in front of her as if it were a sacred religious artifact.

"I am gazing at history," she uttered, her voice breaking with emotion. "I am holding history in the palm of my hand. And I would very much like to be able to utilize an image of this for my —"

"PowerPoint presentation," concluded Rebecca.

"Yes! And also for my book! I would very much like to arrange to have this extraordinary object photographed, and of course I will pay for the expense. Also Pauline's spectacles," she added.

"So now we know they're Pauline's?" Rebecca said. "Is this how scholarship works?"

"It is an educated guess," Ruth said defensively. "A very educated guess. Would you prefer that I omit them? I do want to use the watch, in any case."

"I am sure we can work that out."

"May I ask you some questions now, Rebecca?" Ruth looked at her, her eyes shining with feeling. "You have already been far more generous than I could have dared to hope. This is very unique personal material you are sharing with me. Very, very unique."

"Go ahead."

"Let's begin with the children. I have very good reason to believe, as I told you when we spoke on the telephone in September, that there were children present on the ninth floor that day, but they show up in neither the names of the living nor the names of the dead. I believe children must have died in that fire, but their presence in the Triangle factory was covered up. Did your grandmother speak to you about the children?"

"Yes, she did. But she only said that they were usually there, that there were always poor little girls working in the corner of the ninth floor they called the nursery. We never talked about what happened to them in the fire. My grandmother talked about this when I was little, because I remember her telling me they were my age, but they didn't go to school, because they had to work. She taught me to sew, and we used to sew together and talk about what it would be like if I had to work at it for twelve hours every day instead of going to school or being allowed to play outside. She helped me make clothes for my dolls. She always made the buttonholes — she could make perfect buttonholes in seconds. I always loved watching her do it. She tried to teach me, but my stitches were always uneven."

"Do you recall anything else she might have said to you, more specifically, about the children?"

"Not really. Just that it was called the nursery, that corner. Do you know where it was on the ninth floor?"

"I have ascertained that the area so many survivors of the fire and other Triangle workers reference as the nursery, just as you say, was in the area on the ninth floor nearest to the air shaft, which is where the smoke was very bad within just minutes after the fire broke out. The risk of smoke inhalation would have been greatest on that side of the building, where the air shaft acted like a chimney, venting the fire as it spread beneath them. Of course, this is where the fire escape was, if you could even call it a fire escape. I assume you have seen those photographs?"

"They're in all the books. I know about the fire escapes. People died because of those fire escapes."

"Indeed. I plan on using a very poignant digital image I have located on the Internet, a picture of that useless, twisted fire escape, for my cover image. Can you recall anything else your grandmother told you about the children? Anything?"

"Esther told me the little girls trimmed the loose threads from the finished waists, and some of the older girls sewed in labels, I remember that. They had different labels for some of the stores they supplied all over the country. Oh, and she was friendly with the girl who was in charge of them. I remember her telling me this girl had worked on a farm and loved children, and she would bring them rolls from a bakery where her brother worked, or something, so she got a deal on the day-old —"

"Rose Gottlieb. You mean this woman —"

"I do?"

"You said girl, and I will assume that you actually meant woman for Rose Gottlieb, who was herself nineteen years old when she died."

"I guess I knew Rose Gottlieb died in the fire. You know, I've just never wanted to pore over those books, and you probably have them all memorized. Wouldn't she have been with the children?"

"She was found on the top of the elevator car operated by Joseph Zito. She had jumped into the open shaft after the elevator made its final trip down. There were a number of bodies on top of hers, and beneath her as well. In fact, one of those women who jumped last, Katie Orlovsky, actually survived and testified at the trial, but none of the bodies in the elevator shaft were the children. There is absolutely no record of any child present at the fire, living or dead. My investigation has led me to conclude that there may have been as many as eight children present that day, girls, and in all likelihood a minimum of three. Given that it was a Saturday, even children who did attend school could have accompanied their mothers to work. There may have been an even greater number present."

"That's horrible," Rebecca said in a low voice

"The Triangle fire was a horrible event in our history, which is why I have dedicated myself to this important scholarship," Ruth said, her hand on her bosom for emphasis.

"I don't think I can tell you anything more about this, but it's good that you're pursuing it," Rebecca said. It was hard to keep despising Ruth Zion. "How did they get away with having children work there? Weren't there child labor laws by then?"

"The laws were a joke. They hid the children in the bins of scrap material when the inspectors came. Everyone knew about it. The inspectors were corrupt."

"Did the owners know? Blanck and Harris?"

"Of course they did! Harris walked through the ninth floor several times a day, according to numerous eyewitness accounts. He could hardly have been unaware of the children."

"How did the children vanish?" George asked. "Why were there no survivors and no record of victims, either?"

"Those are important questions," Ruth replied. "I don't know. Is it corruption? If so, what else did the corruption cover up? Were the police paid off? The fire inspectors? Nobody knows."

"I wish I could help you with that," Rebecca said finally, breaking a long silence punctuated only by the faint whirring of Ruth's tape recorder, "but I don't think my grandmother knew anything more than you do. And you've got that in your transcripts. You discussed this with her."

"I agree, in this instance," Ruth said, "that it's another dead end. I could tell when we talked that your grandmother cared about those children, and about Rose Gottlieb — that it was still painful for her to discuss them, as she was clearly very distressed about that aspect of the fire. But as you know, I am convinced that your grandmother did not tell me everything she knew, to say the least, which is why I am here today."

"I'm not going to talk to you about your outrageous theories about payoff money," Rebecca said a little too abruptly and a little too loudly.

"We can return to that, then," Ruth said. "And I can tell you about my three verified secondary sources, which may persuade you to confide in me. I have the interview notes right here." She bent down to extract a folder from her old-fashioned lawyer's satchel of the sort George recalled calling a douche bag in junior high school, because only the nerdiest boys in his class carried their books in such briefcases. It occurred to him that perhaps Ruth was carrying her father's briefcase. "The most significant, I think, is what I have from the granddaughter of Elsa Weiss, who was the bookkeeper for Blanck and Harris for the four years after the fire —"

"We're not returning to it," George said. "She just told you it's not up for discussion. Drop it."

Ruth looked at them, first one and then the other. She opened her mouth to speak, thought better of it, and then, suddenly, she smiled triumphantly. "So, you found it! I *knew* something was there! Where was it? In that safe-deposit box? Did she keep it in cash all these years? Was there a written agreement? I heard there was, but I couldn't verify it."

"What part of 'drop it' isn't in your vocabulary? Enough! It's just not your business, Ruth," said George. "We are only willing to continue this conversation about other things pertaining to the fire if that line of questioning ends now."

"How fascinatingly traditional and unfortunate that here we are again, as if no progress has been made these past decades, with the big man defending his little woman," Ruth said in her smug scholar's voice. George could just imagine her using it to score points, by the hour, in some dreary seminar. "And how very disappointing, I must say, that you, Rebecca, a strong and independent woman, would want to have your man speaking for you about such an important matter, which doesn't concern his family history, but your own. How infantilizing this must be for you! Does he even represent your point of view correctly, or are you just content to let him be the bully and make these decisions for you?"

"That's incredibly insulting," Rebecca said. "Maybe you need to leave now. Do you speak this way to people very much? Do you have any friends? Your feminist agenda is really getting on my nerves now. And I know that's not fair to feminists. Do you even have a life? We invited you here, despite a lot of misgivings, because the fire is important both historically and personally, for me, for my family. I do want to help you get your facts straight, because you're writing about my grandmother. But that doesn't mean you can just snoop around and ask about everything. I just don't want you misrepresenting my grandmother." Rebecca was trying not to shout, but she could hear her voice rising, as it did when she was upset. She was afraid she might start to cry now, but she rode it out, taking a couple of deep breaths before adding, "That's all I care about. That's really why I asked you here, to do what I can to protect her, to have whatever influence I can have over the way you're writing about her."

"Also, we did have some questions we had hoped you could help answer," George said.

"Maybe this whole thing was a giant mistake," Rebecca said.

Joe Green sauntered by and stropped himself against her leg briefly, and Rebecca swept him up into her lap. He struggled briefly but she kept a tight grip, and finally she could feel his bony body relaxing on her thighs. Nobody spoke for another moment. Ruth coughed and cleared her throat, then reached dramatically into her bag for an inhaler, which she placed on the table at the ready.

"I believe we have had a misunderstanding, for which I take full responsibility," Ruth said stiffly, looking away. "I would very much appreciate your willingness to overlook my lack of etiquette. Sometimes I get so carried away with my theories of social organization that I forget myself and forget about the conventions so many other people follow. Please do forgive me."

Rebecca and George both stared at her coldly. She continued blithely, now attempting to make nervous eye contact with each of them. "Shall we proceed from this point forward in good faith that we both — that all three of us, I mean — have the same agenda, which is to say that we want to dialogue so as to discover the truth as best we can about the events that surround the Triangle fire?"

"Let's try for that," Rebecca said, "though you will just have to stop saying 'dialogue' when you mean 'talk.' "

"Fine. My next question, then, concerns the possibility of sexual harassment and abuse in the workplace. Do you know, was your grandmother sexually abused at the Triangle Waist Company, or did she ever say anything to you about her sister, most specifically, or about any other women, other workers who may have suffered from sexual harassment or sexual abuse?"

"Why are you asking this?" Rebecca asked. "Where is this coming from?"

"It has come up in several intriguing places in my research."

"But what could that have to do with the fire?" George asked. He continued to turn the eyeglasses in his hands.

"Well, obviously, as incendiary as the subject is —" Here Ruth broke off and looked at both of them expectantly, hoping that they were as pleased by her wit as she was herself, as it was a remark she was planning to deploy during her PowerPoint presentation. "Of course it would have had nothing to do with the actual ignition of the fire. I do wonder, however, if the socioeconomic hierarchies in place at the Triangle Waist Company did in fact have any actuarial significance in the morbidity outcomes, vis-à-vis access to egress and safety from the fire."

"Access to egress," George murmured softly, picking up one of the coffee spoons to tap it rhythmically to the five syllables, which he continued to do until Rebecca leaned over and took it out of his fingers.

"I was just measuring out their lives in coffee spoons," he said.

"Stop that," Rebecca said.

"Personally, I admire such creativity," Ruth said. "I understand you are very musical, very talented. I do applaud that."

"I used to clap on one and three, now I snap on two and four," George said.

"Quit it!" Rebecca hissed at him. "I mean it. Or leave us alone."

"I'll be good," he vowed, picking up the eyeglasses once again and absentmindedly polishing them with a napkin.

"I'm sorry, Ruth, can you say that in English?" Rebecca asked impatiently. "Do you mean if the women were victims of sexual abuse, they were more likely to die?" Joe Green jumped off her lap and walked over to Ruth's briefcase, which he sniffed cautiously.

"We understand each other perfectly," Ruth said. She took a sip of her now-tepid coffee.

"How would that work?"

"Women who are victims of sexual abuse have lowered self-esteem," Ruth began. "This can lead to —"

"Oh, please! Do you mean to say they were more likely to die because they wouldn't have enough self-esteem to save themselves? That's just insane!" Rebecca burst out.

"It's a working theory," Ruth said stiffly, "though not, as it happens, my own." She bent down to fasten her briefcase against Joe Green's inquisitive nosing.

"What's your theory, Ruth?" George asked, leaning forward. "Seriously, what do you think sexual harassment has to do with anything here, and what do you think Esther might have told Rebecca?"

"Well, since you asked so directly," Ruth said, "and since you both seem to me to be people who want the unvarnished truth of things, I will share with you some of the material in my possession that has raised this rather complicated issue. I have to warn you, it could be somewhat upsetting."

"So what is it?" Rebecca asked irritably.

"First, tell me please, what did your grandmother ever say to you about Morris Jacobs?" Ruth asked.

"I don't remember her ever talking about him at all, and I don't think I ever heard the name, but in your interviews it comes through that she clearly hated him and thought he was a pig. And she saved his obituary. I have that here. So this interests me, and now I want to know why you are asking about him particularly."

Ruth Zion leaned forward and said in a confiding tone, "I owe a great deal to Jonathan Lipman. A great deal. More than I can ever adequately express." She sat back, confident that she had just said something profound.

"Who," George asked, "is Jonathan Lipman?"

"He is the son of Lou Lipman."

"Oh god," groaned Rebecca. "Lou Lipman again. Esther thought he was a pain and a half."

"Is that what she told you? How intriguing! What else did she say about him?" Ruth asked eagerly, pushing the microphone an inch closer to Rebecca.

"Well, she didn't use those words. Those are my words, obviously. But she found him irritating. She said he was a ragpicker."

"I see," Ruth said.

"Is that an insult?" George asked.

"Not necessarily," said Ruth.

"Kind of," said Rebecca. "The way she used the word, it was meant to be. Hey, did you know that ragpicker's disease and wool-sorter's pneumonia are really pretty much the same thing? They're both actually forms of anthrax infection. This guy I know who's doing a postdoc in epidemiology told me about a study he's doing about textile workers, going back into nineteenth-century records in all these little New England mill towns. Of course, he had no idea how hot anthrax studies would be when he picked his topic. He told me he really wanted to do Lewy body dementia. He thinks that's the new frontier in dementia studies, the connection to Parkinson's. But meanwhile, he's been a talking head on CNN a couple of times last week, with all the anthrax excitement."

"Goodness!" Ruth exclaimed. "Such a worry. If it isn't one thing, it's another. I have taken to opening all my mail with disposable gloves. It seems prudent. One never knows, does one?"

"The moment or the place," George said.

"Oh, indeed," said Ruth.

"Fate may be kind," added George.

"Stop it, George. I mean it. So, Lou Lipman?" said Rebecca. "His son Jonathan?"

"Yes, Jonathan Lipman has bestowed upon me the ultimate faith and trust for which a scholar can hope," Ruth explained. "He has provided me with total access to his father's papers, and this includes all of his interview notes with numerous sources, all the people connected to the events with whom he met or corresponded, including thirty-two individuals who survived the fire. Sadly, all of these people are now deceased. And so these notes are quite valuable. Your grandmother, Rebecca, was the very last living survivor."

"I know that."

"But you don't know that he had a great deal of significant material that he chose not to include in his book. Times were different in 1962. Many things were not discussed in polite company, let alone put in print in a scholarly book that was published by a prestigious imprint. There would have been a desire at the time to respect the privacy of the victims, which outweighed the import to our understanding of this tragic event that changed America."

"Maybe he cared more about humanity than posterity," George said.

"That is not the place of the true historian," Ruth sniffed. "He censored a very significant part of the story."

"Like for example?" Rebecca said.

"Well, would it be a shock to you if I tell you that three different women who worked at the Triangle told Lou Lipman that they believed your great-aunt Pauline had been sexually harassed and possibly sexually assaulted as well by one of the men who worked on the floor?"

"Where do you get that?" Rebecca asked.

"Lou Lipman's interview notes. Apparently it was something of an open secret among the workers on the ninth floor that something was going on with Pauline and one of the bosses. It comes up in three different interviews with survivors. I have the pertinent pages photocopied here."

"Who was the man?" George asked. "Did he die in the fire also?"

"I have every reason to believe, given that Lou Lipman used shorthand in his notes and used only initials for this individual, so this can never be absolutely verified, but I do believe that the M.J. in his notes indicates Morris Jacobs — which makes a certain sense when you consider the inevitable access and contact with your grandmother and her sister, given that he was the contractor for whom the Auerbach sisters worked. I have also been unable to ascertain that any other man working at the Triangle in this time period had those initials. There were numerous men with first names starting with M, more than one Max and Melvin, and there was an Isidore Jablonski on the eighth floor, but nobody else matches M.J."

"Really!" Rebecca said. "Morris Jacobs the scheisskopf! The one who tried to close the door on Esther?"

"Exactly. Which brings into question what happened at that door, and why. At the time of my interviews with Esther, I had not read all of the Lipman notes, as he kept very haphazard records in a variety of notebooks and it was very time-consuming for me to go through all of them. But I will always regret that I had not completed the task when I interviewed Esther, because I could have followed up more closely on this topic had I been as certain then as I am now about the identity of the perpetrator of the sexual harassment against Pauline."

"Esther has to have known about it, don't you think?" George mused. "If it happened. Maybe she had words with Jacobs. Maybe Jacobs knew that she knew."

"She would have been the first person to know about anything like that," Rebecca agreed. "They were so close. Well, crap. Did Lipman talk to Jacobs?"

"No, Jacobs died in 1956, and Lipman was just starting his interviews at that time. I can find no interviews with Jacobs at all. The historical record is silent after his trial testimony. A tragedy, really, that he died when he did."

"Maybe the tragedy is that he lived as long as he did," Rebecca said.

"Not from the scholar's point of view, but I understand your animus and take your point," Ruth said. "In any case, the little bit of information I have gathered on him indicates that he had some sort of degenerative illness for several years before he died. Perhaps multiple sclerosis. It's hard to say. And as you know from that obituary, he died in a fire."

"The karma police took care of him," George said.

"Who?" Ruth asked, pen poised over her notebook.

"A joke. Nothing. So I guess maybe now we know why Esther had his obituary saved. So what do you think happened?" George asked. "Did Lipman get specifics from these survivors?"

"Not really. One of them, Tessie Sapirstein, was a finisher who also worked for Jacobs. She worked at a machine in the same row on the ninth floor as the Auerbach sisters. She told Lipman that she had seen Pauline crying on the street one night after work, with her clothing disarranged, and said that she knew Jacobs had been 'pestering' Pauline for several weeks, so she was very worried about this. She said, wait,

I have it here — yes, she said Pauline was 'very attractive and innocent, very young, very pretty,' and on this occasion on the street, 'her hair was coming down, she was holding her cloak around herself, she was crying, and her mouth was bleeding as if someone had hit her. She wouldn't say what was wrong.' "

"When was this?" Rebecca asked.

"It's not clear," Ruth said, "because the questioning was really about the fire. This would have been all for Lipman's understanding of the atmosphere and relationships, so that he could grasp the background socioeconomic sensibilities of the workplace. As thorough as Lou Lipman was, I can only wish he had been even more thorough and less of a patronizing sexist."

"Do you think that's fair?" George asked. "Consider the period."

"So what's your guess?" mused Rebecca. "Do you think something horrible happened to Pauline?"

"Presumably, this data would have been concerning the atmosphere in the weeks and months preceding the fire, as I said," said Ruth. "But there is no way to know the precise date of this occurrence, as Lipman didn't ask. That information is irretrievably lost. But listen to this one, the most incriminating. Another of the women Lipman interviewed — and in his notes he only called her by the initials A.S.— said that Jacobs raped her in the cloakroom one night after almost everyone had left. She told Lipman that Jacobs asked her to stay late to work out a discrepancy in her credit slip numbers, and it turned out to be a trap, and he attacked her. According to the notes, right after it happened, the elevator man — that would be Joey Zito — heard her crying and came to check to see if there was a problem. Apparently Jacobs never bothered her after that, and she didn't know why, but she wondered if Joey Zito had something to do with it."

"Esther liked him," Rebecca said.

"He was a hero," Ruth said. "He risked his life to save dozens of women."

"So that's the evidence on Jacobs?" George asked.

"I have concluded that A.S. is probably either Anna Silverman or Alice Solomon, as both women worked on the ninth floor for Jacobs in that same time period, and both survived the fire."

"They must both be dead by now," Rebecca said.

"Oh, yes, both of them died years ago, and neither of them had family I can trace

— so far, anyway," Ruth said. "But there is also this. There was a third report, someone who worked in the office as a clerk. You have to understand that Lou Lipman didn't even try to put these things together, and that it is my own scholarship that has revealed the pattern of abuse scattered in hundreds of pages of notes made over several years. Maria Santopietro, according to the Lipman notes, here it is, said that 'Isaac Harris shouted at Jacobs in his office, in a meeting behind a closed door, but she could hear some of the words.' She told Lipman that she 'heard Harris telling Jacobs off for taking advantage of the women workers, and told him it had to stop, that this was a decent place of business,' but the notes are not very detailed, so that's all I have."

"It's damning," George said, "but not absolutely conclusive. Especially not about Pauline, who never told anyone her story. I agree that if anyone knew, it was Esther."

"It isn't what we would hope for in source material," said Ruth, "but I am trying to find any other references in all the Triangle sources that might shed further light. And of course we can always wonder how many other women had a story to tell about Jacobs or some of the other men in this factory, and then, when you multiply that by the number of garment factories extant in New York in that time period — well, the mind reels at the possible widespread scale of sexual abuse."

"You don't have to cast your net any wider to be appalled," said George.

"So I must ask you a rather delicate question now, Rebecca." Ruth looked nervously from Rebecca to George and back to Rebecca again. She pushed the microphone another inch closer to Rebecca.

"Yes? What?" Rebecca asked impatiently.

"Could this have happened to Esther also? What makes you absolutely certain that Sam Gottesfeld was the father of Esther's baby? Have you ever had any reason to doubt your father's paternity? Is it remotely possible that Sam Gottesfeld agreed to marry your grandmother because she was pregnant by another man? Could Jacobs have raped both sisters? Have you ever given consideration to these issues?"

"Wow," George said. "No kidding, *rather* delicate!" He picked up the spectacles again, turned them over in his hands a few times, gazing down at them pensively.

"I think I saw that episode of *Law & Order,*" Rebecca said after a pause. She looked at Ruth, who met her eyes for a moment before looking down to jot something in her notebook. "Are you serious, Ruth? I can't believe you would actually ask me this."

"Rebecca and I need a time-out, Ruth," George said abruptly, pushing his chair back from the table. "Will you give us a moment?" Still holding the eyeglasses, he stood.

"I'll put in a fresh tape, and if you don't mind, I will take this opportunity to use your facilities," Ruth said. "I don't usually drink so much caffeinated coffee, because of my reflux."

"Good plan. The bathroom is just beyond the kitchen over there." He held out his hand to Rebecca. She looked at him, puzzled, and then took his hand and allowed him to lead her into the bedroom, which was partitioned off from the rest of the loft by walls of bookshelves.

"What's the time-out for?" Rebecca asked in a whisper once they were alone. He sat her down on the edge of the bed and sat beside her. "A general allergy or something specific?" Rebecca continued. "Because she is certainly a ragpicker on wheels, but —"

"I think you should stop talking to her right now," George said. "I mean *right* now."

"Why?"

"I think she's here with an agenda, which

we anticipated, but I don't think you ought to give her anything else today. She'll just suck up anything you give her. She would suck the marrow from your bones if it would help her next fucking PowerPoint presentation. She really has no idea what she's delving into, and she can't see the difference between solid gold and brass-plated tin, but she's onto some really significant issues, and they're very important to you, and I want to talk about this with you privately before you make any decisions about what you tell anyone else."

"Okay. Go ahead. What is it?"

"I don't mean right this second. I mean alone, after she's left. It's too important. We have to get her out of here now."

"I'm kind of enjoying the conversation, I have to admit."

"What are you saying, Beck, now you like her? You said you couldn't stand her. Now you're sympathetic?"

"Oh, she's totally awful, but I miss Esther so much, and nobody else has ever come along who knew all this or was this interested. I guess I just like talking about my grandmother and her life. But, fine with me — I've had enough. We were going to show her the photo, though. It was going to be the last thing to put on the table, remember?

Where did you leave the engagement photo?"

"No! We can't let her see the photographs," George said. "She's too clever in her own blinkered way. She'll see it. That's why I wanted to talk to you alone. I need to show you something. Suddenly, sitting there just now, I realized. Look at these glasses. Don't you see? Think about the picture, the engagement photo your grandmother kept all those years in that safe-deposit box. She's got these same glasses pinned to her dress —"

"That's what women did. They wore their glasses that way —"

"Yes, I know! Don't you see it, Rebecca? Who is it —"

There was a loud and urgent pounding on the front door.

"What the hell?" Rebecca said irritably. "What's the matter with her? Did she go out in the hall for some reason and lock herself out?"

"We have got to get her out of here right now," George said again.

"Maybe she's already locked out, and all we have to do is not let her back in. That should be simple enough. We can play loud music until she goes away. Maybe just this once you can play your Huntington's piece."

The hammering on the door continued.

"I guess she hasn't located the doorbell," Rebecca said, getting to her feet. "Perhaps she has issues with the gendered space of doorbells in terms of women, servants, and bells."

"Rebecca, listen, I'm serious. We can't let her figure this out. You don't want that," George said as he stood. He opened a dresser drawer and tucked the eyeglasses under some socks, and then he took the envelope containing the engagement photo, which was lying on the dresser beside the framed photograph of the sisters, and he put that in the drawer as well.

"Okay, whatever it is, I want to know. I don't get where you're going with this, but first, what do you think Ruth is really doing out there?"

The insistent pounding on the door now sounded really frantic. George and Rebecca went to the door together just as the flush of the toilet heralded the emergence of Ruth from their bathroom by the kitchen. George opened the door in confusion.

"The window!" gasped the unfamiliar woman standing there, her hand still raised in mid-knock. She was breathless.

"What window?" said Rebecca. "What's wrong?"

"Let me explain —" Ruth began from the bathroom door.

"What?" Rebecca asked her impatiently. "Explain what, Ruth?"

"What are you saying?" George said to the women in the hallway. "Just say it! What window?"

"Your window! Open your window! Hurry! It's your cat! He could fall! Your cat is out on the ledge!" the woman cried desperately, gesticulating wildly. She pushed Rebecca into the apartment and stepped inside with her. "Now! Go to the window! Look! I could see him from across the street! I didn't know what else to do!" She took Rebecca roughly by the shoulders and turned her forcibly to face the window.

George whirled around at the same instant. "What do you mean?" Joe Green was strolling back and forth restlessly on the very narrow sill on the other side of the window, mewing silently. The window was open only an inch, as it had been all afternoon, and there was no way he could have slipped out through the narrow space, any more than he could come back into the room that way. He stopped to put his nose to the crack for a moment and then resumed his agitated patrol of the length of the window ledge.

"Christ! How did he get out there!"
George rushed across the room and flung
the sash up, scooping the little orange cat
off the sill in one swift motion.

"Oh my god," Rebecca said, taking the
woman by the arm. "Thank you, thank you!
If he fell, I don't know what —"

"I am so sorry to barge in —"

"No, come in —"

"No, no, I don't need to, I'll go now, just
so long as your cat is safe —"

"I shall have to claim responsibility for
this error," Ruth said. She stood beside the
bathroom door with her hand on the door-
knob, as if she might go right back in and
lock the door if things didn't work out in
the next moment.

"What happened?" George demanded.
"What do you mean?"

"I felt overly warm," Ruth said defensively,
"and I decided to take you up on your kind
previous offer to open or close the window
for me, in order for me to be comfortable.
Previously, as I say, Rebecca, you had
indeed offered to do just that."

"What are you saying? Just say it! You're
not making sense!" Rebecca shouted at her.

"Please. You are unnecessarily agitated,
Rebecca. I went over to the little window
over there by the piano, you see, just to look

out, and then I opened the window to get a breath of fresh air while I was waiting for you, and then the cat jumped up onto the piano and startled me. I thought it was attacking me, I must admit. I have very acute reflexes. I am very sensitive to sudden motions. Then the cat sprang right at me, I swear it was attacking me, and so I stepped aside, and in my haste I almost twisted my ankle, but I think it's all right, though I should put ice on it later, for any residual swelling, it never hurts to be cautious, and then it jumped from the piano onto the windowsill, you see, and at first I thought it was just looking out, but then it walked out onto the ledge and went all the way down to the other window, and it didn't come back to the open window. I didn't know what to do."

"You opened that window by the piano?" Rebecca shouted in a shrill voice. "What made you feel entitled to do that? That window is never open without a screen, and we only open this big window a couple of inches at this time of year! Are you an idiot? In the summer we always have screens in all the windows! We *never* open a window wide enough for Joe Green to get out!"

"How could I possibly have this sort of complex knowledge of your window policies?" Ruth retorted irritably. "Irregardless, all of this happened in just an instant. I didn't know what to do, and I thought you would come right out, but you didn't, you were in there talking for so long, so I went to the bathroom, hoping that in my absence it would come back inside on its own, and then —"

"You didn't know what to do?" Rebecca asked incredulously. "You didn't know what to *do?*"

"No, I didn't dare intrude on your private conversation, whatever that was about, which was already awkward enough, if I may say so, the way you left me alone in the middle of the interview, and I did need to use the facilities, as I had indicated, so I thought I would compose myself, and then, if you hadn't come back out by then, and if it was still out on the ledge, I thought I could try to call to the cat to tell it to come back to the open window. I didn't think it would fall. I still don't see why everyone is so upset."

"Are you mad?" George said quietly. "How could you think there was no danger?"

"I don't think you are being very sympathetic," Ruth said, edging past them into the room toward the table where her tape recorder and notebook lay. Rebecca took Joe Green from George and held him to her chest. He struggled to get loose, but she tightened her grip.

"I was nervous at that moment," said Ruth, her voice rising in self-defense as she picked up her notebook. "Which led to arguably poor judgment on my part, for which I have already expressed my regret. In addition to some allergy concerns, I will confide in you, under the circumstances, that I am also quite phobic about cats. I really should have said something, you know, when it first came into the room, earlier, but I didn't want to interrupt our interview. Anyway, thankfully, everything is fine now."

"Oh yeah, we're all perfectly *fine*," Rebecca said sarcastically.

"I am so sorry to have barged in here this way, but I was very worried he would fall before you saw him," the woman from across the street said. She was still standing awkwardly in the middle of the room, holding her keys and hugging herself as if she were cold, though she wore a bulky green Irish sweater. "I kept hoping he would find his way back in the open window, but he didn't go back, he just kept looking in the other window."

"Six stories," Rebecca said, kissing the top

of his head. "God."

"Don't they all land on their feet?" Ruth asked. "I always thought they did."

"No!" Rebecca, George, and the woman from across the street chorused together.

"Oh," said Ruth in a small voice. She reached out as if to pet the cat in a conciliatory gesture, and Rebecca turned away with Joe Green to avoid her touch.

"I should go now," the woman from across the street said, pushing her hands up the opposite sleeves to grip her elbows nervously. "I'm Patricia Dolan, by the way, with the cats, you know, across the street."

"The girls! Of course. We're so grateful to you, Patricia," Rebecca said, kissing the top of Joe Green's head. "What if you hadn't been home?"

While they were saying goodbye to Patricia at the door, Ruth had collected her notebook and folders to stow in her satchel. Now she wound the microphone cord of the tape recorder with extra precision and care, and carefully zipped it into a black leatherette pouch before putting that, too, into her briefcase after the tape recorder.

"I look forward to meeting you with you again at a more fortuitous moment," Ruth said. "To continue our dialogue."

"That's not going to work out," George answered. "Don't call us, we'll call you. Ever hear anyone else say that to you before? I'm guessing yes."

"Oh, that is very witty," Ruth said nervously.

"No, it isn't," Rebecca corrected. "It was a literal statement followed by a serious question, followed by a reasonable surmise."

"Well, I do hope you will both reconsider, once you have gotten over your very emotional response to this unfortunate circumstance," Ruth said. "All's well that ends well, that's what I always say. And I will be in touch about documenting your artifacts." She gathered up her things and walked to the door.

George, ordinarily unfailingly polite, threw himself down onto the sofa and sat with folded arms, watching her make her exit. Rebecca sat down beside him, still clutching the now-restless cat, which struggled to break free of her grip, subsided, and then struggled again, but she held him tightly in her lap. Ruth went to the coat closet and removed her beige London Fog raincoat. The belt was safety-pinned to the belt loop.

"May I ask one more question, Rebecca?" Ruth said as she put her coat on.

"What?"

"Was your grandmother dyslexic, by chance?"

"What are you talking about now?" Rebecca snapped. "What does that have to do with anything? Next you'll want to know if she was hypoglycemic or had attention deficit disorder. Is there any cliché you've missed? Was there a lot of anorexia in the needle trades? Why don't you look into that?"

"I have a particular reason for my inquiry, because a careful reading of her various descriptions over the years of her work at the Triangle reveals some apparent confusion between left and right."

"No! She wasn't dyslexic! She knew her left from her right! She was old! Leave her alone!" shouted Rebecca in frustration. George put his hand on Rebecca's shoulder to restrain her from even considering a lunge at Ruth Zion.

"Very well," said Ruth. She took a crumpled paisley scarf from her coat pocket, obliviously dropping a used tissue on the floor as she did so, and wound it around her neck before buttoning her coat carefully all the way to the top. She opened the door, placed her briefcase out in the hallway, and then hesitated. "There is something I want to say to you, Rebecca." She drew herself up and squared her shoulders, as if preparing to make a well-considered statement. "I want you to know," she said in a slightly quavering voice as her emotions overtook her, "that I have forgiven Esther Gottesfeld for her testimony, although I have concluded that it was the turning point in the trial. I just want you to know that." She looked at Rebecca, her jaw squared with a kind of prideful resolve. "I have made my peace with Esther Gottesfeld." With that, Ruth turned away dramatically and closed the door behind her.

"How dare she!" Rebecca fumed, releasing the cat, which sprang out of her arms and shot out of sight into the bedroom. "Who the hell does she think she is to forgive Esther?"

Rebecca ran over to the controversial window by the piano and yanked the sash up high. A cold drizzle had begun to fall on the darkened street, and the sound of wet traffic heading up Sixth Avenue echoed into the apartment. Rebecca leaned out and scanned the sidewalk below. When the beige figure of Ruth Zion emerged a moment later from the building entrance, she stood on the sidewalk beneath the window, fumbling to remove the outer slipcase of a folding umbrella.

"She always thought your poppy-seed cake was too dry!" Rebecca yelled at the top of her lungs, and then she slammed the window shut.

■ ■ ■ ■

PART THREE

■ ■ ■ ■

FOURTEEN

YOU CAN RECOGNIZE A GEORGE BOTKIN COMPOSITION IN TWO NOTES. WHY?
How A Musical Genius Draws His Inspiration from Labor Contractions, Molecular Structures, Birdsong, and a Historic Fire to Create Music Instantly Familiar Yet Thoroughly Unique

by Arthur Wexler
The New York Times Magazine
March 19, 2006

You hear the first two notes of George Botkin's *Echinacea Serenade,* the distinctive *da-**dum*** that jump-starts the piece, and the rest of the melody comes flooding to mind instantly, if you have heard it even once before. Why? What is so magically memorable about the diminished-fifth interval between those two opening notes?

George Botkin thinks that interval has significance, but above all, he says, the instantaneous familiarity of any piece of music probably springs from "the way the melody sits in its key." He hunches over the keyboard of his piano in his Greenwich Village loft on a gray January morning, eager to clarify his meaning, and strikes those first two notes with some of the intense yet playful focus described over the years by the few musicians who have been lucky enough to call themselves his students. Even in this casual exchange, an interruption in his day that could make this a perfunctory conversation, Botkin exudes the quality of perpetual curiosity and eagerness to elucidate that attracts fierce competition for a place in one of his occasional composition classes.

"Listen," he says, sounding a very different but equally distinctive two-note opening phrase. "Do you know this? Sure you do." He plays it again, his long fingers stroking the keys with deft authority. "The first two notes of 'Small World' from the show *Gypsy*. Great show. Great song. Incredible pathos in just two notes.

"Here's another." He strikes three familiar notes. "If you ride any of the newer 2 or 5 trains on either IRT subway line, you hear this every time the train pulls out of the station." He plays the notes again, and the insistent familiarity opens into the first phrase of Leonard Bernstein's "Somewhere," from *West Side Story*.

"Do you hear the tension in the leap?" Botkin asks, playing the first two notes again. "You hear that? It's not just two pure pitches, but the relationship between them that gives it musical meaning. The leap is where we feel the significance. Bernstein's brilliance and generosity drives this, the way it sets the scene and simultaneously telegraphs what's coming next. So that interval, that relationship, manages not only to exist in its own time, while those two notes are played, but it contains information; it lets us know what lies ahead. But I want to tell you why you hear 'Somewhere' every time the 5 train leaves the station," he adds.

Botkin, fifty-six, is a tall man, with a thick shock of unruly gray hair just beginning to recede, but he moves with the impulsiveness of an adolescent. He jumps up from the piano to find a notebook, digging through a pile of dog-eared musical manuscripts before he pulls it out.

"It's an electronic sound, actually, that originates in the propulsion system," Botkin explains, thumbing pages in search of his notes. "I called up the company that makes these train cars to have a chat with them, because it was just driving me crazy." He polishes his eyeglasses on his shirttail and resumes scanning his notes. "The engineer I finally spoke to at Bombardier transportation explained why this sound is unique to the R-142 fleet. They have alternating-current motors that store electricity, instead of depending on a constant feed. But of course all the IRT tracks are set up for the old direct-current trains. So you hear those tones when these new, more efficient trains are gathering speed as they leave a station, because when they hit the higher velocities, which happen to correspond to those frequencies, you hear those notes. The Bombardier guy told me they picked optimal frequencies to make the trains run, but they never thought about what it would sound like."

Botkin closes his notebook and pitches it back onto the table, which is piled high with manuscripts, composition books, and various journals. Is he considering a piece inspired by the 5 train? He laughs. "I did fool with it a little. But it would be difficult to work out, for one thing, without being too dependent on Bernstein, and for another, I have a problem with the R-142

'Somewhere.' The actual notes you hear kind of fall into the cracks; they don't correspond to true pitch. The first one is right between F sharp and G, and the second note is kind of an E, but not quite. If you have perfect pitch, this can really get on your nerves. It's not really 'Somewhere.' It's 'Nowhere.' "

A native New Yorker, the only child of a high school history teacher and a social worker, George Botkin displayed sufficient early musical talent to attend New York's High School of Music and Art, where he flourished. He was graduated with the class of 1968, and he went to Yale to study music and chemistry, to which he says he was drawn equally. Botkin's dual interests came together in his junior year, with the composition of his seminal work, the now-famous *Protein Rhapsodies,* which were inspired by amino-acid sequences he was then studying. From *Parturition* (1981) to the *Echinacea Serenade* (1982) to *Requiem for Stark Whitely* (1986) to nearly two decades' worth of the extraordinary DNA-inspired musical portraits for which Botkin is known (recent commissions have come from the worlds of politics, sports, and Hollywood), the tireless composer has produced a steady stream of work that has won him international recognition, worldwide performance, as many conducting opportunities as he can schedule, and a dazzling list of awards, including a 1987 MacArthur Fellowship at age thirty-seven, and blue-chip composition prizes such as the Rosanoff Award, the Grawemeyer prize, two Agoos awards, a Prokofiev first prize, and the Ryden Medal.

Two days after our conversation at the piano in his Greenwich Village loft, Botkin is at a piano in a vast rehearsal hall on Eleventh Avenue (he says it's the largest rehearsal space in the city) in preparation for the debut of the *Triangle Oratorio,* his most ambitious project to date, which will premiere on the ninety-fifth anniversary of the fire, March 25, in the Isaac Stern Auditorium at Carnegie Hall. Today is the first run-through with the full chorus of 158, which includes a dozen children.

The Triangle Waist Company fire of March 25, 1911, was the most devastating and infamous disaster in New York City before the attacks of September 11 more than ninety years later. In just a few minutes, at least 146 people are known to have died in the conflagration. The *Triangle Oratorio* was inspired by Botkin's close personal relationship with his wife's grandmother, Esther Gottesfeld, who at 106 was the last living survivor of the Triangle fire when she died, on September 7, 2001. He says the Oratorio was not directly influenced by the events of September 11, despite the obvious connections.

"I think that anything we do or make or create in the aftermath of September 11 has that inevitable context," Botkin says, sipping coffee during a break. He is relaxed and expansive despite the demands of the rehearsal. "How can it not? Especially for those of us who were in New York City that day. But everyone has his own September 11 experience, and I am not sure that any single depiction of the events of that day in any form can ever be truly adequate. At the same time, there is a striking parallelity between the two events and the horrific dilemma that so many people faced on both of those terrible days. By various estimates, a third or even half of those who died as a consequence of the Triangle fire jumped from the top stories of the Asch building. And while nobody can ever say for sure, something like two hundred people jumped from the World Trade Center towers. Is it a choice? Is that what we call it? Or is it just human nature, a primitive impulse to preserve the body a few seconds longer? When Esther talked about the Triangle fire and how her sister died, and her fiancé, she would always say the same thing. She would say 'You jump because you want to save yourself. Maybe a miracle will occur and you'll survive. It's human nature. You hope. You jump.' "

Botkin has funded a concert program at the West Village Jewish Home, where Esther Gottesfeld lived for twenty years, and since its inception three years ago the Esther Gottesfeld Memorial Concert Series has brought a variety of performers of all kinds of music to the neighborhood for free concerts each month. On March 25 there are special arrangements for a bus that will travel from the West Village Jewish Home to Carnegie Hall for the *Triangle Oratorio* premiere, and there will be front-row seats reserved for staff as well as residents.

The presence of children in the chorus reflects the likely presence of children working in the Triangle Waist factory, Botkin says as members of the chorus drift back from their break and resume their places. He watches three of the twelve young teenage girls in the chorus as they come through the door together, laughing and holding soda cans. "Many people believe undocumented children worked in the factory illegally, children like those girls, and they probably died in the fire," Botkin says. He reminds the girls gently that they can't carry their soda into the rehearsal space, and they scurry out again. "We can't know how many died, or who they were. We'll never know their names. They have been silenced, so I wanted them to have a voice in the Oratorio."

At the end of the afternoon, walking the forty-odd blocks home as darkness falls, which Botkin says he does habitually after a day of work in a windowless studio or hall, he returns to the question of familiarity and recognition in his music. "Tonal context is probably what you really hear first, and that provides a necessary footing that makes you more able to feel like you've heard a song before. That sets you up to experience the pattern of tension and release. This is really nuanced, and it has to do, I would say, with establishing expectations and then fulfilling or frustrating those expectations. This is what I think about all the time when I am composing. Precisely how a melody relates to its accompaniment is a complex series of tensions and releases, whether it's a basic scale tone or, conversely, a passing tone outside the scale, or a clashing pitch, and that pattern is what makes it unique. Does that make sense?" Botkin is anxious that his explanation has been received and understood.

"By their very nature, leading tones want to be resolved," Botkin continues after a courteous inquiry about the range of the tape recorder microphone that was clipped to his collar before the walk. "Dominant chords want to resolve to tonic chords." He sings, "Why, oh, why can't I?" from "Over the Rainbow." "Ultimately, music that plays with the connection between tension and release can render a very specific and appealing pattern," he explains. "And I think that's what we remember best — our emotional reaction to the interplay. It's like a novel in some ways. Or a great movie. Why do we read novels? Why do we go to the movies? The setup, the forecasting, the anticipation, and then finally a resolution. Or you can have great success with the frustration of not getting the anticipated resolution. And this all functions in fractal form, within a single phrase of music, or across a song, or a symphony, or even a body of work, and it affects us deeply, we respond emotionally."

He has no explanation for the universal

appeal of his own music, calling it a complete mystery. "Really, I can't explain it," he says, crossing Broadway after a pensive pause during which he remains perfectly still, eyes closed. "Some people can't stand the endless questions in Mahler, the way there never seem to be any answers, while lots of other people find that very quality to be provocative. Maybe it has to do with early childhood experience. Or something in our brain waves. Who can say? I think Schubert would have left Beethoven in the dust if he had lived, say, another ten years. But there must be Schubert haters somewhere. I know someone who finds Mozart's delightful problem solving to be too much like algebra. He complains that it's all clean formulas and no mysteries. So I can't really explain anything to you about why certain musical phrases seem to possess universal appeal, though I do have some very ordinary technical explanations, starting with rhythm, which for certain compositions is critical. You know that famous descending major third in the opening measure of Beethoven's Fifth? What's really thematic there, I think, are the upbeat of the three eighth notes followed by the fermata in the next bar. Dum-dum-dum DUM."

■ ■ ■ ■

Two weeks later, Botkin takes a much-needed day away from the ongoing *Triangle Oratorio* rehearsal schedule, which now includes the orchestra. Over a quick lunch he has agreed to explain something of the process he uses to extract inspiration from the natural forms and systems that he tends to build on.

"It's really just a simple paraphrase of the duetted call of the tropical bay wren," he begins, opening a battered folder and laying out a densely inked musical score on the table in the neighborhood restaurant around the corner from his loft. "A friend of mine out in California has devoted her life to studying these little Panamanian songbirds, and she sent me one of her papers a while ago. This is exactly the sort of discovery that inspires me. These amazing little birds sing male and female parts in duet, which is utterly intriguing. The complex two-sex song patterns" — here Botkin interrupts himself to demonstrate with a credible whistled "whopdiddly whopdiddly whopdiddly" tropical bay wren imitation — "pose quite interesting questions for scientists about learning, and about how the males and females know how to sing the right parts of the song, with the boys 'whopping' and the girls 'diddlying.' "

He sings the opening of this work in progress, which he is calling *Whopdiddly Duet for Cello and Piano,* the melody in his reedy tenor a vivid expansion of the simple birdsong into something vigorously endearing and joyful. He sings through the opening bars a second time, explaining the melodic line of the piano first, and then the cello line, taking them apart and then putting them back together. His simple construction strategies for this piece contrast with the *Triangle Oratorio,* which he says he modeled on Felix Mendelssohn's *Elijah* Oratorio in certain ways.

"When you think of oratorio as a form, most people think of Handel or Bach, but Handel and Bach both use solo vocalists for recitatives, with very thin instrumental support. I wanted something that hews more closely to the Mendelssohn model, both for the more overtly dramatic narrative sensibility and also because, as is true of *Elijah,* the *Triangle Oratorio* will be performed by a full chorus — 146 voices, plus the children's choir that comes in at the end — that is almost never without a massive orchestral support." He chose the oratorio form, he says, because "all oratorios carry an implicit morality, and while the *Triangle Oratorio* isn't specifically religious, I did want it to carry that kind of spiritual weight."

Botkin rakes his fingers through his thatch of hair and grins ruefully. He goes on to say, "I have written something that will probably be called theatrical by the critics, who might well say that I am 'not serious,' but I can live with that. Don't forget that when *Porgy and Bess* premiered, Gershwin had to live with Virgil Thomson's accusation of 'fake folklore and gefilte fish orchestration.' I want the story of what happened at the Triangle Waist Company on March 25, 1911, to be felt and understood and honored by anyone who hears this piece. I want listeners to feel it in their bones. And I want it all to flow together — voices, orchestra — to be overwhelming, on the verge of chaotic, which is one of the reasons I use all twelve notes of the chromatic scale. I didn't want to break it into more traditional and civilized distinct pieces, like, say, Bach's cycle of cantatas."

At the end of lunch, when asked to explain the story behind the Botkin composition that will never be performed publicly, the composer explains, "I was working on a

DNA piece in early 2002, a two-part invention that was kind of an overdue twentieth-anniversary present for my wife Rebecca." His tone is guarded. "A piece that was intended to be a wedding portrait, the way the Arnolfini wedding was painted by van Eyck as a wedding document in a certain sense, because we had decided to get married just a few months after September 11, and we did get married, that January — we just took ourselves to City Hall — and so I wanted to write this two-part invention, based on my DNA and her DNA, as a celebration of that. Rebecca was able to finesse getting the data for both of us." (His wife has held various positions in the Clinical Genetics Department at the Yale School of Medicine for twenty years, until June of last year.)

"So," Botkin continues, warming to the subject, "I was using our DNA patterns to build the piece, starting with the beginning, those opening statements where you always want to have a question, something with energy and tension, music with significant expansion of register in the first phrase, which opens it all up to new territory and suggests a future goal, you know?" He pauses to consider his words. "Something that makes people want to hear what's going to happen next, basically," he simplifies. "But what came up in the first movement, as I mapped it out using our DNA sequences in a corresponding musical relationship, the way I work, was this huge surprise — there was this unexpected harmony. Literally. We harmonized. Rebecca and I harmonized in a way that two random, unrelated people just wouldn't. So that became the opening question. Her colleagues in Yale genetics took a look at our DNA and concluded that we had a common ancestor three generations back. And that was the answer. Neither of us had realized this at all, but we figured it out right away once this came to light. So that was a surprise, but it also answered some questions about some important things for both of us. This is private music. I wrote it as a gift for Rebecca."

Leaving the restaurant, Botkin's eye is caught by last night's New York Knicks game being rebroadcast on a sports channel on the television over the bar. "You know when the crowd sings 'air ball'?" he muses. "You know, when the crowd spontaneously sings '*Airrrrrrrr baaaaalllllllll*' at basketball games?" Botkin repeats, demonstrating in his pleasant singing voice. "They always sing the 'air' in A and the 'ball' in F sharp. A minor third. The whole crowd just spontaneously sings those two notes every time. So basketball crowds are inevitably in D major. Don't you think that's interesting?"

Back at his loft, Botkin has agreed to play the *Whopdiddly Duet* on the piano. There is a stroller in the hallway outside his front door that wasn't there earlier. Rebecca Gottesfeld, petite and dark-haired, bearing a strong resemblance to photographs of her famous grandmother, welcomes us back from lunch. She has come home from an outing to Washington Square Park with their twenty-month-old Chinese daughter, Pauline, whom the couple adopted this past November.

Pauline is scooting around on the rug in pursuit of a tolerant orange cat. She is large for her age, possibly of Han descent, Rebecca says, a theory they have developed because of her big bones and also because of her head shape, which is broad and slightly flat. They haven't mapped her DNA. She is an attractive child who radiates a confident intelligence. Pauline, who is named for Esther Gottesfeld's younger sister Pauline, who died in the Triangle fire, cruises over to the coffee table and studies the blinking light on the visitor's tape recorder very seriously, putting her face closer and closer, but she doesn't reach out to grab it or even touch it. When asked why they chose to go to China for their baby, Rebecca's reply is a succinct and rebuking, "because that's where Pauline was."

Still in his duffel coat, George Botkin has sat down at his piano. He rolls an ascending A-minor arpeggio and starts to play the already-familiar opening bars of the *Duet*. Pauline crows excitedly and raises her arms to be picked up, abandoning all interest in the tape recorder now. Instead of picking her up, Botkin reaches for her toy xylophone at his feet, and he drops down to sit cross-legged on the rug beside her, with the colorful xylophone in front of them on the low coffee table. He shrugs out of his coat and hands her one of the xylophone mallets and indicates a note for her to play, an A, which is red. Pauline understands, and as he picks up the other mallet and strikes the neat musical phrases that open the *Duet,* she plays her A note with solemn purpose, in perfect time to the joyful melody. It is indeed a duet.

FIFTEEN

"Music is especially contemporary in significance because it is a thing which exists only in sound, a complex phenomenon of tone combinations organized by a rhythmic pattern in time rather than space. It parades past the senses, leaving no trace save in the listener's mind. Unless he can read musical notation, the listener has no way of apperceiving the music as a whole other than by recreating it in his own imagination."
— from *A Guide to Musical Styles* by Douglas Moore, W. W. Norton, 1962

The critics would, in the days, months, and years ahead, call the *Triangle Oratorio* "a uniquely postmodern amalgamation" with a "melodic inventiveness" and a "powerfully insistent searing narrative impact" that gives it a "bold complexity and authenticity" that honors the lives lost to the Triangle factory fire with a "vigorous affirmation that is at once elegiac and celebratory." There would be comparisons to Gershwin, to Copland, and yes, to Mendelssohn. But on the actual night of March 25, at the Isaac Stern Auditorium at Carnegie Hall, with every seat occupied, the 2,804 souls present have no such fine analytic words. The audience that night has no words at all as the music sweeps over them and blasts them and scorches them.

George Botkin emerges, and the audience applauds. He bows to the concertmaster and then faces the orchestra, baton raised. Then he turns around and smiles at his wife and baby daughter seated directly behind him. He lifts his left hand in a little wave at his daughter, and her happy chirp causes a chuckle to ripple through the first rows. He faces the orchestra again. His baton comes down, and the 146-piece orchestra blares into life with driving blue notes and syncopations as the machinery of the Triangle Waist factory slowly picks up speed and another relentless workday has begun. The machinery charges and pounds and the chorus comes in and the workers cut and sew and stitch and the bosses demand more, and the machines crank and roar and beat on, the tempo increases, the timpani roll, the workers cut and sew and stitch faster and faster, the orchestra shouts, the chorus is chanting, *the presser, the cutter, the wringer, the mangle, the needle, the union, the treadle, the bobbin, the bosses,* and now the whistle is whistling, the workday is ending, and now the machines are beginning to slow.

The baton jabs the air, the chorus is chanting, the machines all fall silent, the clink of money is heard as the bosses circulate among the workers, doling out the week's pay packets, but something is there, something terrible, surging in a powerful undercurrent — a harsh, dissonant, charging, insistent, consuming, growing note, a sustained dissonance, and the tempo increases as it grows, feeding, *sforzando,* looming as the insistent, insatiable presence that it is, *accelerando,* and now with a *boom!* the fire has arrived, and the chorus is chanting Flames! Fire! Fire in the factory! *Sreyfe! Incendio! Ognisko! Szenvedély! Ogon! Fogo! Sreyfe!* Fire! And telephones are ringing and ringing, the orchestra beats on relentlessly in dissonant, oppositional waves of sound, and men are shouting and women are crying in Yiddish and Italian and in Polish and in Russian and there are thundering footsteps and the desperate voices are raised and raised and raised, again, impossibly, and now the orchestra takes off and goes into a gliding orbit around the voices. At once the chorus of 146 voices rages and begs and pleads and rages again, and the glorious, terrible, destroying music soars around them and lifts them up, and the chorus pulls the music down, and down, and down, and the timpani and the untuned bass drums crash together with a *boom, boom, boom,* for each body as it falls, and the bodies fall, down and down and down, and the despairing music darkens the Stern Auditorium, it darkens the very air (many who were there that night would insist all their lives that there had been special light effects, but there were none), and the rolling clouds of black music thicken the air and make it unbreathable and hot, while the chorus gasps and chokes and pleads, and most of the audience grow uneasy and squirm in their seats, and some twist around searching to identify the fire exits, just in case, and then the children's choir joins the noise and adds to the panic, and now come the terrible cries of the violins as the voices of the children and the sopranos in the chorus join in a pure scream of fear and anguish and terror and sorrow, the orchestra is momentarily silent, and a baritone violin tuned an octave low joins the other violins in a double-stopped glissando that builds and rises as fire sirens over the chorus, and then a lone mezzo-soprano rides up the octave with a matching glissando wail, and they ride up and down the siren octave again as the fire trucks arrive, and now the children are silent, snuffed out, invisible, with no more voices, but they stand there mute, moving their mouths, singing rest note after rest note, singing the silences, present in their absence, and the desperate murmur of the helpless onlookers buzzes from the back of the chorus, the full orchestra returns, and the fire rages and the firemen rage, and onlookers mill in the streets, and underneath the noise of it all is the relentless *boom, boom, boom,* of the bodies hitting the pavement one by one, the terrible stopping short of a life is there in the dull weight of each impact, it repeats and repeats, the swoop of the falling bodies and then the finality of that resonant impact, the terrible stillness that ends each fall, again, and again, and yet again, the crashing bodies hit the ground, the overloaded fire escape tears away from the wall, the locked doors hold captive the last of the burning girls. The fire burns in diminishing ripples now, with nothing left to consume, no more lives to be lost, Asch Building to ashes, dust to dust, there is nothing now but the looking back and the remembering, the sifting of ashes that will continue for decades, *this is what happened, this is what happened, this is what happened.*

Sitting in the front row with her arms around her sleeping child, watching the back of that familiar beloved head as George leaps and dances in front of her, whipping the air with his arms and stabbing his baton toward the strings, while with his left hand he beckons and gestures up, up to the wailing horns, bending the blue notes into new notes, Rebecca mourns her grandmother with a fresh and deep grief. Her grip tightens around the hot, trusting little body in her lap and she closes her eyes, inhaling the still intoxicatingly sweet aroma of her baby's scalp. She drifts on the waves of music, and feels her arms around that other little body, that tiny still body in the bed between them on that September day, and she feels in her arms the spirit of her grandmother, as the music surrounds them and floats them and makes her feel loved and held, as she and George surrounded Esther on that last day, the last day, the day her grandmother finally allowed herself to die, as they rocked her and sang their music to her, and they held her and they let her go. Rebecca dozes to the gentle accompaniment of recorders and muted strings as the oratorio approaches the opening of the somber culminating funereal passage; as the streets of the bereaved city clog with thousands of mourners and the chorus keens in grief as the coffins are wheeled down the streets and the crowds following the coffins are silent in their sorrow, there is only the rattling sound on the cobblestones, the clattering, shattering sound of the wheels under the coffins as they roll through the city.

da capo

The wheels of the cart in the hallway make their sound and it rolls through the halls, and in the silence I am hearing in my bed the taxi horns far off in the street and the telephone ringing far off in the hall and now the wheels come nearer and here is the nurse and now comes the squeak squeak squeak of the bulb of the blood pressure cuff again it is on my arm so they can squeeze it to feel the blood is still moving and now the scratch scratch scratch of the nurse writing, and now again the sound of the wheels, the wheels take her out of the room, and I am tired and I am letting go, it is time, it is time, the blood they measure is slower and slower, I feel the pull of the days, thousands of days, the weight of the days is lifting off me on this day, that day, that day, on that day, I am working at my machine, always this is how my days go, that is how this day goes, working at my machine, with only a few minutes left before the end of another day, and I have only those two right sleeves remaining in my pile — my sister, she does the left sleeves and I do the right sleeves and between us we can finish sometimes twenty-four shirtwaists in an hour, three hundred shirtwaists on a good day. We have so many good days, but not enough days. My sister, she is a little faster than I am, always she is in a rush, and her finished pile is higher, because she does her sleeve first and then I take from her pile to do the right sleeve, but I have to say it one more time, my seams are the ones always perfectly straight.

And then when I am done, the waist is finished, and one of the little girls comes by to collect from my pile for sewing on the buttons and trimming the loose threads. Those little girls, they are only ten or eleven years old, and what do they know but working and working?

The day is almost over, and it is payday.

Morris Jacobs makes a very bad day for me. Even before I ever lay eyes on him, he has a reputation as a mean boss to work for, always he is putting the clock back or stopping the hands, to steal time from the girls. He takes pennies from the week workers who are late to sit down at their machines because of the time it takes the freight elevators to carry them up, twenty at a time, to the ninth floor. I hear he is no good before I ever set foot in the door of the Triangle the first time, because of the stories about how he sided with the bosses during the big strike, harassing the picketers, hiring prostitutes to join the picket lines and stir things up.

But when we go to work there, he looks at me in the way a girl knows is trouble, trouble now or trouble some other time. I am tough. I can handle myself better than my sister, even though she is always saying of course she should be the one to be in charge. Maybe to impress me, in between the times of being mean, Jacobs is extra nice to me, so I am always guessing which is it now? Instead of taking from me two pennies because a finished waist had become soiled because it dropped on the dirty floor, he switches that waist into another pile of finished goods so one of the Italian girls is blamed and fined instead. But then another day he takes from me a dollar in his adding of my credit slips for the week, and he just shrugs it off. Another day he counts my stint too much and he touches my bosoms like we have made a deal. I take the money. I should have thrown it in his face and I am ashamed, but I want the money and I take it. I am a greenhorn and I have never been with a man except for Albert Fuchs, and he was a shy yeshiva boy who gives me a kiss on the boat when we are sailing into New York harbor and we see the Statue of Liberty and we are excited, and that is my first kiss, which isn't so much. I wish I could be one of the little girls in the nursery so Jacobs would leave me alone.

And then comes the terrible December day, after Christmas, when the darkness is always early and my fingers have a chilblain on every finger from the cold, and I am feeling lonely because my sister is stepping out now every night, they walk in the streets and they talk, and she comes back to Essex Street with her cheeks red from the cold and red from happiness also, and she tells me what they talked about but still I am left out. I am not feeling it is just the two of us anymore, and I know I have to make room for him in my heart, and Sam is a good man, so I know I can, and I am happy for her. But I feel pushed away, and I make a mistake not to interrupt her happiness, so I don't say to her what I want to say, about what is going on with Jacobs and how every day now he makes me afraid when he passes by my place where I am sitting at my machine, and he touches me and brushes up against me like it is an accident, but it is no accident, and twice when he brushes by me and pushes himself against me I feel his hard thing poking me in my back, and it makes me feel ashamed, like it is my fault because I took that extra money the first time. And I don't tell my sister.

And then comes this night, two days after Christmas, when she is going to walk with Sam, and I tell her I will go home when I am finished with the last waist in the pile, then I see I am the last one in the row and the machines are all quiet, and I hand stitch the last turn to make it right to fix a little mistake my sister made so nobody will ever notice, because I am good at fixing, and then I step into the toilet before I go to the cloakroom, and when I am coming out of the toilet, I feel something brush me in the back and it is Jacobs, and he puts his hot hands on my bosoms from behind me and he starts to rub me and pinch my bosoms through my shirtwaist, and I am pushing him and struggling to get away, but he holds me tighter and rubs himself against me and he kicks the door closed behind him and there we are alone in the toilet and even though I cry out there is nobody to hear me. And he is talking to me, first in a very sweet voice, like a mother talking to her baby, and he says he loves the way I am teasing him always, and don't I want this too, isn't this what I want, I make him crazy with my teasing, and I feel his hardness pushing at my bottom, and he has moved me into the corner by the sink and then he takes my shoulders and he forces me to turn around to face him, and then he pulls me against him, and his hardness pushes into my belly, and we stand in the corner like this, by the sink, and if anyone peeped in we would look like sweethearts, and I wonder for a moment is this what my sister does with her Sam? If it is, what does it matter, they love each other, but I do not love Morris Jacobs.

I am very afraid of him and I hate him, but I don't tell him that, I tell him to please stop it because it isn't a funny joke anymore, and, and I tell him I am a good girl, and I am only sixteen, with no experience with any man, and I think about Albert Fuchs and how he kissed me right after he threw his tefillin from the ship, down into the river it went, and I ask him why did he do this, and he says he wants to start a new life, he heard you got to be an American in America, and we watch the tefillin floating in the water and there are dozens of other tefillin, all flying into the water from the ship, all the men are throwing their tefillin into the river, and they are all just floating there, but they must sink sooner or later, and by now the bottom of New York harbor must be covered with thousands of tefillin, while New York fills up with all the men who want to start fresh, and they don't have tefillin anymore, so they can begin again.

Now I am begging for Jacobs to leave me be, I have tears running down my face and I am wailing and blubbering like a little girl, but he gets excited from this, and suddenly he takes the fabric of my shirtwaist in his two hands and he tears it open right across the front, and then he tears my bodice and I am naked in front of him and he puts those hands on my bare bosoms and he twists my nipples so hard it hurts me. And he pushes me onto the dirty floor of the toilet and he tears at my clothing and starts to push up my skirt, and I fight him, I fight him so hard, I scratch his face with my nails and I try to stick my finger in his eye and I grab hold of his hair, and he roars at me then, and he hits me hard in the side of my face with his fist, so hard I have a ringing in my head for a minute, and the next thing I know he is on top of me and he has his own clothing open, and he is putting himself inside of me, pushing and pushing like the animal that he is, and grunting like the pig that he is, and I am crying, and he rubs his Sabbath beard on my face and I smell the onions in his lunch and I can't breathe, and then he pushes extra hard and he makes a disgusting noise in his throat, a greedy horrible noise, like he is so happy to steal his pleasure from me, and then he is done and I feel the mess he has made on me, inside me and between my legs, and he rolls off me and sits up, and he takes the hem of my skirt and he wipes himself with my skirt, and he makes a smear of blood, and I know this is not the worst thing he has done, but this, this is the thing that bothers me so much, and it makes me feel completely hurt and upset for some reason, and I start to wail, I start to cry like a baby who has been left all alone in the world, and he stands up and adjusts all his clothes and fixes himself to look presentable like the gentleman he pretends to be, and he kicks me with his shoe, and I just keep wailing, lying there curled up on the floor of the toilet, and he kicks me again and he says, Look sister, I got to lock up, so you got to go out now, and you better pull yourself together.

I try to get dressed but my waist is ruined and I say that to him and he goes out and comes back a moment later and he throws a finished waist down to me on the floor where I am, and he says, Take that one, so I put it on, and it's a little too big, but I just button it up as fast as I can go, and that's when I see I have a piece of his hair in my hand, I am still holding it tight, and it's bloody where I pulled it out of his head, and I am glad. I try to make myself look all right in the mirror over the sink, and he is impatient with that, so he turns off the light so I am in the darkness to make me hurry up.

I take myself home to Essex Street in the dark and I wash myself as good as I can with six kettles of water heated on the burner but nothing can make me feel clean like I want to feel, and when my sister comes in, I act like I am already asleep in my bed because I am ashamed of what has happened, even though I know he did wrong and I didn't do anything wrong. I tell myself I will forget this and act like it never happened.

After that night, Jacobs acts like he is a little bit afraid of me and he leaves me alone, so that is something. I try to forget about it, even though at night when I am sleeping in the dark I wake up and think about it, and the tears come, but I stay quiet and I hide my feelings from my sister because now, she and Sam, they are engaged to be married and I don't want to spoil her happiness, but then comes the time when I am feeling sick in the mornings and I sick up into my handkerchief from the smell of a frying egg my sister makes in the morning. I go in the hallway, and the coffee Mr. Gompertz downstairs is always making, a smell I find in the past always delicious and tempting, now it makes me feel the water pouring into my mouth like a river, and I am sick in the hallway all at once. And I have a fear hanging over me in these days that there is a baby, because I know from talking with girls during lunch that when a baby is coming the woman feels sickness like this and I am otherwise healthy, I have no fever, my courses don't come when the time is right, there is nothing wrong with me except in the morning, and now I got a big appetite, too, I am suddenly hungry all the time. So I know, even before I admit to myself, I know.

On the morning of the day of the fire, I am working, and I see Jacobs go into the corner to the place where he sits, and I get up from my machine and I say to my sister I got to discuss with him something about the stint he didn't pay us right from last week, and he is at his little desk, calculating the pay packets to give out. He is angry with me when I tell him I think there is a baby, and he orders me to go back to sewing my sleeves and shut my mouth. Shut up, he tells me, *shvayg shoyn!* And he tells me again, I should *shyavg shoyn* my *pisk,* which is the word for an animal's mouth, not the mouth of a human being. He repeats this, only louder, and one of the girls at the end of the row, Molly Roth, she died that day, she looks up like she heard what he said. *Sha!* He says to me like the way you hush a barking dog, even though I am not saying anything now, and I stand there without moving, and he takes from the desk one of my credit slips and holds it up to me so I see my name clear, and then he tears it up. This is the only way I get money, it is the only proof of the work I have done in the week. I say again to him, What am I supposed to do? And he takes up now one of my sister's slips, and he shows me her name, and then he tears that one in half and drops the pieces on the floor. Hours of hard work that ruin her eyes are gone like that. I ask him to look at me, just look at me in the face like a man, and be a man, I tell him he should be *mentshlekh* and he says louder to me over the machine noise so a lot of girls hear him this time, he says, *Zetsn zikh!* I should sit down, and he takes another of my sister's slips and he tears it into bits. So I go away from him, back to my machine, back to my sister, who has been watching. I tell her everything is okay, and I make up a story that I asked him for a raise and he got mad with me but that was all. Now comes Morris Jacobs with our pay packets, walking down the row. It is almost quitting time. He puts down both our packets and I take them together to put into my stocking to keep safe, so my sister can stay sewing to finish what she got to finish for the week.

Ida Brodsky, she died that day, she was a wonderful friend to my sister and me, she has made a cake for a surprise because of the engagement to Sam, because they have just a few days before said to everyone the secret that they will get married, they didn't even get a ring yet, all they did was get a photograph in Union Square to celebrate when they decided, I was with them, and everybody who heard the news was so happy for them.

And now there is this big noise, right behind me, like nothing I have ever heard, and we turn around, and there are flames! They are outside the window on the Greene Street side, right there behind us. Everyone starts to shout and scream, my sister also, and everyone is in a commotion and the flames are inside with us, coming along the wall and across the floor like water flowing. The next thing you know the flames are all around us, in just an instant, and we can feel this heat like a furnace and at first there is all the screaming but nobody moves, everyone is frozen like a statue for a second, but then all the girls are rushing around, trying to get across the room at once, but they can't do that so simple because of all the machinery on these long tables with no gaps, they take up all the space and people got to squeeze by, which is how Jacobs can make excuses to squeeze by me all those times, so there is no way to pass except at the ends, and some girls try to crawl under but they can't with all the machinery and the oil pans, and everyone is pushing and screaming at the top of their lungs, like animals, girls are climbing across the tables with their skirts getting caught in the machines, and the Italian girls are praying and screaming to each other while everyone is shouting out something different. I am not afraid, even though the other girls are right away afraid. I feel like nothing can hurt me more than I have already been hurt, so I feel curious but like I am just watching all the commotion.

Mr. Grannick, the garment cutter, he stands up on a chair to make us listen but nobody listens to him, his voice is soft, and there is so much black smoke, and people are screaming and coughing and choking and nobody can manage. I see a girl with her hair on fire, and then another one goes running by me with her clothes all burning up. That is when I push past the Italian sisters just standing there screaming and crying without trying to save themselves, like they think Jesus and Mary and the Holy Ghost himself will come get them, it's like they're waiting at a bus stop, I got to say, and their faces are red from screaming and from the smoke, and I push past them and I never see them again, I know they are going to die, they are the first ones I see and I know they will die.

Now I see too many girls at the door, this door that opens in instead of out to save some pennies and make a narrower stairwell, didn't we all know that already, the narishkayt of this door, it's the only way out, every day we pass by the mean little crippled guard with the pinching hands who inspects us to find a thief. The fire is hotter. It is everywhere, creeping on the machines and the tables and all our work is burning up, with black smoke and the terrible smell from the oil, and everyone is choking and gagging, also with the very horrible smell of burning hair, and that smell of burning flesh, you smell it and you just know what it is and you feel so ashamed to be smelling that, and all the girls, they are pushing and pushing together, because nobody could open that door even though they will squeeze each other to death just to keep trying.

I have an idea about this other door on the Greene Street side, and I pull my sister by the hand to go with me that way, but she won't do it, she pulls away from me, she won't go towards the fire and all the black smoke, even though it is our only choice to get out. I am running through the flames and the smoke, and my sister, she pulls back. Now I see Morris Jacobs, and he's got a waist around his face so he could breathe, he is so clever to help himself, and all you can see are his mean, piggy eyes, all red from the smoke, and he is coughing and gagging, and I see him go to this door by the freight elevators, this door that goes to the stairs we aren't supposed to use on weekends, and he has a key, but my sister isn't right behind me anymore by the time I see him unlock the door.

I should have held her hand tighter, but I didn't, because I thought she was right behind me, but of course she goes to Sam, she loves him, they are getting married, and he is at the corner window, helping the girls. Why does Sam stay by that window where nobody can get out? I don't know. I turn around and call out to them, but they don't hear me with all the screaming, and the noise is so terrible from the fire roaring and the little girls are wailing, there are four little girls on this day, and Rose Gottlieb is there with them like always, and she helps them, and she says, *Shah, shah, shah,* as she holds each one of them for a moment, she holds each one and kisses each one and then she breaks the little tender neck with one hard twist for each one, and then she lays them gently into the scrap barrels, and she tucks them into this soft bed to be safe, where nothing will hurt them and they won't be afraid anymore, and nobody will ever find them, and then she goes straight to the open door where the elevator is gone and it is just the open shaft and she steps right in, with her arms at her sides, like for an ordinary ride down, and she halfway turns and I see her face as she drops, and I know Rose Gottlieb can't wait to die.

The flames are catching on my hair and I am getting burned, and I am at this door Jacobs has unlocked, and I am trying to open it but he is holding it closed, and I push harder than he can hold it, and I am almost through the door but he slams it on me so hard, with a rage, and I am caught. I can feel my ribs cracking as he squeezes me in the door with all his strength, he wants to kill me, but I get free and I am inside the stairs with him and then he hits me with his fist in my shoulder to throw me down the stairs, and I fall backwards and hit my head on the rail, but I catch a banister with my hand, so I don't go down except a few steps, and then he is gone, and I can't go down the stairs because they are full of smoke and flames, but I can go up the stairs the same way Jacobs has gone, to get to the roof, and that is what I do, to live my long life and have my baby, and have my Rebecca, and just keep living and living, but I am not going this time.

da capo

This time I crawl up the stairs and I go to that door I struggled so much to get through a moment before. The door has been locked on the inside, the key is still in the lock, the key from Jacobs. He has locked this door so nobody can find me and he doesn't care about anything else, and I unlock this door, and I go back into the fire, and I go back through all the flames and the smoke, and I call out to them, I call out to my sister and to Sam, because I can't see them in the darkness, and I can't breathe and I call out, Wait, wait for me, don't leave me alone, *Vart . . . vart . . . farlawzt meer nisht alain. Dorch der fire ich kum tsu deer . . .* Don't go, I'm coming to you, wait, *vart, vart far meer.* My sister, she calls out to me, and I follow her voice, and I see her then, standing by the window in the black smoke, and I go to her, my beautiful sister with her beautiful smile, and the window in the corner is broken, and Sam is there, standing on the ledge, and he is helping girls. And the music swells once more and the chorus sings its final celebration, culminating in a strangely triumphant *This, this, this is what happened. This is what happened. This is what happened.* The orchestra soars into big punctuating chords of affirmation, a grand, swelling, joyful, noble, reverent new music, imbued with sadness and love and joy.

Sam helps three girls step up onto the sill, one at a time, and it is very narrow, not such an easy place to stand, and the flames are all around us now, and he helps each one of the girls get up to the sill, he holds out a gentle hand, and he helps her stand up straight and calm and steady, and then he lets go each one of them, and each girl falls away, one after the other, with Sam to help them, three times he does this. And then Sam says to me, Pauline, are you ready? And he reaches to help me step up onto the ledge, and I take his hand and I step up, and then he says to my sister, Esther, my love, my wife, are you ready, and he helps her to step up, and he takes her arms and he puts them around his neck like to hold on in the ocean, and he puts one of his arms around me, and she kisses me on one side, and he kisses me on the other side, and then they kiss each other, and we are together, I am not alone, they are with me, we will always be together, and then we jump.

A NOTE ABOUT THE AUTHOR

Katharine Weber is the author of the novels *The Little Women, The Music Lesson,* and *Objects in Mirror Are Closer Than They Appear,* all three *New York Times* Notable Books. She has taught fiction writing at Yale and the Paris Writers Workshop, and is the Kratz Writer in Residence at Goucher College in spring 2006. Her paternal grandmother finished buttonholes at the Triangle Waist Company in 1909.